Captive Fantasy

by

L. Rosario

Captive Fantasy

Contact Information: info@thewildrosepress.com

Cover Art by *R.J.Morris and Lora Darling*

The Wild Rose Press
PO Box 706
Adams Basin, NY 14410-0706
Visit us at www.thewildrosepress.com

Publishing History
First Scarlet Rose Edition, November 2006
Print ISBN 1-60154-026-4

Published in the United States of America

"You aren't leaving, are you?"

"Let's go over here, Becca, and leave the spoil sport to her own devices."

To Sera's horror, Becca allowed Jen to lead her away. Fine, if they didn't want to be with her, she'd leave. She turned back toward the door, only to have her way blocked by a solid male body. She stumbled to a halt, stared at the open collar of his dark brown shirt, then lifted her gaze slowly to his face. Her heart, which most definitely never raced, sped up and flipped over as she recognized Valentino from his pictures on the website. He had been handsome online, in a poster boy sort of way, but in the flesh he was staggering.

"You aren't leaving are you?"

Sera searched for her voice and forced it out past the lump in her throat. "Um..."

Valentino smiled, showing a set of dimples and a mouth full of perfect white teeth. "I'll take that as a no." He reached for her and slipped his fingers around her elbow. "Can I get you a drink?"

"Shouldn't you be working?"

His smile grew, and he jerked his head to toss a few sable locks out of his eyes. His hair had a natural wave to it that was really sexy, and his eyes were deep chocolaty brown. "I have a few minutes before I need to clock in, and I thought I should spend them convincing the sexiest woman in the place to stay a little longer."

Dedication

For Diana, my wonderful editor. Thank you for believing in this story and for wanting to see it in print as much as I did. I'm proud to call you my friend.

And of course, my husband, your love gives me the courage to dream!

Chapter One

"I have a solution to your problem."

Seraphina Scala looked down from her perch high atop the library's shelving ladder and found her friend and coworker, Becca, staring up at her. "What problem?"

Becca rolled her eyes and glanced around before answering. "Your *problem*." She moved closer to the base of the ladder. "You know? The one you told me about the other day."

Oh, Sera knew, and she had regretted that little conversation from the moment it ended. So much for hoping Becca had forgotten about it. Climbing down from the ladder, she met her friend face to face. "I did not tell you about that in order for you to discover a solution."

"Nevertheless, here." Becca shoved what looked to be two tickets toward Sera. "They're for tonight."

Sera took the tickets, read the name emblazoned across the front, then gaped at Becca. "You've got to be kidding?"

Becca shook her head, causing her wild red curls to bounce around her cheeks. "Nope, no joke. We'll bug out of here early and get there before midnight."

Sera shoved the tickets back. "No, we won't." She turned away and grabbed another stack of books. Becca huffed and then jumped between her and the ladder.

"Why so set against it? Don't you want to have an orgasm?"

Sera nearly dropped the books. "Keep your voice down," she hissed.

Never mind that the library was closed, and they

were the only two still here. For two years they had shared the "graveyard shift" as Becca called it. They came in a half hour before the big old library closed and worked through the night to get it ready for the next day. Sera loved the quiet peace of the vacant library. Becca tolerated it, but she took classes during the day, so she didn't have a choice.

"You are too uptight for your own good, Sera, that's why you've never had an—"

"Enough! I get it, Becca, so stop saying it."

Becca giggled behind her hand and stepped aside to allow Sera to climb the ladder. Her voice followed her the whole way up. "We're going tonight, whether you want to or not, and Jen is going to meet us there."

"You'll have to hog tie me and drag me there against my will."

Becca clucked her tongue in disgust. "Finish putting those away and then meet me in the computer room. I'll show you tons of reasons why you will not have to be forced to go to Captive Fantasy." With that, Becca walked away on the tiny tips of her ridiculously high heels.

Sera shook her head. No matter what the website offered, she wouldn't agree to go. Captive Fantasy—although touted as the greatest experience a woman could have in San Francisco—was nothing more than a glorified strip club. She really doubted sitting in a room full of drooling women while a guy gyrated in front of her was going to solve her *problem*. It was a problem she'd had for over 300 years, after all, and things like that didn't get fixed in one night.

But Becca didn't know that because Sera had been hiding an even bigger secret than the fact that she'd never had an orgasm during sex.

She'd been hiding the fact that she was a vampire.

****

Becca was already tapping away at the computer when Sera strolled into the room. She beamed and waved toward the screen. "Come here and take a look. I dare you not to see something that gets your blood flowing faster."

Sera rolled her eyes and moved to stand behind Becca's chair. The computer screen flashed a red scrolling banner with the words Captive Fantasy written on it. Becca clicked on one of the twinkling stars at the top of the page, marked "the men," and another page opened. Tiny thumbnail pictures began to fill the screen, and Becca glanced up and over her shoulder. "Do you prefer light haired guys or dark?"

"Does it matter?"

Becca sighed and turned back to the computer. "We'll say blond, since you're so dark." She clicked on the third row of thumbnails, prompting another page to show the headshots larger. At least a dozen beautiful men stared out from the screen. "See anyone you like?"

Sera wanted to say no and walk away, but she knew how Becca was once she had a bone between her teeth. Squinting at the screen, Sera focused on one guy with bright blue eyes and a slightly crooked nose. "He's cute." She tapped the screen with her nail, and Becca immediately clicked the picture.

"Stefano," Becca read once the guy's face filled more than half the monitor. "Says here, he's good with his hands," she snickered and glanced back. "If I click on the star, we can see him naked."

Sera reeled back from the chair. "Oh my God, Becca, this is ridiculous." She blushed, despite how difficult it was for a vampire to do so.

Becca took it upon herself to click on the star, and in seconds Stefano was displayed in all his glory. No woman, dead or otherwise, could have possibly *not* looked. "Well, I'll be," Becca breathed and leaned closer to the screen.

Sera's blush intensified. If this kept up she'd need a little snack.

"I have never seen a man built like that." Becca moved the cursor and clicked another star. Stefano, in another provocative pose, appeared before their eyes. "Admit he's hot, Sera."

3

"He's hot," Sera said robotically. Of course the guy was hot. He was paid to be hot. That didn't mean watching him strip would make her come.

Becca backed out of Stefano's pictorial and aimed for another blond. "Raphael."

If possible, Raphael was hotter than Stefano. Of course Becca clicked the necessary star to see him naked and Sera gasped. "That can't be real."

Becca glared over her shoulder. "According to Jennifer, these guys are very real and much more impressive in person."

"We'll see about that."

Becca's eyes blazed with triumph. "Does that mean you agree to go?"

Nothing like walking right into a trap. Sera pulled her gaze from Raphael and reached around Becca to take control of the mouse. "Let's see what else there is."

Becca giggled, and they spent the next hour clicking on various thumbnails. Eventually, they each had a favorite. For Becca, it was Raphael. For Sera, it was a dark haired guy named Valentino. Becca shut down the computer. "Let's hope they're both working tonight."

"Let's hope Mr. Henry doesn't figure out how we were using the computer." That would be beyond mortifying.

"He never comes in here," Becca assured her. "Let's get the rest of the shelving done, so we can bug out early enough to go home and change."

Sera glanced down at her practical black slacks and white blouse. "What does a girl wear to a place like Captive Fantasy?"

"Something sexy." Becca left the room without looking back.

Sera had been afraid that would be the answer. She didn't do sexy.

****

Jennifer was waiting for them in front of the club. She was dressed in tiny cuffed shorts, a halter top, and a pair of killer stilettos; all in black. With her long blonde hair, big brown eyes and wide smile, she looked exactly like Jessica Simpson. Damn her. She frowned at Sera. "You've got to be kidding. Jeans?" She then looked at Becca, who was dressed in a sparkly, emerald-green, mini dress. "You let her wear jeans?"

Becca shrugged. "It was all she had, trust me."

Sera saw nothing wrong with her outfit. The dark wash jeans were tight and low cut, she'd allowed Becca to convince her to leave several of the buttons undone on her black blouse, and her black lace bra peeked out as a result. Surely she didn't look *that* bad? Her boots even had heels. "I promise to go with you the next time you guys make a run to sluts are us, okay?"

Jennifer was not amused. She spun around and headed for the door.

Becca shot Sera a dark look. "Must you irritate her?"

"Must she belittle me?"

"It's her way."

"Well I don't like it," Sera admitted.

Jennifer glanced back with an impatient look as she reached the door. "Coming?"

Becca grabbed Sera's hand and dragged her toward the entrance. "Try to have a good time, okay?"

Sera began to nod, then froze as she came face to face with fantasy land. The club was not at all what she had expected. There were no large round tables, no bar, and no stage. Where did the guys dance then?

Women, all dressed in the same vain as Jennifer and Becca, milled around with drinks in their hands. Their mixed voices caused a low drone of noise that actually hurt Sera's sensitive ears. This was why she avoided clubs. The sounds and smells were just too much for a vampire, not to mention all the heartbeats.

As a rule, she didn't drink from humans, but at one time, she had. It was too easy to remember the feel of flesh pinched between her teeth and warm blood dripping down her throat. The need to escape this place increased by the second.

Becca tugged her hand and she had no choice but to move deeper into the club. The sharp smell of incense clogged her senses and made her flinch. Piled on top of the droning voices, she could hear liquid dripping and wood scraping against wood. Other sounds reached her as well, but she refused to identify them. The thought that there might be rattling chains somewhere left her more than a tad uneasy.

"They are with me," Jennifer said to the doorman.

Sera pulled her gaze from the unusual environs and focused on the large man holding his hand out for their tickets. At first glance she thought he was naked, but then she noticed the flesh toned pouch cupping his genitalia. Good God! She yanked her eyes away, and Becca laughed softly at her side.

"Do you recognize him?" she whispered in Sera's ear.

Sera refused to take another look, so she shook her head.

"It's Stefano."

A quick peek out the corner of her eye confirmed Becca's observation. He had his longish blond hair pulled back in a low ponytail and it changed the angles of his face just enough to make him slightly unrecognizable. He felt her gaze and looked at her with his bright blue eyes. Sera ducked her head and the sound of low masculine laughter poured over her.

"Enjoy your night, ladies," Stefano said.

"Oh, we will," Jennifer piped back.

Sera wasn't so sure that all three of them would. She hadn't even made it past the door and already she felt horribly uncomfortable. Maybe she'd slip away once Jen and Becca were distracted by the performers. She looked around the club, but didn't see any. Hmm. Her senses were definitely picking up the unmistakable musk of man, so she knew they were here somewhere. Maybe they filed out together in a parade of sorts? Maybe the show just hadn't started yet?

"I'm going to get a drink," Jen announced, then

headed away without waiting to see if Becca or Sera might follow. They didn't.

"So what do we do now?"

Becca scanned the club and gave a little shrug. "I don't know."

Just then, the buzz of conversation shifted. The strong flavor of anticipation hung in the air, and Becca and Sera looked around to see what had caused the commotion. A guy, dressed in a black tuxedo, strolled into the center of the milling women and lifted a microphone to his lips. He was gorgeous enough to be the first performer, and Sera realized she was holding her breath.

Would the tuxedo come off a piece at a time? Would he take the clip out of his long black hair and let it drift down over his bare shoulders? Would he find her hungry gaze among the crowd and dance his way in her direction? She blushed as the last thought formed.

"Welcome to Captive Fantasy, ladies," the man announced. A smattering of clapping followed, and he waited for silence. "I do hope you've all had ample time to glance through your brochures."

Sera met Becca's gaze and mouthed, "What brochure?"

Becca shrugged then slid her glance behind Sera. She motioned with her head, and Sera turned to find Stefano at her back. He held out two shiny brochures. "You forgot these." He winked and slipped away.

Sera looked at the brochure and saw all the same headshots that had been on the website. Good lord, it was like a catalogue.

"Do we just choose and point, do you figure?"

She didn't know, so she let Becca's question go unanswered. The man with the microphone pulled their attention back to the center of the club.

"If it is your first visit tonight, I suggest you take the time to allow the gentlemen to get to know you, before making your selections. For those of you who have been here before, you know where to go and what to do." He lowered the microphone and gave a little bow.

Sera looked away from the women splitting up into tiny groups. "This place is creepy."

Becca shrugged. "Let's stick around long enough to see the guys, okay?"

"Where did Jennifer go?" Sera didn't see anything that resembled a bar, but obviously the drinks had come from somewhere.

"She comes here all the time, so she must know where to go and what to do."

"I'm right here," Jennifer said behind them. She smiled at their startled expressions and held up her little glass. "I told you I was getting a drink."

"Where?" Sera demanded. "There isn't any bar."

"Are you going to question everything that happens tonight, Sera?" Jen's tone made it clear how annoying the prospect was.

Sera bit her tongue and looked away.

"Let's go over here, Becca, and leave the spoil sport to her own devices."

To Sera's horror, Becca allowed Jen to lead her away. Fine, if they didn't want to be with her, she'd leave. She turned back toward the door, only to have her way blocked by a solid male body. She stumbled to a halt, stared at the open collar of his dark brown shirt, then lifted her gaze slowly to his face. Her heart, which most definitely never raced, sped up and flipped over as she recognized Valentino from his pictures on the website. He had been handsome online, in a poster boy sort of way, but in the flesh he was staggering.

"You aren't leaving are you?"

Sera searched for her voice and forced it out past the lump in her throat. "Um..."

Valentino smiled, showing a set of dimples and a mouth full of perfect white teeth. "I'll take that as a no." He reached for her and slipped his fingers around her elbow. "Can I get you a drink?"

"Shouldn't you be working?"

His smile grew, and he jerked his head to toss a few sable locks out of his eyes. His hair had a natural wave to it that was really sexy, and his eyes were deep chocolaty brown. "I have a few minutes before I need to clock in, and I thought I should spend them convincing the sexiest woman in the place to stay a little longer."

Sera tried to stay immune to the heavy dose of charm but failed. She blushed and licked her lips. "Considering the reaction my friends had to the outfit I'm wearing, I know I am far from the sexiest woman here."

Valentino arched a brow and began to lead her back toward the club proper. "Let me be the judge of that, all right?" He led her past the milling women, and Sera realized there really was a bar. It was tucked into a shadowy corner and unnoticeable until you almost slammed into it. Valentino stretched his free hand across the polished surface and slapped a little bell. Then he glanced over at her. "What do you drink?"

Blood. Not that she dared to say that out loud. "Um...water?"

His eyes widened, as did his smile. "All right, water it is." The bartender appeared, and Sera tried not to stare as Valentino ordered an ice cold water and a beer. The tall, muscular, nearly naked man nodded his head and walked away.

"You seem overdressed." Sera longed to die the moment the words slipped out, but wait, that wasn't an option. She felt Valentino's gaze on her profile, but refused to return it. His fingers squeezed her elbow, and his soft chuckle crept under her skin.

"We're allowed to wear clothes when we're not working, but if you'd like, I can get into uniform for you."

Maybe the floor would open up and suck her into the pits of hell? She stared at the ceiling, and Valentino chuckled again.

"Here's your water." He pressed the glass against her arm, chilling her through the thin sleeve of her blouse.

Sera avoided his gaze as she took the glass. He

released her elbow to take his beer from the bartender. "Thanks, Mike."

"Mike?" Sera echoed. The name sounded too normal for this place.

Valentino sipped his beer and nodded. "Yep. Actually his name is Michelangelo, but he prefers Mike."

"And do you prefer Val?"

He looked impressed. "You know my name."

Sera carried her drink to her lips to hide her embarrassment. She sipped the water, really wishing it was something else. Valentino's blood, to be exact. The thought rocked her. She didn't do humans. It was a code she lived by, and it wasn't one she planned on breaking. The little bags of blood waiting in her fridge were good enough, and she'd snap one open the moment she got home. Her strange little craving was probably just a result of not drinking enough before Becca picked her up.

"Does that mean you've been on the site, 'cause I know I've never seen you here before."

Sera pushed away the thought of blood. "I was on the website, yes."

"See anything you like?"

He was teasing her, and she knew it, but still she felt compelled to answer. "Maybe." It wasn't like her to play coy, but if ever the time seemed right, it was now.

"I see," Valentino mumbled then took another swig of beer. "Only seems fair to tell me your name."

Surely there was no harm. "Sera."

"Just Sera?"

Sera nodded. "Yeah, just Sera."

"Okay. Sera. Have I convinced you to stay a while longer?"

She laughed, surprising both of them. "A glass of cold water is supposed to convince me to stay?"

Valentino set the beer bottle down and turned to lean a hip against the bar. He crossed his arms and steadied his gaze on her face. "What if I told you I could make all your deepest, darkest fantasies come true?"

Sera suppressed a shiver and looked anywhere but into chocolate depths of Valentino's eyes. "You sound like a commercial I've heard on the radio."

He chuckled. "But it's true."

Sera risked a glance at his face. "I'm not the kind of girl to harbor deep dark fantasies."

He looked her over then shook his head. "I don't believe that. You strike me as someone with a great deal of depth."

The observation unnerved her. After another sip of water, she placed her glass on the bar. "I think I'll go now." His arm snaked around her waist to stop her from moving away. In that instant his scent nearly overwhelmed her. It was a mixture of rain and dewy grass. Odd, but pleasant. It took a lot of willpower not to lean into the solid wall of his body.

"I didn't mean to offend you. I'm sorry." He looked so sincere, she instantly nodded. His gaze softened and he reached up to feather his fingertips over her lips.

Sera jerked at the contact and pulled against the arm at her waist. She was strong enough to break free, just one of the perks of being a vampire, but something stopped her from doing so. She stared into Valentino's eyes and stilled as he made another pass over her mouth.

"Why are you here, Sera?"

She licked her lips and tasted the flavor of his skin. "My friends forced me to come."

"But you'd rather be at home, I take it?" He sounded offended.

"Maybe."

"I want you to stay. I want to perform for you."

Her stomach did a little flip. The visual of this guy peeling his clothes off for her, and her alone, did mighty strange things to her insides. "Um…"

He smiled and tightened his arm to snuggle her flush against his chest. His body was all hard muscle, and it felt really nice through her jeans and blouse. It would feel even better if they were both naked.

Good God! Where had that come from?

"Is that a yes?" he teased.

"Um…"

"I say it is." He touched her lips again then set her away from his body. "I'll make sure you don't regret your decision to stay, Sera." He finished his beer, and then left her with a bright smile on his mouth.

Sera collapsed against the bar, staring at the mouth-watering sight of Valentino's ass in snug dark jeans. She didn't know what had just happened, but she'd stay, if for no other reason than to see what happened next.

Chapter Two

There had been no music playing when they arrived, but now the sound system pulsed with a rhythmic beat that brought to mind a roaring fire and writhing bodies. Sera had danced around such a fire a long time ago while celebrating All Hallows Eve. It had delighted her to mingle with the local townsfolk, though her father would have exiled her to a convent had he known. The night had not ended well, but now was not the time to revisit such memories.

She focused her gaze on the center of the room as the guy with the microphone reappeared.

"It is with great pleasure, ladies, that I introduce Valentino." He stepped back with a flourish, and the female voices hushed.

Sera held her breath, then let it out and gripped the edge of the bar as Valentino appeared. He was in *uniform*, if that was what you could call the tight black shorts clinging to his lower body. The rest of him was gloriously bare, smooth, and tan. The shorts left little to the imagination, but thanks to the website photos, she knew exactly what was inside anyway. Every other woman probably did as well, and that bothered Sera a little bit more than she would have liked it to.

Valentino strolled among the women, allowing several to reach for him, but he never stopped to let them grab him. Every now and then he caught the beat of the music and did a sexy little move that made him look like he was made of molten bronze. How did a body slither from the ankles up?

Sera stood mesmerized then caught her breath when Valentino's gaze slammed into her. He stopped midstride and smiled. The music pulsed louder and he lifted his arm and crooked his finger. Several women turned to fire daggers in Sera's direction, but she ignored them all. Entranced, she stepped away from the bar and made her way across the floor. Valentino's smile grew with every step she took.

Becca's sudden appearance shattered the moment. "Sera?"

Sera blinked and looked into her friend's wide green eyes. "What do you want?" Her voice had a hard edge to it. Very unlike her.

Becca blinked, then began snapping her fingers in front of Sera's face. It was so annoying, it actually worked. Sera forgot all about Valentino and glared at her friend. "I thought you wanted me to enjoy myself?"

"Yeah, sure, but you look odd." She glanced over her shoulder toward Valentino. "I saw you talking to him."

"So."

"*So*, what did he say?"

"He said he wanted to perform for me."

Becca's mouth fell open. "*Oh my God.*"

Sera narrowed her eyes. "Is it really that big of a deal?"

Becca nodded. "I should tell you what I've discovered in the past few minutes about this place." Her tone suggested whatever it was, it was *big*.

Sera wasn't sure she wanted to hear it, but she arched a brow and waited.

"This is not a strip club," Becca said softly. She glanced at Valentino again. "Perform does not mean dance, Sera."

"Then what does it mean?" Valentino still stood in the center of a group of women, staring at her. Some of the bolder women had moved closer to him, but they seemed too awestruck to attempt to lay hands on him. He ignored them all while wearing an expression that told her he'd wait all night for her to come to him.

"It means sex."

Those three words snapped Sera's attention back to Becca. "*What?*"

"Jennifer suggested I bring you here because the guys have sex with the women. Valentino wants to have sex with you."

"You told Jennifer my secret?"

Becca rolled her eyes. "Will you listen to what I'm saying?" She gestured over her shoulder. "He's waiting to have sex with you."

"In front of everyone?" Sera's stomach rolled for a much different reason now.

Becca shook her head. "No, there are rooms. That's what the guy with the mic meant when he said that some of the women knew where to go and what to do. Their selections were waiting for them."

Sera didn't believe Becca. These guys couldn't have sex with the women. Wasn't that against the law? Wasn't it prostitution? "I don't believe you."

Becca opened her mouth but then snapped it shut. She stepped out of the way and swept her arm out. "Fine. See for yourself."

****

For one heart stopping moment, Valentino feared Sera would not come to him. Her curvy redheaded friend spoke sharply and gestured wildly, making Sera's lovely face contort into an expression of doubt and disbelief. What was she saying, damnit?

"I was hoping I could have you tonight, Valentino," a voice purred close to his left ear.

He turned to meet a familiar amber gaze. "Hello, Tabby."

The woman's name was actually Tabitha, but she hated it with a passion and claimed to adore the way he said her nickname. She came here almost every night if her big shot lawyer of a husband was out of town. Tonight was the third night this week, and Valentino wasn't looking forward to the feel of her sharp nails raking down his back.

Tabby flicked her chestnut hair over her shoulder and moved closer. Her breasts brushed his arm through her thin camisole, and her smile turned feline. "What do you say?"

"I've already been spoken for. Sorry."

Her eyes narrowed dangerously, and she glanced toward Sera. "She appears to have changed her mind."

Valentino glanced over as well and bit back a smile when Sera brushed by her friend and started his way again. "No, it looks like she knows exactly what she wants."

Tabby snaked her hand down his chest and snagged her fingers in the waistband of his shorts, but went no further. Even she knew better than to grope him on the main floor. She pressed closer and found his ear with her lips. "I want you when she's done. Is that understood?"

Valentino refrained from commenting as he gripped her wrist and eased her hand away from his body. She did nothing to hide how unhappy she was as she flounced away, but his full attention was on Sera, and he didn't care how ruffled Tabby's feathers were.

He had told Sera she was the sexiest woman in the place, and it was true. Unlike the others who were dressed in various "hooker" type outfits, she wore jeans and a silk blouse. The tight denim hugged her long, lean legs and the simplicity of the outfit was the perfect compliment to her unique beauty.

Her eyes were icy blue and slightly slanted at the edges, her nose was long and narrow, and her lips were plump. High cheekbones and slashing brows gave her a fierce exotic look, and the choppy black hair framing her face added to the illusion. She looked like a lost gypsy. As she moved across the floor, her blouse shifted to show little glimpses of her lacy bra. Fire shot to his groin, and he wondered if she had on panties to match. He'd know soon enough.

He reached for her when she was still a few strides away, and she accepted his hand. He wanted to pull her forward against his body, but rules were rules. Placing her palm to his chest, he began to move to the music. Her eyes widened, and her lips parted. "Dance with me, Sera."

For several beats, she didn't move, but then her hips started to swivel. She licked her lips and began to move a little faster.

Valentino nodded and stepped closer. On every other beat his body brushed lightly against hers. "I'd be honored if you would join me for a private session."

Her pale cheeks turned a faint shade of pink. "Um…"

Valentino grinned at the little sound. "I'll take that as a yes." He tucked her hand around his elbow and led her away from all the other women and the pulsing music. They passed Tabby on their way into the narrow hallway leading to the private rooms, and he felt the heat of the woman's anger.

Sera must have sensed it as well because she said, "I think you've upset someone."

"She'll recover." He wouldn't allow Tabby's possessiveness to ruin his time with Sera. He flashed a smile. "It looked like your friend was trying to convince you to stay away from me."

"She was." Her gaze fell away from his. "She said you guys have sex here." She looked at him again. "Is that true?"

Valentino didn't answer. He focused straight ahead and stayed silent the whole way to the room reserved for him and his guests. He motioned Sera inside and gave her a moment to take in the lush surroundings. His favorite color was red, and every shade imaginable decorated the bed, the walls, the floor, and the ceiling.

Sera's eyes were huge when they focused on his face. "I've never seen anything like this," she breathed.

Valentino carefully reached back to close the door. One false move might be enough to send her fleeing, and he didn't want that to happen. "Do you hate it?"

She shook her head. "No, I don't. I actually really like it." There was something odd about her tone, but he let it go. Her gaze fell upon the bed.

It was a large ridiculous thing with heavy red drapery and mounded pillows, but it was decadent to sleep in and women adored it. What did Sera think of it though? He'd ask after she'd spent some time in it.

"You said your friends forced you to come here tonight. Why?"

She pulled her gaze from the bed and ran her hands up and down her arms. "I'd rather not say if that's all right?"

"You aren't getting married tomorrow are you?"

"No," she said with obvious surprise. "Why?"

Valentino shrugged. "This is a popular place for brides to spend their last night as a single woman."

"Have you entertained many brides to be?"

He met her gaze. "Do you really want to know?"

She lowered her lids without answering and took a step back toward the door. "I won't have sex with you," she said softly. "If that's what goes on here, I won't be a part of it."

"Nothing will happen that you don't ask for, Sera."

She looked irritated by his reply. "I keep hoping you'll deny the fact that you have sex here night after night, and you haven't done that yet."

"I won't deny the truth."

She studied his face for several moments then swept her gaze down his body. He was accustomed to being stared at, but she didn't look at him as if he were a slab of fresh meat. Her look was more intense, more searching. Incredibly intimate.

His body stirred as a result, and he hardened against the tight confines of his shorts. Sera's gasp filled the thick air and her eyes flew to his face. "Sorry," he offered. "You can't hope a guy won't respond to such a look."

"Aren't you paid to respond?"

He shrugged. "If that's all you want from me, then yeah."

She crossed her arms and cocked her head. "So if I say I want you to stand there and let me look at you, you'll just do it?"

"Yep."

She shook her head. "That's ridiculous."

"I agree, especially since you've looked your fill on the website." His words filled her face with color.

"Just because I know your name doesn't mean I looked at all your pictures," she protested.

Valentino couldn't resist pushing her a little further. "Did you look, Sera?"

More color crept into her cheeks, and her gaze strayed toward the bed. "Maybe."

"I'm better in person."

Her mouth fell open, and her eyes flicked back to his face. "I cannot believe you just said that. In fact, I can't believe any of this. It's too odd." She turned from him and reached for the door. "I need to leave now."

"I'll let you go after you tell me why your friends dragged you here. You aren't getting married, so what is it then? A bad break up? A bad husband?" He glanced at her left ring finger, but there wasn't a ring or a mark indicating there ever had been.

Her hand tightened around the doorknob, but she didn't turn it. "I told you I'd rather not say."

"But knowing will help me figure out how to behave around you. It might explain why you're so touchy."

She shot a glare over her shoulder, and the fire in her eyes made her nearly irresistible. "I am not touchy."

"Yes, you are." Most women begged to stay longer, the fact that Sera longed to flee, intrigued the hell out of him.

She let go of the knob and turned to face him. "Fine, Mr. Stubborn, I'll tell you exactly why I'm here tonight."

Valentino resisted the urge to hold his breath.

"I made the mistake of telling my friend that I've

never had an orgasm during sex."

He admired her ability to say all of that with a straight face and dead-on eye contact. "You've had one on your own though?"

"Excuse me?"

"You said, during sex. It implies you've had one without sex."

She shook her head, and the razor cut ends of her hair slapped against her jawline. "I've never had one, all right?"

"Of course it's all right, and not the least bit abnormal."

She rolled her eyes and tossed her hands in the air. "Oh my God, don't play Dr. Ruth with me. You don't look the part."

Valentino grinned and held out his hand. "I'm not trying to play Dr. Ruth. Come here."

"No," she snapped.

He dropped his hand. "I'll give you an orgasm, Sera, but it would be easier if you let me touch you."

Her mouth opened and closed, and her eyes narrowed. "Does that mean you can give me one *without* touching me?"

"Sure." He did his best to keep his tone casual. No telling how she would react if she realized how eager he was to touch her. "But I'd prefer the traditional way, and you would too, trust me."

Chapter Three

The traditional way?

Sera was more confused than she'd ever been in her life. Even waking up with a sudden craving to drink blood hadn't confused her this much. What the heck did he mean, the traditional way? And how could he give her an orgasm without touching her?

Damn him for making her want to know the answers to those questions.

She stared at him, and he stared back. Surrounded by all the blood red layers of the room, he was almost too glorious to look at. She hated the fact that she wanted to see him naked on the bed. She wanted to see his golden skin against the crimson comforter and his dark hair spread out over the red pillows. She wanted to lick drops of blood from his skin...

Sera forced the dangerous thoughts away. What had gotten into her tonight? If she wasn't careful, she'd attack someone on the way home. Becca and Jennifer were high on the list. It would be just payment for having them drag her into the current situation, after all. How dare they?

"Sera?"

The sound of her name yanked her back into focus.

"Tell me what you want me to do for you?"

Good God, he sounded like something out of a dream. She backed against the door, feeling a little better with the solid wood pressed to her spine. She could pull it open and leave at any time. Valentino didn't seem inclined to force her to do anything against her will, so surely he'd let her leave.

"What do you want, Sera?"

If he didn't stop talking to her in that buttery voice, she'd lose her mind. "I don't know what I want, but I refuse to have sex with you."

"Fine. No sex." He stepped toward her, and suddenly the solid door at her back was a trap.

"Wait!" She held up her hand to stop him before he could press his chest to hers. He stopped, and she curled her fingers into her palm to resist touching the skin that was oh so close. On the dance floor he had laid her hand against him, making her want to pet him from head to toe. "What are you going to do to me?"

"You make it sound like I'm about to eat you."

Muscles that had always failed to stir, stirred now with a vengeance. Her body grew moist, and her jeans chafed against her crotch. She shifted her stance, but it didn't ease the sensation.

"Unless you'd like me to eat you," Valentino drawled.

Sera jammed her fangs into her tongue. The pain did nothing to lessen the awareness of what his voice did to her nether region. She struggled to breathe, hating the way he reduced her to behaving like a normal mortal. She was stronger than this, damnit!

"Is that what you want, Sera?" He moved a step closer, the heat from his body pressing in on her, but still not touching her. "Do you want my mouth on you?"

"Oh my god..." She didn't mean to say the words out loud, but there they were. He smiled, and her body clenched deep down inside. This could not be happening. It was going to take more than a seductive voice to end her three hundred year old drought. Wasn't it?

Valentino licked his lips slowly and lifted his arms to brace his hands on either side of her head. He still didn't move close enough to touch her, but her awareness of him drove her crazy. His scent wrapped around her, his heart pounded in her ears, and she could smell his blood.

"Does that sound good?" he asked.

Sera caught herself as she began to nod. "No."

"Ah, the magic word." Valentino lowered his arms and stepped away.

Sera reached for him without thinking and dug her fingers in the muscles of his upper arms. "No," she said again. "I won't do sex, but...I want..." God, she had never been good at voicing this sort of stuff.

Valentino eased close again and placed his hands back against the door. The position forced her to release his arms, and she rested her palms against his chest. His heart beat sure and steady beneath her right hand. She tried not to follow the rhythm, but doing so became too difficult. She dropped her hands. It made things easier if she didn't touch him. "You have to tell me what you want, Sera, or I have to let you walk out this door."

"I can't." She shook her head and lowered her gaze. "I can't talk about stuff like this." Becca told her it was one of the reasons she couldn't fully enjoy sex. Yeah, maybe, but knowing it was a hang-up didn't make the words suddenly spill off her tongue.

"Then I'll ask the questions and you can say, yes or no."

She looked into his eyes, wondering if he was this wonderful with all the women. Not a good thought to have at the moment. "Okay." She could manage a yes or no.

"Do you want to take your clothes off?"

"Oh my god."

He smiled and flicked his hair back from his eyes. "Yes or no?"

"Not yet."

"All right. Not yet." He nodded, and the hair slid forward again. "Can I kiss you?" His gaze moved to her mouth as he asked the question.

"Um..."

"I need a definite yes or no here, baby, or I'll get into a shit load of trouble."

Sera stared at Valentino's mouth. His lips were sinfully full. Maybe too full for a guy, but at the moment it didn't matter. "Yes."

Very slowly he closed the space between their mouths. Was he giving her a chance to change her mind? When his lips hovered a breath away from hers, his eyes flicked up. "Tell me now if you don't want my tongue in your mouth."

Sera's knees buckled, and Valentino quickly clasped her shoulders. "Do you need permission to do everything?" Her voice shook.

"No," the devil smiled, "I don't, but I love the way your face reacts to my words. I think I could talk you straight into your first orgasm."

She thought maybe he was right, but he didn't give her a chance to say so out loud. He licked his lips then kissed her. Aside from his hands on her shoulders, his mouth was the only part of his body touching her, which meant there was nothing to detract from the sensation of his lips moving over hers. They were full and soft, but at the same time, they possessed a firm masculinity that made her melt. His tongue snaked out, and she parted her lips to allow him to slip deep inside. He licked the roof of her mouth and danced around her tongue, then slid back out to suck on her bottom lip.

Sera gasped when she felt the harmless prick of Valentino's teeth sink into her swollen flesh. The sound caused the kiss to end, and he eased back to look her in the eye. "Too much?"

What would he say if she admitted it wasn't nearly enough?

She swallowed and shook her head. "No, it's fine. Ask me another question."

He took his hands from her shoulders and put them back against the door. "All right. Do you want to take off your clothes now?"

Sera chuckled. She couldn't help it. "Not yet, lover boy."

"Then let me unbutton your blouse."

"That's not a question," she pointed out.

"No, it's not."

Valentino's eyes darkened until they were nearly black, holding Sera mesmerized. "You may," she whispered. Who knew what had gotten into her, but it would be interesting to see how long this bold little attitude of hers lasted. Long enough? Lord, she hoped so.

He didn't unbutton the blouse. He ripped it open. Holding the sides wide apart, he stared down at her black bra and swept his tongue over his lips. "Let me touch you."

"How?" she croaked. The look on his face was killing her. Such hunger did not normally grace the face of a mortal, and it had awakened her own. She braced her hands against his chest, once more concentrating on the beat of his heart.

He lifted his gaze. "It doesn't matter how. If you want my hands on you, say so. If you'd rather have my mouth..." He broke off with a shrug.

Sera's nipples hardened behind the lace, and she swallowed a moan. She recalled the feel of his teeth pricking her lip, and she knew what she wanted. Now she just had to find the courage to say the words out loud. She closed her eyes, and rested her head back against the door. "I want you to kiss me through my bra."

She barely had the words out before Valentino's hot mouth closed over her left breast. He sucked the hard tip and swirled his tongue back and forth until she arched against him with a strangled gasp. His teeth tugged at her and ripped through the delicate lace, but it felt too good to worry about the damage to her clothing.

Sera lowered her hands from Valentino's chest and flattened them to the door. Doing so gave him total access, and he took advantage. Once he had rendered her left breast numb with intense pleasure, he moved over to torment the other one. The first scrape of his teeth made her whimper, and he pulled back.

"No," Sera moaned. "Please, it feels good, I swear it."

He lowered his head and sucked her back into his

mouth.

Sera clawed at the door with her nails. She tried so hard to be normal everyday and suppress the vampire in her so that others would have nothing to question. She was very good at hiding the monster, but the feel of Valentino's teeth scraping her nipple made her want to take hold of his hair, rip his head back, and sink her teeth deep into his neck. She shivered as the need for blood—fresh blood—nearly forced her to her knees.

Valentino lifted his head and leaned his body against hers. The smooth skin of his chest teased her sensitized nipples, making her shiver again. She forced her head away from the door to look at him. "What now?" she croaked.

"That's up to you, but you haven't done what you came here to do yet."

Sera shook her head. No, she hadn't had an orgasm yet. "I might have if you hadn't stopped what you were doing."

That made him flash that deadly smile of his, the one showcased so beautifully on the website, the one that probably got a million hits a day from lonely, frustrated women—like her.

"Where do you want me to kiss next?"

Sera groaned. It was a long, drawn out sound that would make someone giggle if they heard it through a wall, but she didn't care. She jumped when Valentino brushed his finger over her lips.

"Here?" he asked. He trailed his finger down to tease the underside of her chin. "Or maybe here?" He continued on, stroking the line of her throat and making her swallow again and again. "Do you want to feel my lips here?"

Yes...

He pressed his finger to the hollow of her throat. "So calm," he said. "I would expect your pulse to be racing, Sera. Am I doing something wrong?"

"No." Lord, what could she say? *I'm sorry, Valentino,*

but my pulse can't race. It hasn't been able to race for over three centuries, but if it could...

His fingers moved down into her cleavage, then hooked around the fastener of her bra. "May I?"

Sera did not enjoy being naked in front of men, or anyone, for that matter. She knew there was nothing wrong with her body, but that didn't mean she needed to display it. She shook her head and Valentino slid his finger away.

A frown pulled at his lips, but he didn't give into it. "Okay, but you aren't making this very easy, you know?"

"You said you could do this without even touching me, so I can't imagine clothes are an impediment."

ꞏ "They aren't, but I want to see you naked. Not because you need me to do something for you, but because you're a gorgeous woman." The look in his eyes matched the sincerity of his tone.

Sera swallowed the urge to grant him what he wanted. "Thank you, but I'd prefer to stay dressed."

Valentino nodded once then braced his hands on the door. He leaned closer, and she felt the hard line of his flesh trapped against his shorts. Instinct screamed at her to rub against him like a cat in heat, but she resisted. Resistance was something she was really good at. Another reason she never enjoyed sex? Yeah, probably.

"One orgasm coming up, with minimal bodily contact."

Sera frowned. "Do you have to make it sound like I'm going through the drive-thru?"

"You're the one keeping things impersonal, baby, not me," Valentino fired back. He pressed closer, and she gasped as his penis throbbed against her belly. "I would be more than willing to make this all about pleasure instead of business."

Sera gritted her teeth and closed her eyes. "Just do it, okay?"

"You have to relax," he said directly into her ear.

Sera did her best to relax.

"Keep your eyes closed," his honey voice instructed. "I want you to focus all of your energy on listening. Can you do that?"

Sera nodded, and Valentino's lips brushed over her ear. The contact made her shiver.

"Let's go back to me asking questions, and you saying, yes or no, okay?"

Sera nodded again.

"Do you enjoy receiving oral sex?"

Under different circumstances the question would have offended the hell out of her, but having it purred in her ear wasn't so bad. "Um...sometimes?"

"Sometimes is all right, but I could make you crave it."

Oh, she didn't doubt that.

His lips brushed her ear and he eased his body away so that only his mouth touched her. "Can you picture me on my knees for you?"

Thanks to the photo online of him kneeling on a bed, yeah, she could. It was nice, to say the least. She nodded.

He licked the upper curve of her ear, making her gasp. "I'd have to hold you still, so should I put my hands on your hips, or your ass?"

Oh... "Hips," she said quickly.

He flicked his tongue against her again. "I'd rather hold your ass," he murmured.

Sera's muscles tightened. "All right." It was all pretend anyway, so what was the harm?

"You feel good. Real good," he said into her ear. "You taste even better."

"Um..."

"Hush."

Sera snapped her mouth shut.

"I don't think kissing and sucking at you will be enough, Sera. I want to take your little clit in my mouth and sink my teeth into it. Would you like that?"

Something happened in that moment, making Sera arch away from the door with a tortured moan. She reached for Valentino and gripped his shoulders. He lifted his head to look at her, and she blinked rapidly to bring him into focus. Down below, her muscles were going crazy, and the air around them filled with the sharp scent of female arousal. Hers.

"Tell me what's going through your mind, baby."

She couldn't begin to put it into words. She shook her head and dug her nails deeper into his shoulders while rocking her hips forward. She brushed over his erection, liked it, then did it again.

"Everything I just said, I can do, Sera. Just say the word, and I'll get on my knees and suck you so hard into my mouth—"

Her groan drowned out his words.

He pressed his body hard into hers and put his lips back to her ear. "The thought of getting a little rough turns you on, doesn't it? Did you know that about yourself?"

She shook her head against his mouth. She'd never admit it. She was a librarian for God's sake; rough sex was not something librarians did.

"What turns you on more? The thought of being spanked, or the threat of my teeth tearing into you?"

"Teeth," she rasped. "God, I want you to bite me." Lord, had she said that out loud?

He dragged his mouth down her ear and nuzzled the crook of her neck. "You want me to bite you, huh? Where?" He opened his lips over her skin and licked her. "On the neck? Do you want to play vampire, baby?" His teeth pinched at her, and when she moaned, he bit harder. He tugged at her skin, and she bucked her hips forward. He took the hint and began to grind his erection against her.

It was too much to bear. "Harder...please."

He increased the pressure of his bite and his movements. Even with her jeans and his shorts separating them, she could feel each pulse of his erection. He pressed hard against the apex of her thighs until she was saturated with her own lust. Her muscles tightened and relaxed in a rhythm she wished would never end. Oh, this was nice. Real nice.

Valentino bit harder and shook his head, as if trying to rip the flesh from her bones. He growled and palmed her breast. His hips continued their circular torment, and his heart pounded against her chest. Sera shuddered and ripped at his shoulders until she smelled blood. The fragrance shoved her head first over the edge, and she screamed as her first orgasm ripped through her.

Chapter Four

Valentino flicked his tongue over Sera's neck as she convulsed in his arms. He wanted to fuck her. He wanted to rip off her clothes, wrap her legs around his waist, and impale her against the door. His dick throbbed painfully as she continued to rub against him, and he was afraid he'd break the cardinal rule of Captive Fantasy and lose control.

That couldn't happen. His livelihood depended on it.

Eventually, Sera calmed and she shifted her hips back against the door. He missed the feel of her the way a fish would miss water, and he wanted to take hold of her hips and yank her forward again. Instead, he kissed the side of her neck and pulled his mouth away. Without a doubt, his bite was going to bruise. Already the skin was red and angry looking.

Sera rolled her head against the door and met his gaze. "Oh my God."

Valentino smiled at the unintentional compliment. Normally, he'd say something flip like "it's what I do," but looking into Sera's clear blue eyes didn't make him feel very flip. He leaned down to kiss her without asking and she didn't protest. He kept the gesture brief. "It was my pleasure."

She smiled a brilliant smile that transformed her features. She'd been gorgeous before, but now she was breathtaking. She lowered her lids to hide her eyes and ducked her head. "I need to go, I think."

He knew she'd run. He lowered his hands and

31

stepped away. Rules were rules, and no matter how much he wanted her to stay, if she wanted to leave, he had to let her. She slid away from the door and looked down at her torn blouse. For several moments she tried to secure the sides together then gave up with a frustrated whimper.

Valentino took pity on her and reached out to brush her hands away. She looked at him as he gathered the hem and tied it in a knot over her belly button. It wasn't perfect, but it covered her bra for the most part.

"Thank you," she said quietly. "For everything."

He nodded. The ache in his groin was making him a little crazy, not to mention, frustrated. If there were no rules to follow, he'd beg Sera to stay and finish what had been started here.

Sera skimmed her hands over her hair, licked her lips, and flicked her gaze around the room. She looked ready to speak, but she never did. With a brief glance in his direction, she reached for the door, pulled it open and walked out.

Valentino cursed under his breath and slammed the door shut. He'd been in agony before after a client had opted not to have sex, but nothing that felt like this. Bracing one hand on the door, he dropped his head, closed his eyes, and shoved his hand down the front of his shorts. He hissed as he took hold of his erection, and it took only a few pumps of his fist to coax a climax. He came fast and hard, not caring about the damage to his shorts or the fact that he'd have to waste time taking a shower.

The next time Sera stepped into his world, he hoped to God it was her hand coaxing the cum from his dick. Or better yet, her mouth. *If* she ever came back. He wasn't sure she would.

A knock on the door made him jump back. "Yeah?" he called.

"Open up, Val."

Recognizing Stefano's low voice, he pulled the door open. The big blond stepped in the room and gestured for him to shut the door. Valentino did so, growing more and more curious by the moment. "What's up?"

Stefano searched the room, then faced Valentino. "You had that exotic raven-haired beauty in here, didn't you? The one that came with the curvy red head and the bombshell blonde?"

Valentino hadn't noticed a blonde with Sera, but he nodded nonetheless. "What about her?"

Before he answered, Stefano took a minute to skim his gaze over Valentino. He gestured toward the stain on his shorts. "That answers one question."

Valentino didn't bother to glance down. "Why would you come in here to ask if I had sex with her?"

"You need to report to the lab," Stefano told him.

Valentino's blood ran cold. "Why?"

What had he done wrong? He leaned back against the door and replayed every second of his time with Sera. He had backed off when she said no. He hadn't forced anything on her. He'd given her exactly what she had come here for. What then? Why did he have to report to the fucking lab?

Stefano shrugged. "Wish I knew, buddy, but orders are orders. I was sent back here to tell you to go downstairs, and I've done it."

"Did you see her as she left?" There was no need to explain he meant Sera.

Stefano nodded. "Yeah."

"And?"

Another shrug. "She looked upset." Stefano moved toward the door and eased Valentino aside. "Whatever you did to her, it didn't make her happy, and that might be the reason for the invitation."

"I assure you she was happy."

Stefano pulled the door open and stepped into the hall. "Whatever you say, buddy, but she left alone and it looked like she was crying." He waited until a departing woman cleared the hall, then continued. "Or at least trying really damn hard not to cry." Another shrug. "Just get your ass to the lab, all right?"

What Stefano wasn't saying was that if Valentino refused, his friend would have no choice but to take him there himself. Despite their friendship, a personal escort wouldn't be as pleasant as it sounded.

****

The lab was a heck of a lot more high tech than that one little word implied.

Valentino looked through the glass door and was motioned in by a middle-aged man wearing a long white lab coat. Dr. Sven Reynolds was the brain child behind Captive Fantasy and worried incessantly about something going wrong. He set aside his clipboard, pushed up his reading glasses, and watched Valentino stroll into the room.

"You are out of uniform," was his way of a greeting.

Valentino shrugged. "I figured I was done for the night, so why not shower and change?" He'd slipped back into his jeans and button down shirt.

Dr. Reynolds didn't look happy, but he merely waved his hand toward the metal examination table. "Strip and lie down."

As always, Valentino cringed at the no nonsense command, but he knew better than to disobey. While the doctor slipped on a pair of rubber gloves and readied an array of instruments, Valentino shed his clothes and stretched out on the cold table. He closed his eyes and images of Sera floated into his mind.

Where was she now? In bed, thinking of him? His body stirred at the prospect.

"I won't even ask what is on your mind, young man," Dr. Reynolds commented dryly before the feel of rubber gloves touched Valentino's bare chest. "Take a deep breath," the doctor commanded.

Time passed slowly as Dr. Reynolds did a routine checkup. Blood was drawn, heart rate was measured, height, weight, you name it, he did it. When the last test ended, Valentino swung his legs over the side of the table, ready to get his clothes and get the hell out. The doctor had other plans.

"Not so fast." He set aside the tube of dark, almost purple blood, then pulled off his gloves. He pinned Valentino with a speculative look. "Tell me all about your client this evening."

Normally, there would be no hesitation. Valentino would rattle off the woman's name, her occupation, her blood type, anything he might have learned while making her sexual fantasies come true, but for some reason he didn't have any desire to say a word about Sera. His hesitation to obey was met with obvious disapproval.

"Listen, CF19," he used Valentino's lab code instead of his name, "you'll tell me what I want to know, or I'll simply have the men investigate on their own."

As far as threats went, it was a good one.

Sera wouldn't stand a chance if "the men" tracked her down and interrogated her. He was backed into a corner, and the gleam in the doctor's eye irritated the hell out of him. "Her name is Sera."

With a nod, Dr. Reynolds picked up his clipboard and flipped pages. "Go on. Last name?"

"She didn't say."

The doctor looked up over the top of his glasses. "Did you ask?"

"Of course I asked, but given how skittish she was, I didn't dare push her."

Dr. Reynolds scratched his pencil over the page, while nodding again. He asked the next question without glancing up. "Age?"

"I don't know."

A sigh. "Occupation?"

"Again, I don't know."

The doctor glanced up with a frown that didn't bode well for Valentino. "Your unwillingness to do your job properly is only one reason I had CF14 send you down here before the night was over. I'll not tolerate rebellion. Need I remind you how special the situation here is? Do you no longer wish to be a part of the ground breaking

technology that is Captive Fantasy? If that is the case..."
He nodded toward a sealed steel door.

Beyond, lay the gas chamber. The place where every single one of Dr. Reynolds' creations eventually ended their existence. Some because of age, others due to disobedience. It was a threat that hung heavy over Captive Fantasy.

Valentino shifted on the cold table and thought of the pile of clothes lying nearby. He might be just a number to the good doctor, but no man should have to undergo an interrogation while naked. For a brief moment he allowed himself to fantasize about stripping the doctor's clothes off and strapping the annoying SOB to a cold table. No doubt the man would squawk like a trapped chicken.

He almost laughed out loud at the vision. Almost. One did not laugh in front of Dr. Reynolds. "I have never been unwilling to do my job," he countered.

"Is that so?" Reynolds set the clipboard down and crossed the lab. He killed the lights and pulled a large screen down from the ceiling. "Explain this then, CF19, if you would be so kind." With that, the doctor pushed a button on a remote and the screen filled with images of Valentino entertaining a woman in his red room.

Not just any woman. Tabby. Damn.

Wishing he could be anywhere but here, Valentino watched the events unfold on the giant screen. With a toss of her chestnut hair, Tabby crossed the room and stretched out on top of the bed. She crooked a finger at him, but he remained standing by the door. Frowning, she began to remove her clothing, one item at a time, until she lay on the bed dressed in red stockings and black heels. Again she crooked her finger, and again he didn't move.

Dr. Reynolds snapped the lights on without warning, and Valentino blinked against the sudden glare. "It looks to me as if you are refusing to service a client. Care to explain why?"

"She eventually got what she wanted," Valentino bit

out.

"Eventually is not what we do at Captive Fantasy. I have noticed an increase in hesitation with you, and it does not make me happy. Now, once and for all, tell me why you know nothing about the woman you spent over an hour with."

The images still flickered on the screen, harder to see now with the lights on, and Valentino averted his gaze. "I told you, I didn't ask. The woman was one wrong word away from running like a scared rabbit, so I didn't want to risk it."

"I've watched the tape," Dr. Reynolds announced without emotion.

Valentino cringed. Damn. Sera would freak if she knew their little encounter was immortalized on film. At least she hadn't gotten naked for him; a dim silver lining, but one nonetheless.

"It did not appear as if the woman was a moment away from fleeing. You could have had her in your bed, had you coerced her a little bit more."

Valentino opened his mouth to spit out something in his defense, but the doctor went on.

"Since you failed to do your job in its entirety, you will remain down here for the rest of the night and you will volunteer to test out my new serum." Reynolds crossed the lab again and then spun around with a medium-sized bottle in his hand. His smile was not comforting, nor was the rather thick, pinkish colored liquid in the bottle. "I am unable to test this particular brew on the rats," he explained while moving back toward Valentino. "It must be consumed by a man to see if it will have the hoped for effect on your skin."

Valentino couldn't take his eyes off the bottle. "What it supposed to do?"

Dr. Reynolds uncorked the bottle and thrust it under Valentino's nose. He gagged at the smell. "Drink it without asking questions. That is the way things work down here, CF19."

Valentino took the bottle, pinched his nose, and drank. God willing, he wouldn't sprout wings or a tail. He doubted very much that Sera would appreciate the addition of either.

Chapter Five

"Well?"

Sera knocked the computer mouse off the table as Becca's voice shattered the silence of the room. She bent over to pick the thing up, hoping her friend would stay put and not discover what website she had been surfing. No such luck.

Becca strolled into the room. "Ah." That one word, or sound or whatever, held a wealth of meaning.

Sera snatched the mouse off the floor and quickly used it to exit Captive Fantasy's site. The damage was done, however, so she braced herself to face Becca's insatiable curiosity.

"So tell me all about Valentino."

The mention of his name made her hot all over. She'd had a great deal of blood before coming to work, but not enough to make her feel *this* warm. She gave a little shrug. "There's nothing to tell."

"Oh, come on!" Becca moved closer, pointing toward Sera's neck. "Then what's this peeking out of your turtleneck?"

Damn. Bruises didn't heal as fast as open wounds. Sera cupped her hand over Valentino's bite mark and slammed the door on the recollection of how it had gotten there. Now was not the time to relive that heavenly moment. "Did you get lucky with Raphael?"

"I'm not going to let you change the subject."

Sera gave up with a sigh. "Fine." She spun around in the computer chair and crossed her legs and arms. "You can consider my problem solved, which I'm sure will give you something to crow about for years."

Becca beamed. "Oh, that's fantastic!" She clapped her hands and beamed some more. "So I was right about the guys having sex with the women?"

"Does that mean you never hooked up with Raphael?"

"He wasn't working, but I want to hear about Valentino. Did you guys...you know?" Becca made an infantile gesture with her fingers and wiggled her brows.

"No," Sera said simply. One would think the clipped tone would be enough to alert Becca to drop this, but it had never worked in the past. Why now?

Becca plopped down into another chair and spun it around. She leaned forward, causing her short skirt to ride way up her thighs. Why she wore such impractical clothing to a library was a mystery Sera knew she'd never solve. "But obviously something happened in order to produce that shiner of a hickey," Becca pressed.

"You know I'm not good at talking about this stuff, so can we just leave it alone?"

Becca shook her head without an ounce of remorse. "Nope." She leaned forward and peered closely at Sera's neck. "Are those teeth marks?"

Sera groaned and prayed for patience while tugging her collar higher. "Maybe."

Becca's eyes widened. "He *bit* you?" She sat back in her chair with a little sigh. "God, that's hot."

Sera rolled her eyes and got up to leave. "I'll leave you to enjoy the fantasy of whatever it is you think happened."

"But he made you come, right? You said your problem was fixed, right?"

Sera nodded and kept walking. Becca's heels tapped loudly behind her.

"Do you want to go again tonight?"

Sera stopped, nearly causing Becca to slam into her, and turned. "I don't see any reason to go back." Though that didn't mean she didn't *want* to, but Becca didn't need to know that. Just looking at Valentino's pictures on the website had made her wet and ready, seeing him again would undoubtedly be another trip into bliss.

"You don't see any reason to go back? Are you nuts? Why were you looking at his pictures? Are you regretting the fact that the two of you didn't screw? Or was that a lie?"

Sera turned away from the rapid fire questions and headed for the shelving cart. "We have a job to do, Becca."

"Screw work, I want answers."

Sera escaped up a shelving ladder with a pile of books in her hand. Unfortunately they were all sex manuals. Lovely. She tried not to look at the covers as she quickly slid them into their little spaces.

Becca rattled the ladder below. "Hey, don't ignore me, bitch."

"Is such a thing possible?" Sera mumbled. Having shelved the last book, she started down the ladder to slide it to the next section.

Becca grabbed her ankle and halted her several rungs up. Their gazes clashed. "Why won't you give me any details? I just want to know if the pics on the website are photoshopped. Surely you can tell me that much?"

Sera shook off Becca's hold, calling on just a little vampire strength to do so, and jumped off the ladder. "I don't know if they are photoshopped or not."

Becca narrowed her eyes and crossed her arms. "How can you not know? You were just gawking at Valentino's naked dick two seconds ago, did it or did it not, look like that in real life?"

"Did your mother teach you to talk like that?" Sera turned away from her friend's irritated glare.

"Fine," Becca huffed. "Don't spill any of the juicy details. I'll just go back tonight and see for myself."

Sera pivoted so fast she got dizzy. "What do you mean by that?" She didn't care for Becca's crooked grin. Not one damn bit.

The redhead shrugged and leaned her shoulder

against the shelves. "It means I'll go back to the club and select Valentino from the handy brochure and see for myself. Should I write it down, or do you get it now?"

Oh, Sera got it all right, but she didn't like it. The thought of her friend going anywhere near Valentino made her skin crawl. Lord, was this jealousy? She was jealous over a guy who got paid to screw women? She must be losing her mind.

"You look a little green, Sera," Becca pointed out. "You aren't jealous, are you? Does the thought of me licking all that fine flesh of Valentino's make you want to rip my tongue out?"

Sera gritted her teeth. If she admitted how she felt, Becca would never let it go.

"I'll tell you this," her friend went on. "If he does pack the weapon they show online, I'll take great joy in trying to shove it down my—"

"Enough!" Sera yelled. "I get it, okay? I fucking get it!" She spun away and stalked toward the end of the aisle.

"I take it that little outburst means you want to go with me tonight?" Becca yelled the question from where Sera had left her.

Sera growled low in her throat but didn't answer. She'd walked right into Becca's little trap and they both knew it.

****

"You've got to be kidding?" Sera stood in the cramped women's restroom of the library, staring at the black dress Becca had just pulled out of a shopping bag. "I'm not wearing that."

Becca ignored her. "Are you wearing boots?"

"Yes, but I'm not wearing *that*." Sera pointed at the skimpy dress and shook her head.

"Put the damn thing on and shut up, Sera." Becca tossed the garment across the small distance and then rummaged into the bag for her own change of clothes. She pulled out a blush-colored cami and a red mini.

"Aren't redheads supposed to avoid colors like that?"

Becca shrugged and exchanged her racy "work" outfit for the racy "club" outfit. Sera didn't see much difference. "Put the dress on, so we can get out of here."

With a sigh, Sera gave in. She took off her black trousers and charcoal gray blouse and folded them neatly before rolling them up to put in her large purse. She stepped into the tight dress and slid the straps up her arms. The neckline was too low and her black bra showed. She glanced at Becca. "I won't wear this in public."

"You look amazing."

Sera moved in front of the mirror. Her kitten-heel boots hugged her legs, all the way to the knee, and there was a good length of leg exposed before the hem of the dress started. Technically, the dress was nothing more than a long tank top, only it lacked a back and a great deal of the front. "I look like a whore."

"Maybe," Becca conceded. "But a gorgeous whore bound to get laid by the equally gorgeous Valentino." She tossed over a tube of lipstick. "Now put some of this on, so you don't look so dead."

Sera fought back an ironic grin and uncapped the blood red lipstick. Why was she not surprised? After putting the lipstick on, she had to admit she looked hot. Would Valentino agree? Her heart thumped a little faster as she thought about seeing him. Maybe she'd ask him to make her come with his mouth this time.

Her vaginal muscles flexed at the thought, and she swallowed a moan.

"Good lord, girl." Becca's gaze met hers in the mirror. "You look like you're about ready to go off right now."

Sera's face heated, and she slid her gaze away while handing Becca her lipstick. "Are we taking my car, or yours?"

Becca turned away to repack her shopping bag. "We'll drive separate, just in case," she said over her shoulder. She glanced up after a few moments. "Okay?"

"Yeah, whatever." Sera grabbed her purse and

followed Becca out of the restroom. They made sure everything was in order for tomorrow morning, then set the alarm, and left. The heavy doors of the library slammed shut behind them.

****

Captive Fantasy was packed.

Sera hung back behind Becca after they paid the gorgeous guy at the door their entrance fee. It wasn't Stefano tonight, but tall, dark, and handsome was just as nice to look at. He winked at her, and she stopped staring.

"I wonder why there are so many women here tonight," Becca called back over her shoulder. There was not only music playing, it was loud music.

Sera shrugged and scanned the crowd. Instantly she recognized the woman who had shot daggers at her last night, the one who had pawed at Valentino before she could get to his side. The woman looked away from whatever was going on in the middle of the floor, and her gaze locked with Sera's.

Animosity flared. She turned away and disappeared among the throng of shrieking women. Sera tried to track the woman's progress, but there were just too many others.

Becca grabbed her hand and coaxed her forward. "I think one of the guys is dancing or something, but we can't see from here."

Sera had no choice but to follow or be pulled like a rebellious child. They moved closer to the writhing group of ecstatic women and a sharp odor smacked her in the face. She pulled her hand free to cover her nose. "Ugh."

Becca stopped and turned around. "What is it?"

Sera lowered her hand. "Don't you smell that?" It was obvious that Becca didn't. Her friend frowned and continued on. The smell intensified the closer they got to the pack. She knew now what she smelled. Arousal. Sharp, feminine arousal.

Sera's eyes watered, and she wanted to turn tail and run.

But before she could there was a break in the crowd, and she caught a glimpse of what all the fuss was about.

Valentino.

Her breath caught in her throat and the foul odor was forgotten.

"Ooh," Becca breathed into her ear. "There he is."

There he was, indeed. Tonight he had on white shorts, and if possible they were more provocative than the black ones had been. Maybe because she could see a shadowy swath of skin through them? Yeah, that had to be it. She yanked her attention up to his face and her mouth fell open. Oh God, this man was beyond gorgeous.

He had his head tossed back and his hands on his chest. He touched himself while moving to the pulsing beat of the music. When he pinched his left nipple the women shrieked.

Sera's nipples pushed against the lace of her bra, and she crossed her arms.

"If you don't screw him tonight, I'll kill you," Becca hissed.

She wanted to do more than just screw him. She wanted to lick him from head to toe. She wanted to taste every inch of his glowing skin and then sink her teeth deep into the hard muscle above his left nipple. She wanted to gnaw on him until he begged for mercy, and then she'd drink his blood.

"Hey, earth to Sera," Becca interrupted.

Sera blinked and focused on her friend. "Sorry."

"Wow, this guy really does it for you, huh?"

Sera looked back at Valentino and gasped to find his gaze focused in her direction. He wasn't dancing anymore. Without looking left or right, he sliced through the crowd of women to come to her. He halted too far away for her to touch him and smiled.

"I didn't think you'd come back."

Words escaped her.

Valentino held out his hand. "Come with me."

Sera nodded and didn't even give Becca a parting

glance as she slipped her hand into Valentino's. He pulled her forward, and she flattened her hand to his shiny chest. She had assumed it was sweat, but his skin was dry. It shouldn't surprise her that he glowed like some unearthly god.

"Say you'll come to my room with me."

Sera nodded, but Valentino shook his head and repeated his request. She knew what he wanted. "I'll come to your room with you." The quiet words earned her a bright smile and a tight squeeze.

He shifted her hair away from her ear to place his lips there. "Tonight I'm going to fuck you."

Chapter Six

Valentino laced his fingers with Sera's and led her away from the crowd of women. She followed with none of the hesitation she had displayed last night, and he couldn't help but smile to himself. God, he was thrilled to see her. More thrilled than he had a right to be, but that couldn't undo how he felt. He'd have to be cautious though, or Dr. Reynolds would pick up on it and no doubt ban him from Sera's company.

That he wouldn't tolerate. He might drink vile brew that made his skin shine with some artificial glow and take a shot here and there, but he wouldn't let the doctor deny him Sera.

She squeezed his fingers as they reached his door, and he looked over his shoulder. "What happens tonight, Valentino?"

He didn't answer until they were in his room with the door closed. He eased her back against it and gripped her shoulders. "Ask me to kiss you."

"You haven't answered my question."

He leaned closer. "Oh yes, I did. I told you out on the floor exactly what we were going to do tonight. Weren't you listening?"

She lowered her lids and licked her lips.

Valentino growled at the sight of her little pink tongue. "Damnit, Sera, ask me to kiss you."

Her gaze lifted, but instead of saying the words, she nodded. For him, the gesture was enough. However, rules were rules. "You have to say it out loud, baby."

She licked her lips again, making the blood red lipstick shine. "Kiss me, Valentino."

He did.

Tasting lipstick, tongue, and heavenly woman, he took her mouth and delved deep inside. He released her shoulders to take hold of her head, and her silky hair slithered between his fingers. He arched her back, pressed his body hard into hers, and deepened the kiss until he could feel the back of her throat. She clawed at his back but returned the embrace with equal fervor. God, he could eat her alive.

Valentino ended the kiss with his forehead pressed to Sera's. She looked up into his eyes and smiled while licking her lips again. Most of the lipstick hadn't survived his kiss. No doubt he was wearing it now. "What do you want now?" He struggled to force the question out and barely heard it over the sound of his heart racing in his ears.

"Please," she whispered. "I'm not good at this, you know that. Please don't make me say out loud what I want from you."

He cupped her face and stepped back. If it were up to him he wouldn't force the issue, but Dr. Reynolds had made his wishes known last night, as well as what would happen if Valentino failed again tonight. The latter didn't bear further thought. "Should we do the yes and no again?"

"Um...okay." She gave a little nod within the cage of his hands.

"Did you think of me at all once you left here?"

Her eyes widened at the question. "Um..."

"I want to know," he prompted. "I *need* to know."

"Yes," she admitted with a little nod.

"I thought of you all night long. To call it torture would be a gross understatement." That made her blush lightly and flick her gaze downward. "Look at me, baby." She did. "Do you want to fu—make love tonight?"

"I d-don't know if I do or not." She shrugged and slid

her gaze away again. "I'm not what you would call casual."

Which was exactly what he loved about her.

Valentino went very still for several heartbeats as the thought slid in and out of his mind. Love? Odd choice of words, and one that would get him into a shitload of trouble. He shook off the feeling of dread crawling up his spine and focused on the ethereal beauty of Sera's gaze. He'd never seen eyes like hers before. They were so clear and so blue. "You have gorgeous eyes."

She blinked. "Th-thank you."

Her confusion made him smile. "It's hard to stay on track with you, so forgive me if my questions and comments seem all over the place."

"It's all right."

With a smile, he took her hand and led her across the room to the bed. "Would you like to sit down?"

Instead of answering, she slid her hand free and perched on the very corner of the mattress. She crossed her legs, drawing his attention to how sexy her high boots looked with the short dress. Seeing her dressed in such a provocative manner had shocked him, until he realized underneath she was still very much the shy lady. The contrast had the power to kick any guy right in the gut. It hit him double time.

He hunkered down in front of her and braced his hands against the bed. Doing so trapped her between his arms and put his chest close to her legs. Their eyes met. "Do you know what I want to do to you?"

She shook her head and shifted to rest her weight on her hands behind her. The action pulled the skimpy top of her dress further away from her lace bra.

Valentino focused on the hard nub of Sera's nipple through the thin veil of her bra and then tracked his gaze down her body toward her lap. She shifted again as if he had actually touched her. "I want to shove you onto your back, spread your knees wide, and bury my face between your legs." He heard her catch a breath, but he didn't take his eyes off his target.

Very slowly, she uncrossed her legs, brushing his chest with the leather of her boot. "I'd like that."

Valentino looked up, almost afraid to believe that she had actually said those words. "Say it again."

She licked her lips and took a deep breath. "I'd like you to do what you just said. I'd like it very much."

He might be guilty of making Tabby wait too long for what she wanted, but he wouldn't be accused of doing the same with Sera. Eagerness rushed through him, and he planted a hand in the center of her chest and pushed. She fell back with a little gasp, then gasped louder when he shoved her knees wide open. Shifting to kneel, he scooted closer and slid her dress up to her waist. She had on a pair of black lace panties to match her bra, and instead of removing them he leaned forward and placed his mouth over the fabric.

She jerked under the contact and writhed around a little bit. He put his hands on her hips, and she calmed. She smelled good. Good and ready, to be precise. He nipped at her through her panties, then pressed his tongue over the spot. Mmm...she tasted good too.

He wanted more.

"Can I take your panties off, baby?" He asked the question without lifting his mouth, and every word made her gasp.

"Um..."

"Looking for a yes or no, here."

"Yes."

He tore the lace with his teeth and had her clit in his mouth before she could finish tangling her fingers in his hair. She arched high off the bed and moaned long and low. He sucked at her until she whimpered, but he didn't release her. He knew what she liked, even if she'd never admit it out loud, and he was going to give it to her. Clasping her between his teeth, he shook his head and pressed his face closer. He growled, knowing the rumble would vibrate through her body.

"Oh...Val...oh..."

He flinched as she tugged on his hair a little too hard. He released her and looked up the length of her arched body. "Easy, I sort of like my hair."

Her fingers relaxed, but she didn't let him go. She wiggled her hips under his mouth, and he didn't make her ask twice.

Sliding his hands under her ass, he lifted her off the bed and licked her from back to front. She quivered, and he did it again. By the third pass, she was tearing at his hair again and panting his name. "Put your heels on the bed," he ordered her.

She did.

Access granted, Valentino went in for the kill. With his hands pressed against the back of her thighs, he shoved her legs toward her chest, opening her fully to his gaze and his mouth. He looked at the close-cropped black curls for a moment then blew lightly on them. All the glorious, wet, pink flesh exposed to him clenched then relaxed. He blew on her again, and she tore at his hair.

"No...you're teasing me."

If not for that magic word, he might have continued. Still holding her wide open, he licked her then plunged his tongue inside. She convulsed around him and he tasted the sweet flavor of her cum. He sucked it out, swallowed, and went back for more. All the while he rubbed his nose over her clit. Each clench of her muscles grew tighter and tighter as did the grip in his hair. The room was eerily quiet, and he realized she must be holding her breath. He wanted to hear her scream.

Sliding his tongue out of her passage, he licked upward, then caught her clit between his teeth. Her breath whooshed out, and her hands fell free of his hair. He pulled at the sensitive skin for several moments then bit down.

Not only did she scream, she saturated his chin with a healthy dose of cum.

Valentino didn't relent until he heard Sera choke

back a sob. She gripped his hair with limp fingers and pulled ineffectively at his head. He moved away and shook free of her grip. Instead of waiting to see if she'd be able to lift her head, he got off his knees and stretched out on top of her, careful to keep his weight braced on his hands and his body away from hers.

Her lids fluttered to reveal her stunning eyes. Were they darker?

"Oh my God," she exhaled.

Valentino hid his pleased smile. "Just imagine what I could do if you let me take all your clothes off."

She shook her head. "Not yet, okay?"

"You make it tough for a guy, don't you?"

Her expression slammed shut, and she shoved at his chest to get him to roll off. He had no choice but to let her sit up and eventually leave the bed. He rose to his elbows and watched her peel her ruined panties off before tugging her dress down to her thighs. She balled up the little lacy confection then looked over to meet his gaze. "Relationships, especially ones that involve..." She waved toward the bed. "I don't do well at."

"We aren't having a relationship, Sera."

"Yeah, that might be the problem." She crossed her arms and turned her back.

"I don't think it is."

She glanced over her shoulder and frowned at him. "Are you a psychologist now?"

Valentino chuckled and sat up. "You've had two pretty intense—if I do say so myself—orgasms while in my company. Perhaps your relationship hang-ups are the reason you can't say the same when in the company of other men? Maybe actually being in a relationship scares the sexual shit out of you."

"So I'm letting go with you because I know I can walk away?"

He shrugged. "Yeah, why not?"

"That's just wrong." She headed for the door, and he flew off the bed.

"Hey, where do you think you're going?" He jumped in front of her and pressed his back to the door. She tried to stop a stride away, but he caught her waist and pulled her against him. "I'm not done with you yet."

"But I didn't say you could do anything else."

Damn. He flicked his gaze over her shoulder toward the camera hidden in the ceiling tiles. If she insisted on leaving, he had no say in the matter. He couldn't even seduce her into staying. He settled his gaze on her face. "You really don't want anything else from me tonight?" *Like the feel of his hard dick inside her?* If she said no, this night was going to end exactly the way last night had, with his hand in his shorts.

Her gaze drifted down from his face to settle in the vicinity of his throat. She licked her lips and a strange expression flitted over her features. She dropped the panties to the floor and flattened both palms against his chest. "There might be something else I want," she said very quietly.

"I swear to God, anything you ask for, I'll give you."

She glanced up with a strange little smile curling the edge of her lips. Her eyes were definitely darker now. "Are you sure you're willing to give me *anything*?"

Hell, her voice had darkened too. It seemed strange to describe it in such a way, but he couldn't think of anything better. Her tone was normally soft and hesitant, but now it was just...darker. He nodded and narrowed his eyes. "What exactly do you want me to do to you?" He'd had women that liked it rough before, and he could recall a time or two when blood had actually been drawn. He wasn't so sure he could make Sera bleed because the thought of causing her too much pain made him want to cry.

She seemed so damn fragile, though that wasn't exactly an accurate description at the moment. Right now she looked pretty dangerous.

She licked her lips and focused on his throat again. "I want your blood, Valentino."

His blood?

She went on in her dark, sultry tone before he could speak. "I want to taste the flavor of it on my tongue." She licked her lips again and leaned closer to sniff at him.

He stiffened and moved his grip to her shoulders. "Sera?" Something was wrong here. Hell if he knew what it was, but his instincts were literally screaming in his ear.

Chapter Seven

Sera had just entered the danger zone, but knowing it didn't make it any easier to back out. The feel of Valentino's smooth skin beneath her palms, the rapid beating of his heart, the smell of him, the knowledge that he was full of warm fresh blood...all of it added up to make it damn hard for her to walk away right now. She had never felt so hungry. Maybe years of suppressing her true sexual desires had somehow suppressed her hunger for blood as well, and now that Valentino had ripped the lid off the former, the latter wanted to come out and play as well.

It would be so nice to lean into his hard body, place her mouth at his neck, and bite—

"Sera?"

His voice broke through to her, and she lifted her gaze to his. He looked concerned and maybe a little bit scared. She didn't want to scare him. In fact, that was the one thing she hated the most about being a vampire. The fear she caused in others. "Don't be afraid."

He blinked and cupped her face. "I told you I would give you anything you wanted, so if you want me to bleed for you, I will."

Oooh, that sounded nice. She licked her lips and pressed closer to rub her breasts against his chest. "You have to promise not to be afraid."

He seemed unsure as he nodded. "Maybe we should move back to the bed?"

It didn't matter to Sera where it happened as long as

she got to drink this man's blood. Soon.

He took her hand, and she followed him to the bed like a good little girl. Once there, he turned to her and settled his hands over the straps of her dress. "Can I take this off?"

"Yes."

He didn't give her time to change her mind, not that she wanted to. He stripped the good for nothing dress off her body and left it pooled at her feet. He reached for her bra next and arched a brow. She nodded, and lacy garment drifted to the floor.

"I might risk a lot by asking this, but I need to know." He talked while staring at her exposed breasts. His hands were at his sides, and his chest rose and fell in great gulps of air. "Why are you letting me do all of this now? Where did the shy Sera go?"

Did she dare tell him that her hunger had consumed that other personality? Would he understand, or would it only bring the fear back into his eyes? She chose the safer route and lied. "I guess you just make me comfortable."

He lifted his gaze and narrowed his eyes. For several moments he stared hard at her, but instead of calling her out, he nodded toward the bed. "Care to lie down?"

Sera flicked her gaze toward the expanse of red satin. "I would prefer it if you lie down first." She wanted to be in control.

With a nod, Valentino walked around the bed and stretched out on top of the red coverlet. He propped his hands behind his head and bent one knee. "Now what do you want?"

Sera stared. Valentino's physical perfection almost made her forget about his blood. The white shorts, doing little to hide his state of arousal, stood out against the blood red fabric, as did his shiny golden skin and dark chocolate hair. His gaze never wavered from her face as she continued to gawk at him.

"You can touch me if you'd like," he said softly.

Sera swallowed hard. Tearing her gaze from the man

sprawled on the bed, she reached down for the zipper of her boot.

"I'd like you to leave them on, but it's up to you."

She glanced up and nearly fell over under the impact of Valentino's wicked smile. She took her hand away from her boot and walked around to the side of the bed. A tiny part of her brain tried to remind her she was naked in front of a man, and that this wasn't something she normally did, but she shoved the annoyance away. When Valentino held out a hand to her, she took it and allowed him to pull her across his body. His smile grew with every inch of her skin that touched his.

He wrapped his arms around her and held her close. "Are you always so cold?"

"Maybe you're just too hot?"

His laugh shook her, and he angled his head up to kiss her forehead. "Silly."

Sera ducked her face into his neck and inhaled the flavor of his skin. He didn't smell like anyone she'd ever been this close to before. The earthy aroma she had detected the first night seemed stronger, but the smell of fresh cut grass was gone. Maybe he had used a different soap tonight?

"So what now, baby?"

She nuzzled his neck before answering. "Now I want blood." With that, she opened her mouth, and sank her teeth into human flesh for the fist time in nearly three centuries. It shouldn't have surprised her when Valentino jerked with pain and tried to throw her off. She *was* out of practice, after all.

She pulled her fangs free and soothed his neck with her tongue. "I'm sorry."

"It's fine." His voice was lower than normal and his hands moved lightly up and down her back. "Do it again."

With pleasure.

Sera shifted her position to squeeze her knees tight to Valentino's thighs. Pressing her hands into his shoulders, she slid her fangs into him again. This time, her bite was gentle. He sighed, and his blood began to flow into her mouth.

Oh, sweet heaven, he tasted divine. Either she had really forgotten what it was like to drink directly from the source, or there was something incredibly different about Valentino's blood. Never before had she experienced such sweetness. He was like a liquid serving of dessert.

Sera altered her bite to sink her fangs deeper. She hadn't used them in so long it actually hurt to tear at Valentino's skin. He whimpered a little, and the sound made her pull back and lick her lips. He blinked at her as she sat up. The look on his face was a sexy mixture of pain and expectation. She ignored the expectation. "Did I hurt you too much?"

He shook his head and grabbed her hips. "I can take it." He pulled her forward a little and moved his hips. "So now what?"

Clearly he wanted sex, but Sera believed he wouldn't take it without her consent. Stalling sounded good. She glanced at the wound on his neck. She'd been messy, and it was bleeding. The strange color of his blood drew her closer.

"You're blood isn't red." She flicked her tongue out and his body stiffened as she licked a few drops away. It still tasted super sweet, even outside the body. She swallowed and scraped her fangs over the wound. More blood pumped out, making her moan.

His fingers flexed on her hips. "I'll give you all the blood you want, but please give me something in return."

Sera lifted her head enough to see Valentino's face. "It's been a very long time since I've had sex, and you are not small." That was likely the understatement of the millennium, but she doubted he needed her to stroke his ego. Of course, the pictures on the website might be fake. Though he felt large.

"I swear to God, I won't hurt you." He sounded ready to beg. "If it's too much, just say stop, and I stop. It's that easy."

She knew she could trust him. With a little nod, she eased off his lap. Immediately, he began to peel his tight shorts down. She looked away as he shifted his hips off the bed, and his chuckle brought heat to her face. Let him laugh. She refused to stare like an idiot. No matter how desperately she wished to. Her vampire hearing picked up the provocative sound of the shorts hitting the floor. Oh dear.

He reached for her and clasped her hips to guide her back across his lap. "Look at me."

Sera met Valentino's gaze as he lifted her hips to position the head of his penis at her opening. She swallowed and braced her palms on his chest. He closed his eyes and eased her down on top of him. His movements were slow. Very slow, and she felt every thick inch of him slide deeper and deeper. Eventually she simply couldn't take anymore. "Stop."

He did, and his eyes flew open. "You're almost there, baby."

Sera glanced down to see a healthy length of Valentino not imbedded inside her. She couldn't possibly take it all. Maybe if he weren't so thick.

"It'll be easier if you're on your back," he said.

She nodded, and he rolled her over with an impressive maneuver. Still buried inside her, he settled between her thighs and gave her a little nudge. She gasped as her body took another increment of hard cock.

He brought his face close, until his lips barely touched hers. "Bite me."

Sera hadn't expected that. She looked into his strained face and then at his neck. "Now?"

Valentino nodded. "Put your mouth on my neck and hold tight." He lifted off of her and braced his weight on his hands. "Can you reach, little vampire?"

She shook her head and gripped his shoulders to pull him back down. She wasn't sure if the nickname was a tease, or if he really knew what she was. She'd ask later. Settling her lips over the wound, she licked him a couple of times then touched him with her teeth. "You taste so good."

"I can't possibly taste as good as you feel." He gave her the rest of what he had to offer in one thrust.

Sera tore into Valentino's neck as he filled her completely and unmercifully. His blood pumped down her throat, and his cock burned the walls of her passage. Each thrust coaxed a soft moan from her throat.

His lips brushed over her ear. "Am I hurting you?"

She didn't know how to answer. Part of her brain registered the pain of being filled by something entirely too large, while another part begged her to let go and give into the glorious sensations coursing through her body. The feel of fresh, warm blood on her tongue helped her decide which half to listen to, and she shook her head in response to Valentino's question. "Feels good," she panted.

He growled in her ear and thrust deeper and harder.

Dear God, she could feel him all the way to the bones of her lower back.

Taking her mouth from his neck, she dug her nails into his shoulders and arched to meet his next thrust. The friction of his movements burned, but she didn't want him to stop. Not when she felt the stirrings of an orgasm. How heavenly it would be to come around this thick invasion. A drop of blood dripped from his neck onto her lips, and she lashed her tongue out to lick it away. Another followed, then more as Valentino increased the tempo of his movements.

"You're close, aren't you, baby?"

Sera nodded, not caring that he couldn't see her. His blood continued to drip onto her lips, and she fed without having to make any effort whatsoever.

There'll be no going back now, her inner voice hissed. *You've tasted heaven again, and you won't be able to pretend you don't enjoy it.*

No. After tonight everything would go back to normal. She'd have her little bags of blood to erase the memory of Valentino's taste, and she'd never come here again. Time would pass, as always, and she'd shove this moment to the very back of her mind. She'd store it there with the rest of the memories she never took out. In time, she might even forget.

"Oh Jesus..." Valentino breathed in her ear. "You have to finish before I do, so tell me you're close."

She clenched around him as he thrust again, giving him the answer he sought without speaking a word. His thickness stretched her so wide, she barely felt the contractions of her orgasm, but she had no trouble feeling the hot rush of his release as he let go inside her.

Too soon it was over, and Valentino collapsed on top of her. His neck and the wound were out of reach, so she buried her face in the lovely fragrance of his hair. The strands were like silk against her cheek and nose. "Please tell me I didn't hurt you."

He shook his head against her cheek. "Just give me a moment to catch my breath."

Sera would gladly hold him all night, if that was what he wished, but she kept the sentiment to herself; along with the fact that for the first time in over three centuries, she felt at peace. A scary condition to be in considering the man on top of her was a male prostitute and she was a vampire.

Even Dr. Phil couldn't make this relationship work.

Chapter Eight

It took longer than usual for Valentino to recover, but eventually he lifted his head from the curve of Sera's shoulder to look her in the eyes. She blinked, and there was no mistaking the darker shade of blue staring back at him. Her cheeks held a hint of more color as well and the realization that his blood was responsible for these changes was a bit too much to process.

She was a vampire. Shy, reserved Sera was a frickin' vampire.

"You probably should have mentioned what you were the first time we were together." He kept his voice pitched low so the microphone on the camera couldn't pick it up. *This* he did not want to hear about later. Hiding the bite marks would be enough of a challenge.

She frowned. "I've never been sure how to bring such a thing up."

He braced himself over her and shook his hair out of his eyes. "A quick flash of fangs would have sufficed." He looked at her full lips for a moment, then back into her eyes. "Can I see them now?" He'd already felt them, after all.

She curled her lips back into a smile that only revealed the sharp tips.

"Kind of sexy," Valentino mumbled, and Sera's smile grew. He met her gaze. "We'll keep this between us, okay? Not sure how my boss would feel about you ingesting my blood." Dr. Reynolds would probably go through the roof before running a series of uncomfortable tests.

Sera nodded and squirmed beneath him. "Do you mind?"

He pulled out of her and rolled away, keeping his eyes on her face the whole time. "Why don't you take your boots off and slip under the covers for a little bit?" He didn't want her to leave him. Not yet.

She shook her head and scooted to the edge of the bed. "I should go." She glanced over her shoulder. "Could you let me get dressed without staring at me?"

Ah, shy Sera was back.

Valentino nodded and closed his eyes. "I promise not to peek."

The bed shifted, and he listened to the sounds of Sera slipping back into her clothes. Her boot heels clicked across the floor, and he slit his eyes open just as she reached for the door. "Hey." He shot off the bed and caught her before she could finish her little escape.

"I said I need to go."

Valentino pulled her into his arms, but she kept her gaze focused on his chest. "I'm not going to see you again, am I?"

She jerked her head up and the answer swirled in her eyes. The color had shifted back to the clear, icy blue. She licked her lips and shook her head. "It's for the best if you don't."

"And if I say I want to? Does that matter?"

"Don't do this," she said softly. "Just let me leave, okay?"

Valentino released her and stepped back. For several moments she stared at him, and he silently begged her to stay, all the while knowing she wouldn't. With a little noise that might have been a sob, she turned away and yanked the door open to run out of his life. Once the sound of her retreat faded away, he closed the door and leaned his forehead against it. It was wrong to feel such a loss, but for some reason he had formed an attachment with Sera, and the thought of never seeing her again burned more than the wound on his neck.

Maybe she'd change her mind? Maybe she'd miss the taste of his blood and come back for more? Maybe he'd find a way to rewind time and alter what they both were? Yeah...maybe, maybe, maybe.

****

Sera drew to a halt in the center of the main floor as Becca stepped in front of her.

"Where are you racing to?" she asked.

Sera prayed there was no blood on her lips. "I'm done...I mean...um...I'm heading home."

Becca cocked her head and slid her gaze from Sera's eyes all the way to her feet then back again. "You look odd. Are you all right?"

Sera nodded and grabbed her friend's hand to pull her with her as she headed for the exit. "I'm fine. Just tired."

Becca giggled at that, but made no comment as she followed Sera out of the club and to their cars. The silence didn't last. "Did you do it?"

Sera dropped her keys, cursed, then stooped to pick them up. "Um...yeah." She fumbled to unlock the door but finally managed. She looked toward Becca and forced a smile. "See you at work tomorrow night?" Before Becca could do more than gape, Sera slid into the driver's seat and slammed the door. The old Mustang roared to life and she peeled away from the curb without a backward glance.

Dear God, what had she done!

She licked her lips and tasted Valentino. She swallowed and tasted Valentino. Even sighing brought the taste of him back. She needed to get home and drown herself in some good ole fashion synthetic blood. Her stomach twisted at the prospect.

"Well, get used to it," she said out loud. "I don't plan on losing control ever again."

The shrill ring of her cell phone nearly sent her off the road. After taking a deep breath and checking all her mirrors, she reached over to pop open the glove box. She pulled out the phone and flipped it open. "Hello?"

"Welcome back, Seraphina," an all too familiar voice purred in her ear. "I've missed you."

Ice cold shock slithered down her spine, and she pulled off the road to park in front of a small barber shop. She turned off her car and gripped the wheel as tightly as she gripped the phone. "What do you want, Constantine?"

"For a moment I was afraid you wouldn't recognize my voice."

Sera gritted her teeth. She didn't believe for an instant that it was a coincidence to hear from her maker on the very night she had tasted human blood again. But why? Constantine had made it very clear he wanted nothing to do with a "weak, pathetic excuse for a vampire" the night he had literally kicked her out of his home. If he had called only to gloat, she wasn't in the mood. "I'll hang up if you don't tell me why you called."

"Careful, my pet, I am the only one in this little relationship powerful enough to issue threats."

Her knuckles turned white against the black steering wheel. "We have no relationship." To be honest, they never had, even in the very beginning when she believed he had loved her.

"Tsk, tsk, my pet. Would you believe me if I told you I merely wished to touch base after all these...centuries?"

"No," she ground out.

Constantine's seductive chuckle vibrated in her ear. It was a sound she had never wished to hear again. "Very well," he went on. "If you wish to know my real reason for calling, I shall tell you."

She waited with her breath lodged in her throat.

"Tell me why you caved, my pet? Why after all this time did you allow yourself the ecstasy of a real feed?"

Sera released her pent up breath and dropped her head against the seat. "I don't know why." Of course, Constantine would see right through the lie.

"Oh my dear, dear Seraphina, you cannot lie to me. Have you forgotten that?"

"No," she said between her teeth.

"Then tell me the truth." The tone of Constantine's voice warned her not to disobey.

"I lost control, but I'm not sure why."

"Perhaps the sex is to blame?"

She stared hard out the windshield as Constantine's words echoed in her ear. How could she have forgotten how easy it was for him to step into her thoughts? Too late she attempted to erect a mental wall between them, but his laughter showed her the futility of her ways. "My life is none of your business," she snapped. "You kicked me out, remember? You didn't want me anymore, remember?"

Her raised voice bounced around the interior of the car. God, she sounded like a harridan. "You said I was too weak and pathetic, remember? So what difference does it make to you if I decide to fuck every guy in this town?"

"My, my," Constantine purred. "Such language, my pet. You shock me."

Sera hissed into the phone then snapped it shut, ending the call. Knowing Constantine, he'd call again and keep calling until he had all the answers he wanted from her. Well, he could go fry in the sun for all she cared. Rolling the window down, she threw the phone into the other lane and watched a yellow cab run it over. "Take that, you bastard."

****

Sera arrived home and unlocked her door to the sound of her phone ringing. She rolled her eyes and answered it without turning on any lights. "You can't take a hint, can you?"

Constantine laughed. "I believe you were telling me about your sex toy before we were rudely cut off."

With a sigh of defeat, she plopped onto her couch and stared into the darkest corner of her tiny living room. "Why does any of this matter?"

"Listen, my pet—"

"Please stop calling me that."

"How nice of you to say please."

Sera rolled her eyes. "I'm tired, Constantine, can we get this conversation over with before dawn?"

"You realize, my pet, if you had shown this much spunk while we were together, I might have kept you."

"Yea, for me."

He chuckled in her ear. "Had you thought to call me, I would have warned you that losing control in any aspect of your life would awaken your instinctive hunger."

She blinked at the sudden rush of information and sat up a little straighter. "Will it happen again?"

"Do you plan on losing control again? Sexually or otherwise?"

"I'm not going to answer that."

"No need," Constantine said smartly. "If you keep your distance from Valentino, then you should be able to once again suppress your desires."

Sera had gone very still at the mention of Valentino's name. "How did you know his name?" The question echoed around the room and came back sounding strained.

"My dear," Constantine chided. "Do you believe you must live under my roof to maintain our bond? You cannot be that naive. With very little effort I can see your thoughts and even experience what you do. Your eyes, when I wish them to be, are mine."

She clenched the phone. "Well, before you get all excited by the prospect of using my life to get free kicks, you should know I'm not planning on losing control ever again."

"So you say."

"What does *that* mean?"

It was Constantine's turn to sigh. "You have tasted his blood, my pet. Doing so will not allow your hunger to subside as easily as it once did. You'll crave him now, and in time, you will return to him."

"You're wrong." She'd stay far away from Captive Fantasy. She'd have to come up with a valid reason to do so once Becca started asking questions, but she'd deal with that later. "If you're done spouting dire pronouncements in my ear, I'd like to go to bed."

"One more thing, my pet." After a moment of silence, Constantine went on. "If you need me, do not hesitate to call."

"I will never need you." With that she hung up.

Unfortunately she couldn't hang up on the memories Constantine's voice stirred. Images of a long ago night filtered into her mind, and she lay down and curled up as they demanded to be seen. Candles flickered, voices murmured over the sounds of music, and Constantine bowed over her hand. She flinched as she watched herself accept the gesture. How could something so innocent looking lead to such disaster? If only she had known better.

They danced all night long, scandalizing everyone present at the masked celebration, but she felt safe behind her disguise. Come morning, she need only pretend that she had never left her bed. Her father would never know the truth.

The final dance ended, and Constantine escorted her away from the heat of the fire and deeper into the crisp night air. He offered his long black cloak when she shivered, and she wrapped herself in it and inhaled his scent. He watched her with a smile on his lips.

"You are more beautiful than any other woman here tonight."

His voice made her shiver all over again. She blushed under her mask and dipped her chin to her chest. She'd waited a long time to hear such things.

He lifted her face with a single finger. "Do not be shy." He stepped closer, and his hand slid to her nape. "Do you kiss with as much elegance as you dance?"

The question rendered her speechless.

He pressed his mouth to hers. She parted her lips and let his tongue push inside. She could taste the lingering flavor of champagne and something else...something strange and metallic. Had he cut the inside of his mouth somehow?

Her thoughts could not compete with the thrill of being kissed, so she let them go. His possession of her intensified and the embrace became heated. With her back pressed to a rough tree trunk, he cupped her breasts through her stiff bodice and kneaded her aching flesh. All the while, his tongue stroked her mouth with languid movements that brought a strange fire to her loins. She could barely catch her breath as he pulled back to end the kiss.

He nuzzled the side of her neck. "How much are you willing to give me, my pet?"

She didn't know how to answer such a question. Focusing on the spill of black hair over his pale cheek, she shook her head and whispered, "Your behavior confuses me, and I find myself at a loss." Was this love?

He lifted his head and stared at her through coal black eyes. No mask hid his features from her and the beauty of their perfection continued to mesmerize her. "Grant me one more kiss, and I'll see you safely back to the celebration."

Dare she?

He touched her lips lightly with the tip of one finger. "Just one more kiss, my pet. It is all I ask, and then I vow to let you go."

She nodded and leaned her head back against the tree. She tipped her face up, but he did not aim for her mouth. His lips touched the side of her neck followed by a sharp stinging pain. She gasped, but before she could push him away, the pain turned to unbelievable pleasure. It coursed from her neck down to her loins and she trembled under the force of it. His strong body pinned her to the tree and she could feel the hard press of his arousal against the front of her gown. With a little whimper, she shifted her hips forward and the world exploded behind her lids in a spray of white light...

Sera jerked her eyes open and looked around.

Regardless of how vivid the memory had been, she was safe and sound in her apartment. On shaky legs, she headed for her bedroom, knowing the images of that fateful night would be hard to wipe away. Damn Constantine for bringing them all back. No doubt it would thrill him to know she recalled the pleasure of his first bite, and how it had brought her to orgasm. Her first and last orgasm, until Valentino stripped away her defenses with his expert touch. Not to mention the sweet taste of his blood.

She wouldn't think of that. Everything would be just fine if she avoided men in general from now on. How hard could that be? She slept all day and worked in a closed library all night. Yes, that's what she'd do. No more men. Ever.

She crawled into bed, chanting the new mantra over and over again.

Chapter Nine

"Hey, Val, you need to wake up."

The voice sliced into the dream Valentino was having, but it did little to rouse him. He mumbled into the pillow and chased after the retreating images of Sera sprawled in his bed.

"Val! Let's go." A rough hand on his back accompanied the voice this time. It shook him until he had no choice but to lift his head off the pillow. "You need to get up now or you'll miss your chance to catch a ride."

Once a month the employees—if you could call them that—of Captive Fantasy were granted one day of leisure. They could do anything they wished, as long as no one left the club alone and everyone returned before curfew. Valentino always spent the day with Raphael and Aiden, but he didn't feel much like carousing today. The moment his head left the pillow, a sharp pain sliced through his neck.

With a moan, he gave into it and landed face down.

"Hey," Raphael said. "Are you sick?"

Valentino lifted his head again, and the pain returned. *Jesus.* Rolling to his back, he blinked up at Raphael then rubbed the sleep from his eyes. "I feel like shit."

"You don't look so good either."

Valentino lowered his hand. "Really?"

"Really," Raphael nodded. "You've got a hell of a mark on your neck, and I don't want to be you when Dr. Reynolds sees it."

His neck? He felt around under his tangled hair and discovered a large section of puckered skin that was really hot to the touch. Despite the pain that now traveled from his neck down to the rest of his body, he sat up and shook his hair back. "It's the bite," he mumbled.

Raphael arched a golden brow. "Excuse me?"

Valentino ignored his friend's curiosity. "Where were we headed today?"

"Wherever," Raphael said with a shrug, though he was dressed in sweats and a tank top. Clearly, he had the neighborhood gym in mind.

Of course, Captive Fantasy had its own facility, but Raphael wasn't alone in his desire to workout without cameras tracking his every rep.

Still holding his hand over the wound on his neck, Valentino forced himself out of bed and stumbled toward the bathroom. "You and Aiden can do whatever you want, but I need to pay someone a visit."

"Who?"

Valentino gripped the side of the bathroom door for balance as a fresh wave of pain and a healthy dose of nausea rolled through him. What the fuck had Sera done to him? He glanced back across the room to meet Raphael's concerned gaze. "I need to find the woman I spent last night with."

"Shouldn't be hard. You have her name, age, and occupation—"

"No, I don't." Valentino silenced Raphael with a sharp shake of his head before the other guy could give voice to any questions. "Don't ask, okay? I've already been read the riot act from the good doctor, but that doesn't change the fact that I need to know how and where to find her. And fast."

"Did she come alone?"

Valentino shook his head. "Both nights she was with a curvy little redhead."

Something shifted on Raphael's face. "Was the friend wearing pink and red, by any chance?"

"Might have been." Valentino searched his memory, but to be honest, once Sera caught his attention other women faded into the background.

"Well, if that's the redhead that came with your client, her name was Becca and she works at the downtown library."

A library? Somehow that seemed like the perfect place for Sera to work as well. "Then we'll assume it's her, and you guys can drop me at the library on your way to wherever."

"And if your client doesn't work at the library?"

Valentino stumbled into the bathroom, the tiled walls spinning around him. "Then her friend will know where I can find her."

"Aiden and I will stay with you."

Shaking his head caused the room to spin faster. Valentino reached out toward the wall and missed. He heard Raphael swear then felt his friend's arms around his shoulders.

"What the fuck is the matter with you?"

Valentino didn't know, but he needed Sera, and he needed her now.

****

After much arguing, Raphael and Aiden agreed to drop Valentino off in front of the library. He promised to get back to the club before curfew, and they had no choice but to believe him. Their expressions weren't happy as they drove away.

The library was a huge towering monstrosity of brick and stone, and although Valentino had been aware of it being here, he'd never stepped foot inside. Not that he didn't like to read, he just preferred to buy his books, rather than borrow them. He pulled the heavy front door open and was instantly assailed with the smell of old leather and stained wood. The building had a homey feel, despite its size and ominous appearance, and he could easily imagine Sera flitting around between the tall stacks of books.

A quick survey of the place didn't reveal her though, so he headed for the center circular desk and the unfriendly looking man behind it. "Excuse me," Valentino whispered.

The man jerked his head up from whatever task he was doing on the computer and scowled over the top of his tiny reading glasses. He had to be at least ninety years old, given the amount of wrinkles and age spots on his face, and his wild nest of hair was pure white. He shoved his glasses up his nose and scowled some more. "I think you're lost, young man."

The reply forced Valentino to step back. He almost glanced down at himself just to see what it might be that proclaimed him unfit to step foot in a library, but he knew there was nothing strange about his blue jeans and red t-shirt. With a smile, he chose to ignore the old man's rudeness. "I was hoping you could help me locate someone."

"This is a library, not the police department." With that, the old troll gave the computer his full attention again.

Valentino refused to be deterred. Leaning his elbows on the countertop, he dangled a hand over and gripped one of the man's fragile wrists. The guy looked up and arched a fluffy white brow, but he didn't seem the least bit cowed.

"I suggest you take your hand off of me, young man."

Valentino kept his hand just where it was. "I'm looking for a woman named Sera who might work here."

"I'm not entitled to give out personal information." Surprisingly, the old guy pulled free of Valentino's grip. "And before you ask," he went on, "that doesn't mean she works here."

It was obvious he wouldn't make any headway by continuing to badger the troll. With a nod and a sarcastic thank you, Valentino spun around and headed for the exit. Damn. Now what? Before he could shove the door open, a woman sidled up to his side and put her hand on

74

his arm. He looked over, thinking the gorgeous blonde looked vaguely familiar.

"Did I hear you asking about Sera?" she whispered.

Valentino's heart raced. "I did, yes. Does she work here? Is she here now?"

The blonde smiled and slid her hand off his arm to extend it toward him. "My name is Jennifer."

He shook her hand, anxious to have his questions answered. "I'm charmed."

Clearly the response didn't please Jennifer, and a frown replaced her bright smile before she answered him. "Yes, she works here, but only at night."

Of course! If he'd taken a minute to think this plan through, he would have realized vampires sleep during the day. Way to go, genius.

"I can give you her address though," Jennifer stepped close to whisper. "I'm not allowed, but..." she shrugged and lowered her gaze to his chest. She licked her lips, and Valentino's instincts kicked into high gear.

The information was going to cost him, but he'd deal with that later. "I'm listening.

Jennifer glanced up, her smile back in place. "Are you working tonight?"

Valentino sighed. "Yes."

"Make sure I can have you, and I'll give you Sera's address."

He didn't agree or disagree, he simply winked, but it was enough for Jennifer. She rattled off Sera's address, and he left before she could coerce him into more favors.

Sera's apartment was a short walk from the library, so it only took Valentino a few minutes to get there. He didn't have any trouble convincing a young woman to buzz him in to the lobby, nor did he have any problem locating apartment number sixty-nine on the sixth floor. The number made him chuckle and visualize a lovely fantasy.

He knocked on the door, not sure if he should expect a response or not. Did vampires really sleep like the dead all day long? If so, he could knock until his knuckles bled and she'd never hear him. Stepping back, he glanced up and down the hallway before lowering his gaze to the mat under his feet. On a whim, he hunkered down and turned up a corner to find a spare key. He'd have to warn Sera not to be so obvious.

Once inside, he placed the key on a nearby table then shut and locked the door. Her place was exactly what he might have expected, had he taken the time to give it any thought. White slipcovers with tiny red roses covered the couch and two oversized chairs. Mismatched throw pillows were haphazardly arranged on all three pieces of furniture and larger pillows were stacked in the corner next to a wooden, TV armoire. The apartment walls were painted very pale blue and the carpet on the floor was off-white. All in all it was peaceful and really girly.

He liked it.

A small area, set aside for eating, separated the living room from the kitchen, and branching off of the kitchen was a narrow hallway that led to a floral bathroom and a closed door. He assumed the closed door led to Sera's bedroom, and for a moment he debated whether or not he should invade her privacy.

The moment didn't last long.

He turned the knob and stepped into the pitch black room. Christ, wasn't there a window? Carefully, he picked his way inside until the bed bumped his shins. Part of him was a little freaked out about being in a dark room with a vampire, but he needed answers about the bite she'd given him, and he doubted she'd actually harm him.

"Sera?" The sound of his voice echoed around the room, but he heard nothing in response. Feeling his way along the side of the bed, he reached out and encountered the unmistakable hump of a female hip. So, she *was* sleeping the day away. He'd just have to wait until she woke up. He turned to make his way back to the living room, but the nausea from earlier rolled in his stomach and stopped him in his tracks.

Maybe it would be best to lie down?

He stripped out of his shoes, jeans, and tee and then decided to just leave them where they fell. The room was too damn dark to attempt to move around in. Fighting down another wave of nausea, he stretched out on top of the blanket Sera was snuggled under and prayed vampires didn't wake up too hungry to think straight.

Chapter Ten

Very little could disturb a vampire's slumber, but the sound of a steady heartbeat and the warmth of mortal flesh certainly did the trick. Sera's fang dug into her bottom lip as her senses reached out toward the warm body at her side. In addition to the steady beat of a heart, she smelled the musky fragrance of male skin. She moaned quietly and shifted closer, keeping her eyes shut just in case it was all a dream.

Sliding her hand forward, she touched the warm solid mass of a bicep, then kept moving until her fingers were splayed out over a bare chest. Beneath her palm, the heartbeat continued to thump regularly. It was still early in the day, the feeling of sluggishness told her that much, but that didn't mean she wasn't waking up hungry. She scooted even closer and finally opened her eyes. Her gasp sounded loud in the quiet room.

Valentino? What was *he* doing here?

Seeing him only intensified her hunger. The taste of his blood still lingered in her mouth and her memory, and the hardest thing in the world she'd ever done was roll away from him and get out of bed. She needed a drink fast, or he'd wake up to the feel of her teeth in his neck. Immune to the complete darkness of the room, she located her robe, shrugged into it, and headed for the door. An unexpected pile of clothing tripped her, stalling her just long enough to give Valentino enough time to stir.

"Hey," he called out.

Sera gripped the door knob and looked over her

shoulder. Oh God. He'd removed all of his clothing except a pair of navy boxer briefs, and the sight of him stretched out on top of her red toile sheets was too much. He shifted onto his elbows and narrowed his gaze. She knew he couldn't really see her in the dark.

"Where are you running to?"

Sera swallowed, hoping to alleviate some of her hunger. It didn't work. Her fangs throbbed, her tongue worked the roof of her mouth, and her veins cried for fresh blood. "I need to get something to drink." She didn't offer anything more as she ripped the door open and fled the room.

Once in the safety of her kitchen, she unsealed a fresh bag of blood and filled a mug. Valentino appeared, looking a little rumpled and way too sexy, just as the microwave dinged. Sera tried to ignore him as she snatched the hot mug out. She burned her lip with the first sip and swore softly. After blowing on the contents for a few moments, she drank almost half without stopping. All the while, Valentino watched her.

"Can you shut the drapes in the living room?" she asked, without looking at him. She wasn't technically supposed to be awake, and her apartment was annoyingly flooded with sunlight. Already her eyes burned.

Valentino glanced over his shoulder, then nodded and did as she asked. Sera took the opportunity to stare as he strolled away. The boxer briefs cupped his backside and accentuated the muscles in his thighs. Hell, even his spine was sexy.

Great, now she was hungry and horny. She tore her gaze from Valentino's glorious body and drank more blood. Why wasn't this working? A mug full should more than take the edge off her hunger, but it wasn't. Her fangs hit the rim as she tossed back the last drop then headed to the fridge for more. She'd feel like a glutton if she drank another bag, but Valentino wouldn't know the difference.

"Is it safe for you to be awake?" He inquired from

across the room. Without being asked, he came back into the kitchen and shut the curtain over the sink. Propped against the counter, with his arms over his chest, he watched her prepare a second mug of blood. "Do you always drink this much?"

She ignored the second question. "As long as I avoid the windows and the lovely sun, I'll be fine." Sera slammed the microwave door and hit the numbers. Damn, her hand was shaking. She glanced toward Valentino, and his expression left little doubt that he had noticed the state she was in. Did he realize he was to blame? "Why are you here?" She shook her head. "*How* are you here?"

"I did a bit of investigative work." He flashed a triumphant smile that nearly knocked her over. "It would have been easier if I knew your full name and what you do for a living."

Sera watched the green numbers on the microwave. Why were they going so slow? She began to tap her nails on the counter. "Seraphina Scala, and I work at the library downtown."

Valentino chuckled. "Yeah, aside from the full name, I knew the part about the library."

She jerked her gaze up. "How?" The microwave finished, but she ignored it and waited for Valentino's answer.

He shrugged and lowered his arms to brace his hands on the counter. Doing so pulled her attention to the perfection of his chest. He didn't seem to realize the display he was putting on. Though why would he? He was paid to display his body. "A friend of yours spent the evening with a friend of mine, and he told me where she worked. I figured if you didn't actually work with her, she'd at least tell me how to find you."

Sera glanced at the clock on top of the fridge, then back toward Valentino. "Becca doesn't work this early, and I don't believe for a second Mr. Henry gave out any information."

"Is he the old troll behind the desk?"

The description was dead on. Sera laughed and finally took her mug out of the microwave. The first sip wasn't so painful this time. "Yeah, that would be my boss."

"Friendly guy." Valentino's tone said otherwise. "You're right though, he didn't help at all. But Jennifer did."

Sera hid her irritation behind her mug. No doubt Jennifer had only helped after exacting some price from Valentino. One didn't need to be a genius to figure out what, either.

"She told me where you lived, and here I am." He spread his arms as if to say, come and get me.

Sera lowered her mug and cradled it in both hands. "And what do you owe her now? Or should I say, how many nights?" The jealous edge in her tone bothered her, but she was still too hungry to focus on tempering her mood.

"Does it matter?"

Did it? Should it? Sera took another drink instead of answering.

Valentino sighed and crossed his arms again. "Look, it doesn't matter what I had to agree to, to get Jennifer to help me, what matters is that I'm here and I need to ask you some questions."

"I'm listening."

Valentino cocked his head to the side, drawing attention to the angry mark on his neck. "Is it supposed to look like this?"

Sera stepped closer and stared at the puckered flesh. "I have no idea." It was nasty looking though. Maybe she'd been too violent?

"What do you mean, you don't know?" He glared at her from behind some roguish strands of sable hair. "I doubt I'm the first person you've fed off of."

"Maybe you are," Sera mumbled on her way out of the kitchen. She headed back into the dark sanctuary of her room, her mug still clutched in her hand. Maybe

Valentino would take a hint and leave? She didn't want him here, looking good enough to eat, nor did she want to talk about being a vampire. Yes, the bite she'd given him looked spooky, but she'd never heard of any mortal dying from one little bite. It took more than that. Didn't it?

Wonderful. Now she was hungry, horny and scared that her bite might actually harm Valentino. Was it too late to pretend she'd never woken up?

****

Valentino was too stunned to move for several moments, but eventually he shoved away from the counter and followed Sera. He stepped into her room just as she was settling into the center of the bed. He left the door open to allow some light to filter in. She sipped her blood and completely ignored him. Despite the cold shoulder act, she looked damn cute wrapped in her big terrycloth robe with her hands wrapped around the mug that read "My ex-boyfriend is a vampire."

The irony wasn't lost on him.

"How long have you been a vampire?"

She answered without looking up. "Three centuries, give or take a decade or two."

Jesus, she was over three hundred years old? It took a moment to digest that. "How can I be your first?"

She lifted her cup and her gaze. "Synthetic blood is a wonderful invention."

Valentino frowned. "That couldn't have been around three hundred years ago." How would Dr. Reynolds feel if he discovered he hadn't cornered the market on engineered blood?

"No, it wasn't around until just a few years ago. In the beginning I fed off of animals."

Valentino tried not to flinch, but he failed, and Sera dropped her gaze again. Cautiously, he approached the bed, aware of her watching him through her lashes. "I thought vampires had to feed off of humans?" She stiffened, and he regretted the question. "But I could be wrong."

She looked up and shook her hair off her forehead. "We don't have to, but those of us who choose not to are considered outcasts."

The pain in her voice drew him closer to the bed. He wanted to snuggle up next to her and hold her. He wanted to offer comfort, instead of sex, but he sensed she might refuse. He stayed where he was, feeling helpless and more than a little out of his element. "Outcasts from what? Do you have like a coven or something?" He'd seen movies and read books, after all.

With a resolved sigh, she reached across the bed to put her empty mug on the little nightstand. "You aren't going to stop with the questions, are you?"

He shook his head and took a seat on the bed. He didn't miss the way her gaze roamed over his body. Yeah, he wanted her, too. "I'm sorry if my curiosity bothers you, but you're the first vampire I've met."

"You can't know that for certain. I'm just the first one to bite you."

Okay, he'd concede that point. He directed her gaze toward his neck with a gesture. "So, why does it look this bad, and why did I feel like shit when I woke up this morning?"

"I really don't know, Valentino." Regret oozed from her reply and her gaze as she swung her eyes to meet his. "I'm sorry." She licked her lips and lowered her attention to his neck again.

It was hard to misinterpret the look on her face. "Are you still hungry, Sera?" Lord, was he offering to feed her?

She nodded without meeting his gaze and licked her lips again. Each pass of her tongue might as well have been over his dick. He shifted to alleviate the weight of his erection. "I'm not so sure another bite is a good idea."

Her focus flew to his face. "Then maybe you shouldn't make the offer," she bit out. He'd never seen her angry, and the glow in her eyes was mesmerizing.

"I didn't."

With an enraged snarl, she crawled off the bed and

83

stood glaring down at him. He decided not to tell her that her robe was gaping open. "Just being here, in my room, looking like that," she waved at him and shook her head, "is a damn invitation to bite you."

"Sorry."

"Ugh!" She whipped around and headed back out the door. This time he caught her before she could escape. She spun around in his arms and fisted her hands against his chest. "Let me go!"

"Calm down, Sera."

She lifted her burning eyes to his face and her nostrils flared. "Calm down? I can't calm down, for your information. In fact, telling me to *calm down* is like telling a grizzly about to attack that you don't mean it any harm."

"You aren't a wild animal." Though she sort of looked like one, with her eyes blazing and her jaw clenching and unclenching. The hint of fang peeking over her bottom lip didn't help either. Maybe he should go?

"No, Valentino," she said in a surprisingly calm tone, "I'm not a wild animal." She spread her hands open over his chest and pushed him toward the bed. He went a little too willingly, his body still eager and rock hard to have her naked and shrieking his name. "I'm a monster."

One good shove and he was flat on his back, and she was crawling over him. He barely had time to grip her hips before she encircled his throat with her cool hands and lowered her face close to his.

"You have no idea what I'm capable of," she warned.

He knew she expected a spark of fear to show in his eyes, but damnit, he'd never been so turned on in his life. "So show me."

Her lids drifted over her icy eyes, and she curled her lips back enough to flash more than just the tips of her fangs. He probably needed therapy for thinking she looked sexy.

She swept her tongue over her pointy teeth, then across her bottom lip. "I've never done this."

"Done what?" Valentino had to force the words out over the loud cadence of his breathing.

"I've never pinned a mortal down to feed from them." Her gaze locked on his neck.

"You like it, don't you? You like having me at your mercy. I can tell by the look in your eyes." Maybe it was dangerous to taunt her, but if she didn't bite him soon, he'd beg for it.

She dragged in a deep breath of air and tightened her hands around his throat. "I don't want to do this," she ground out. "I want you to get the hell out of here, so I'm not forced to do this."

"No one is forcing you, and I want it."

Something snapped. It was hard to say if it was in her eyes, or in her entire body, but he felt a change come over her. Her fingers flexed at his neck and her thighs tightened around his waist. At some point, the robe had come completely undone. Maybe when she'd crawled on top of him? It gaped to reveal her breasts and flat belly, and he had to curl his fingers into her hips to resist fondling her.

"What's it gonna be, baby?" he prompted. "Are you gonna bite me, or should I just flip you onto your back and fuck you?"

Chapter Eleven

Sera's whole body shuddered with the force of her groan. Valentino certainly knew right where to hit a girl. She stared down at him, trying to ignore the pulse of his tendons under her fingers. Easier said than done. Every time he swallowed, his skin pulled against her fingers, making her fangs ache. What would be the harm in biting him? She'd done it once and they'd both survived.

Her gaze strayed to the mark just barely visible above her hand. Why *did* it look so angry?

"Plan on answering in the near future?" His voice pulled her attention to his face.

He grinned, and she wanted to growl at him. "I do not want to bite you." It was true. Sort of. Her fangs certainly wanted to sink into his skin, and her veins all but wept for his blood, but her conscience did not want to do it. Acting like a monster had never been her gig.

"How 'bout option number two?" The grin turned down right naughty.

Sera's body melted in a pool of lust, and she stretched out on top of Valentino to seal her lips over his. He kissed her long and hard while his fingers dug into her hip bones. Between her legs, his erection strained against the flimsy confines of his underwear to tease her exposed sex. The smell of her arousal was sharp in the air.

Breathing harder than ever, she pulled back from his kiss to look him in the eyes. "What is it about you?" she whispered. His questioning gaze made her elaborate. "Why do you have this effect on me?"

His hands slid from her hips to cup her bottom. He squeezed her through the thick robe. "You're just lucky, I guess."

She doubted luck had anything at all to do with it, but she let the matter go.

"Take your robe off, baby."

Again, her body pulsed in response to his smooth voice, and she was helpless not to obey. Sitting back up on his lap, she shrugged the robe off and left it pooled over his thighs. Very aware of his wandering gaze, she held still and tried not to let her anxieties get the better of her.

Constantine had enjoyed looking at her in the beginning, but then his gaze had turned ugly and disinterested. She'd never survive seeing the same change come over Valentino. Not that she cared to analyze why that was.

She looked away from his face to focus on the safety of her closet door.

Valentino cupped her breasts and shoved them together. His low sound of approval captured her attention, and he winked when she caught his eye. "Come here." He urged her forward with the grip he had on her until she hovered over his mouth. He bit her left nipple without so much as a warning lick, and Sera squeaked at the pleasure. "Too bad I don't have fangs," he murmured, before taking another bite.

"They get in the way," Sera forced out. God, she wanted to press down and rub against the hard line of Valentino's teeth. She wanted to bleed. She wanted him to have fangs as well. The thought made her groan, and she squeezed her eyes shut and dug her hands into the bedding near Valentino's shoulders. He continued to pull at her sensitized nipple, and just when she thought she'd climax as a result of the fixed attention, he moved to the other one.

The first nip of his teeth caused another squeak. She sucked air through her clenched teeth and considered begging him to stop. The words never came.

He stopped his biting and licked her for a few moments before taking his mouth away altogether. "Let me get naked."

Oh man...were there four more beautiful words in the English language?

Sera scooted off Valentino's lap, still a little uneasy that she was allowing this to happen. Constantine had warned her about losing control again. Was it possible not to with Valentino? He removed his boxer briefs by lifting his hips off the bed, then he looked her way as he dropped them over the side. Naked and glorious, he held out his hand to her.

She was in serious trouble.

Sera took Valentino's hand and straddled him once more. He reared up between her legs, parting her feminine curls and tormenting her swollen sex. The only way to stay in control would be to take control. But did she dare? Did she even know how? Tamping down her nerves, she reached for his penis. He flexed within her grip, and she watched his face as she stroked him from root to tip.

"Is it all right if I set the pace?"

He nodded, clearly unable to speak. His adam's apple bobbed up and down with every hard swallow, and his nostrils flared in time to the tick in his jaw.

Still holding onto his thick erection, she got to her knees and put him at her opening. A little experience would have been nice right about now, but she assumed some things were just instinctive. Pressing down, she slid her hand away and took as much of him as she could. Turned out that was about half. With a gasp, she stilled and fell forward onto her hands. Doing so put her breasts over Valentino's mouth, and he didn't hesitate to take advantage.

While her thighs quivered and her vagina did its best to stretch, he cupped her and laved at her with his tongue. "Oh God..."

Unconsciously, her body accepted the rest of his

length, and she climaxed the moment he was fully imbedded within her. Hanging her head and closing her eyes, she rode out the pulses of her orgasm. There was no end in sight as Valentino continued to suckle her breasts.

His hands found her hips, and he coaxed her to move. He released her nipple. "Ride me."

Sera dug her fangs into her bottom lip and complied. The moment she did, Valentino latched back onto her nipple and sucked it deep into his mouth. He bit her rather hard, awakening the one urge she didn't need right now. Behind her tight lids, she saw her face aiming for his neck. In her mouth, she tasted his blood, only to realize it was her blood.

Her fangs had torn her bottom lip.

With a little groan, Sera licked the blood away, hoping it would erase her desire for Valentino's. No such luck.

He deserted her breast and gripped her waist to move her upright. Their eyes locked, then she watched his gaze lower toward her mouth. A little frown indicated he'd noticed the blood staining her lip. "You're bleeding."

Sera nodded, not sure what to say. She licked her lip again, knowing the wound would close before long. There was really no need for Valentino to look so concern—

He reached for her and cupped the back of her head to pull her face down to his. He kissed her hard, and his tongue feathered right over the slit in her lip. If she didn't know any better, she'd say he actually sucked fresh blood from the wound. But he wouldn't wish to do that, would he?

****

Wanting to taste Sera's blood was a surprise, but Valentino didn't regret his actions for one second once his mouth was sealed over hers. He sucked and sipped at her wounded lip until fresh blood pooled on his tongue, then he swallowed it down after savoring the odd flavor of it. It reminded him of the time he'd placed a penny between his lips while digging in his pocket for more change. Lost in the recollection, he didn't realize Sera meant to pull away until her mouth was no longer crushed to his.

"Stop it," she breathed while struggling to sit up on his lap.

He blinked up at her and slowly ran his tongue across his lips. It didn't escape his notice how she watched the action like a hungry hawk. If she wanted to bite him so damn bad, why not just do it? He wouldn't mind. Maybe if he arched his head back and begged for it, she'd relent?

Or she'd slip off of him and make a beeline for the door?

That would be beyond annoying considering how incredibly good it felt to be sheathed inside her. The thought centered his focus on the joining of their bodies and he moved under her until she gasped adorably and bit her lip. If she wasn't careful, she'd bleed again.

"Do you want me on top?"

She blinked, looking a little confused by the offer, then shook her head and spread her hands over his chest. "No...I...like this."

So did he.

Concentrating his efforts with renewed purpose, he held her hips immobile against his pelvis and thrust up into her, determined to watch her climax again. When her lips parted and her lids lowered, he knew he almost had her. "Gonna come for me, baby?"

Her eyes sprang open, and she dug her fangs into her bottom lip. The nod she offered was barely discernable, but he had no problem feeling the first powerful clench of her inner muscles. She gripped tight enough to nearly undo him, and he gritted his teeth and did his best to ignore the tightening in his balls. It didn't matter if he ended before she found her pleasure, but old habits were hard to break. He wanted her panting and happy; not because it was his job, but because he couldn't think of single thing lovelier.

Her nails raked over his chest, and she tossed her

head back with a stifled gasp. Around his thrusting dick, she convulsed a few times and then liquefied with a single shudder. He couldn't take anymore. Closing his eyes and arching his head back into the bed, Valentino bucked up one more time and spilled his seed deep inside Sera.

Before the dazed bliss of his orgasm had a chance to wear off, the sharp sting of teeth pierced the skin just below his right ear. Sera's soft hair tickled his cheek, and he could feel the sporadic rise and fall of her breasts where they lay crammed against his chest. Not wanting to scare her away, he relaxed into her bite as the last pulse of his climax faded away.

****

It wasn't until the sweet flavor of Valentino's blood touched the back of her tongue that Sera realized her control had snapped. By then, it was too late. His skin was trapped between her teeth, and his hands had gone limp against her hips. It was surrender, pure and simple, on both their parts, and she didn't have any desire to stop.

She drank until her skin grew almost too hot to bear. She'd never felt like this before. Even her first time feeding from Valentino hadn't felt this...right. Not really wishing to, but knowing she must, she slid her fangs free and eased her mouth away from his tempting skin. His eyes slid to hers the moment she lifted her face. "Sorry," she mumbled.

He shook his head and wrapped his arms around her waist to flatten her atop his body. "I told you it was all right. There was no reason for you to fight the urge as long as you did."

He'd never really understand, so she let it go. "What time do you have to go?" she asked against the steady pulse in his throat. Now that she was gleefully full of blood, the rhythm soothed instead of taunted.

"Curfew is at eight."

Sera lifted her head. "Curfew? You mean for the club? Do you *live* there?"

Instead of answering, he rolled her off him, then

snuggled up to her back. "We'll talk about all that later, okay? How about we just enjoy what's going on here for the moment."

Sera stared across the room, focusing on the front of her chest of drawers. "What is going on?"

Valentino sighed behind her, ruffling her hair and sending a little shiver down her spine. "I don't know."

Yeah, neither did she.

After a few moments, she couldn't take the silence. "Valentino?"

"Hmm?"

"How long have you worked at Captive Fantasy?" He shifted his arms around her and she wondered if he might refuse to answer. It was a harmless question, wasn't it?

"A little over a year."

"Do you like it?" Sera bit her lip and stared hard without seeing a damn thing. No matter how he answered, it would irritate her. So why the heck ask the question?

He kissed her ear before answering. "It's a job, Sera." Again he squeezed her tight. "Until you..."

She held her breath, but he didn't elaborate. He sighed and nuzzled her hair, and she wanted to beg him to finish what he was going to say. Until her, what? None of the other women mattered? She was different? With her, it wasn't just sex?

"It feels good laying here with you."

The unexpected words made her press her eyes shut. It did feel good. Scary good.

How long they lay together, pretending everything must be right with the world, Sera didn't know. Eventually, Valentino stirred and mumbled his desire to take a shower before heading back to the club. She pointed him in the direction of the bathroom, then tried not to stare as he walked naked from the room. Reaching for her robe, she wondered how one developed such a blasé attitude toward nakedness.

The phone rang just as Valentino turned on the

water. Sera jumped off the bed to answer it without giving a single thought to who it might be. She instantly regretted her eagerness.

"Did it again, I see," Constantine drawled.

"Why don't you leave me alone?" She sat down hard on the bed and stared out into the hall toward the bathroom door. Valentino was humming over the sound of the water.

"It's my job, you might say, to make sure you conduct yourself accordingly and it delights me to no end to finally watch you giving in to your true nature. I should seek this Valentino out and shake his hand."

The thought sickened her. "Don't you dare."

"Why? He obviously knows what you are, and it hasn't scared him away. Quite the opposite, I'd say."

"Did you call for a reason or just to irritate me?"

Constantine clucked his tongue. "I must admit, I don't really care for the attitude that has come along with the change in you. We'll have to temper that, I believe."

"*You* bring out the worst in me, Constantine. It has nothing to do with whether or not I drink fresh blood." Or did it? A frown tugged her lips down.

"Believe what you must, my pet." His tone told her how wrong she was. "There really was a reason for my call, however."

Sera waited out the silence, refusing to appear eager.

"You'll be expected to take your place among the coven now that you've embraced what you are."

"No." She wanted no part of coven life. Her brief stay at the manor house in Nottingham, England had shown her such an existence was not for her. Just the mere thought of having to take a human servant turned her stomach.

What if it was Valentino?

She shook the annoying thought away, refusing to acknowledge its appeal.

"Regardless of what you might wish for, my pet," Constantine went on. "Your American master will expect your presence at the coven. If you do not show yourself, I'll be forced to take you there. Neither of us really wants that, do we?"

Lord, no! She could happily live out the rest of eternity without laying eyes on Constantine again. "I'll think about it," she halfheartedly conceded before hanging up. With a sigh, she closed her eyes and rubbed the ache in her temples. Only Constantine could give her this sort of headache.

"Who was that?"

Valentino's voice jerked her gaze toward the door. How long had he been standing there? Why the hell hadn't she heard him? And, Jesus Christ, could he look sexier?

His hair was ten shades darker, now that it was wet, and it clung to the side of his neck and dripped down over his shoulders. The fresh bite she'd given him was hidden, but the old one stood out against his skin, still looking angry and nasty. He had on nothing but one of her oversized, red bath towels and that was clutched precariously low on his hips. Lord, help her.

"Sera?"

She pulled her gaze from his body. "What?"

"Who was on the phone? You look upset."

She shrugged. "It was only work. No big deal."

He narrowed his gaze but didn't challenge her answer. "Do you have a razor I could borrow?"

The question drew her attention to the light dusting of stubble along his jaw and it occurred to her that it was the first sign of facial hair she'd seen. "How old are you?" The question sort of spurted out, but once she asked, her curiosity eagerly awaited the answer. Surely he was over eighteen?

Valentino frowned and took a moment to tighten the red towel around his hips. When he answered, he did so without meeting her gaze. "Twenty-two."

Oh Lord, that was young. Of course, in mortal years—ick, that made her feel like a dog or something—

she was only twenty-five, but she felt centuries older. She *was* centuries older. What was she thinking to allow someone as young as Valentino into her life?

You were having a mind blowing orgasm, you weren't thinking.

Her inner voice was fast becoming as annoying as Constantine's phone calls.

Sera became aware of Valentino's gaze. He looked unsure all of a sudden, as if he feared she'd point to the door and kick him out. Looking like that? Not bloody likely. "I'll grab a razor for you." She stood up, making sure her robe stayed tightly closed. "I hope you don't mind disposable?"

Valentino caught her as she tried to slip past him. His fingers were hot through the sleeve of her robe. "Does it matter how old I am?"

Somehow she'd known he wouldn't let this go. She shook her head. "Not at all. It's not as if you're my next boyfriend or anything."

He released her as if she'd burned him. "Yeah, right."

Damn.

Without another word, which was probably for the best, Sera hurried toward the bathroom. Valentino followed silently behind. Her hand trembled as she handed over the pink razor and she pulled back before his fingers had the chance to brush hers. "There's shaving cream above the sink, but it smells like watermelon."

His smile seemed forced. "Maybe it'll make me a hit tonight."

Okay, she deserved that, but it didn't make it hurt less. The thought of Jennifer being the one to enjoy his company tonight clawed through her insides like an angry virus. Sure, he hadn't admitted that it would be Jen, but Sera just knew. "Well, I'll let you do your thing." She motioned toward the sink and backed toward the door. "If you need anything else, just holler."

Valentino set the razor down and reached for her. Had she tried to dodge his grip, he wouldn't have been able to snare her wrist. Why hadn't she tried? He pulled her forward against his damp chest, and she inhaled the sharp scent of her body wash. Strange how the fragrance smelled entirely different on him.

"I don't want this to end here, Sera."

Neither did she, but admitting that seemed really dangerous for some reason.

He hooked a finger under her chin to force her gaze up. "Come to the club tonight, and I'll make sure you're the one I spend the night with."

"You promised Jennifer." Ugh, saying it out loud hurt more.

"I don't care. Come, and I'll be yours. I swear it."

"I can't." This had to end; they both realized that, didn't they? Better here and now, than later, after another glorious night of sex. With a shake of her head, she slid out of his grasp and hurried from the bathroom. Despite the churning in her stomach, she believed this was the best course of action.

Maybe someday Valentino would look back on this moment and agree?

Chapter Twelve

Valentino slammed the passenger door of Sera's Mustang and turned back to say good-bye. She peeled away from the curb without giving him the chance, and he could do nothing but stare after her. Damn, damn, damn.

The brief ride from her place to Captive Fantasy had been nothing but strained silence. He'd wanted to say something that would clear the air between them, but her tight expression had convinced him to keep his mouth shut. It made him wonder why she'd bothered to offer a ride, if she hadn't meant to utter a single word. Though, he could have ignored her erected wall and spoken at any point. Why the hell hadn't he?

Regret was going to be a tough pill to swallow now; especially if he never saw her again.

Shaking his head, Valentino stepped into the club and spotted Raphael waiting for him. His friend was already showered and dressed for work. Shit. So much for making curfew.

"Where the fuck have you been?" Raphael fired the question in lieu of a greeting. "We went back to the library, but there wasn't any sign of you, Becca, or the chic you were looking for. After asking the old guy at the desk if he knew anything, I figured it would be safer to leave before he decided to call the damn police. I suggest you start explaining right now."

Valentino brushed by his friend and headed through the empty club toward his room. Maybe it was the way he'd left things with Sera, or maybe it was the upcoming night and the commitment he'd made to Jennifer, but something was making him feel not so good. He wanted a nap before he had to clock in, which meant Raphael's annoying questions would have to wait.

"Not now, Raphael, okay?" Valentino tossed a look over his shoulder as he spoke and his hair slid away from his neck.

Raphael cursed under his breath. "Please tell me that isn't another bite?"

After shaking his hair forward, Valentino reached for the wound. Just like with the first one, it felt hot and sore, and it probably looked just as bad. He'd have to think of a way to cover both of them up. Too bad he hadn't thought to borrow make-up from Sera, not that she looked as if she needed any. He suspected her flawless complexion was the result of a very strict vampire diet instead of high-priced cosmetics.

"Did she bite you again, Val?"

Halting in his tracks, he turned to confront his friend. "Do I really owe you any explanations? Unless you're secretly working for Dr. Reynolds now in some capacity other than a sex slave, what I do is my business and not yours." Regret, nausea and anger made his tone harder than he intended.

Raphael looked taken aback by the mild attack. "Wow, I take it things didn't go as planned with your girlfriend?"

"She's not my girlfriend." Nor would she ever be. Sera had made that perfectly clear. Valentino turned his back and headed for his room again. This time, Raphael wisely chose not to follow.

Once inside his room, Valentino quickly stripped off his clothes and crawled into bed. He didn't have a lot of time, but he just wanted to close his eyes and let his stomach settle. The moment his head hit the pillow, however, he knew something was really wrong with him. Behind his lids, the world began to spin until his stomach decided to join in for the ride. Without a lot of warning, bile surged up the back of his throat and filled his mouth. The blanket fought him as he tried to get out of bed, and the room titled dangerously the moment he put his feet on the floor.

He passed out on the way to the bathroom.

****

"I swear I have no idea where they came from."

The defensive tone of Raphael's voice pulled Valentino back to awareness. He blinked the bright lights of Dr. Reynolds' lab into focus and barely managed to stifle a groan. What the hell was he doing here? And why the fuck was Raphael being interrogated? Instinct told him neither answer would be pleasant.

"You were with him all day, CF16, or do you deny that too?" Wow, Dr. Reynolds sounded really angry.

"Actually," Raphael began with obvious reluctance. There was no need. Valentino would never blame him for being honest with the doctor. None of them really had a choice. "I wasn't with him all day. Aiden and I dropped him off downtown and then spent the rest of the day at the gym."

Silence descended upon the room like an oppressive storm cloud. Valentino held his breath and began to count the ticks of a nearby clock as he waited for the doctor to respond...or explode.

"*Where* did you drop him off?" It wasn't quite an explosion, but the doctor's temper was clearly simmering.

"The library," Raphael responded in a voice that said he knew the doctor would never believe him. He was right.

Dr. Reynolds snorted, then cursed, before finally responding in a very predictable fashion. "I would appreciate the truth from you, CF16, or you will join your friend in the gas chamber."

Jesus, the gas chamber? What the fuck?

Just as predictably, Raphael supplied all the details. "There was a girl..."

Valentino stopped listening. He simply tuned out the

sound of his friend's voice and focused his slit gaze on the ceiling. Clearly the doctor had decided to end his employment. Why else mention the gas chamber? Would it be tonight then? Was this it? Not caring anymore if Dr. Reynolds discovered he was conscious, Valentino rolled his head and glanced toward the vault-like door that led to the gas chamber. Would it hurt?

"...vampire."

That regained Valentino's attention.

"I swear I didn't know what she was," Raphael insisted. "I knew she'd bitten him, but a lot of the clients like freaky stuff."

"You may go, CF16, and do not speak a word of this to anyone. Do I make myself clear?"

"Yes, sir." The door sealed behind Raphael, and Valentino tensed as he listened to the doctor nearing the table. Would he be given a chance to defend his actions? Could he claim rape of some sort?

"You have a great deal of explaining to do, young man."

Valentino lifted his head to see the doctor hovering at the foot of the table. "I didn't know what she was until it was too late."

Under the loose shoulders of his white lab coat, Dr. Reynolds shrugged. "Regardless, the damage is done, and nothing I can do will reverse it."

"Which means what?" It was hard to keep the panic out of his tone or his gaze from straying toward the chamber's door.

The doctor sighed, and for a moment, he looked almost regretful. "You will have to be disposed of, Valentino."

That was that then. Dr. Reynolds would never call him Valentino under other circumstances. *Jesus.*

"Would you like me to explain exactly what is going on inside you that I cannot reverse?"

God, did it matter?

Obviously it did, because Dr. Reynolds went on

without waiting for Valentino to reply. "You see, when I created the concept of Captive Fantasy, I made sure my creations were filled with blood that could withstand all of the known viruses and diseases. Not only that, but your blood allows you to age twice as slowly as a normal man. You believe you are twenty-two, but you are actually closer to forty-five."

What would Sera think of that? Her horror at his age had been pretty evident. Not that it mattered now.

"The blood I created was not perfect though," the doctor went on, beginning to pace around the lab as he spoke. "I had to sacrifice some elements in order to gift all of you with a heightened libido, not to mention sustained arousal, and impressive proportions."

Right about now, none of that mattered to Valentino. He'd always sort of wanted to be normal anyway. Just once, he wanted to know what it was like to finish too early, or fail to get an erection. The closest he'd ever come to feeling normal was with Sera. With her, he almost lost control.

"What exactly did you sacrifice?" His question caused Dr. Reynolds to halt in his tracks and spin around to face the table. Valentino shrugged. "You might as well tell me everything, doc."

"Your blood, and that of all the other captives, is susceptible to only one thing. The bite of a blood-sucking mammal. They secrete a venom-like substance that—well, none of that matters, really." A humorless chuckle escaped the doctor's narrow lips. "I considered San Francisco to be a fairly safe place due to the lack of vampire bats."

Under different circumstances, maybe Valentino would have summoned a chuckle. But there was not a goddamn thing funny about any of this. Had he the strength, he would have leapt off the table and strangled Dr. Reynolds. Then they could all be free.

"It never occurred to me that you would be forced to entertain a vampire." The doctor shook his white head. "It never occurred to me that they actually existed. And you've been bitten twice." His eyes narrowed, and he approached the table. "The second one was voluntary, wasn't it? Why would you wish her to do such a thing?"

Valentino refused to share a single detail of his time alone with Sera. Tight-lipped, he stared up at Dr. Reynolds and arched a brow.

"You are right. I cannot force you to tell me a thing." The doctor turned away and began to pace again. "Perhaps it will comfort you to know that I'll use your DNA to create a clone." He stopped and glanced back. "Would you prefer I not reuse the name Valentino?"

"I can't see how it matters to me what the hell you do."

The doctor looked displeased by the retort, but he let it slide. With a nod, he headed for the door. "I injected you with a drug that should stabilize the effects of her bite. You shouldn't get sick again, but the drug will not last for long. I suggest you stay calm and move around as little as possible. Of course her photo and name have been posted at the door, and she'll be banned from entering this establishment. You were one of my best captives, and I'll not risk her ruining another."

"When will you do it?" He had a right to know, didn't he?

Dr. Reynolds answered with his head down, and his hand poised over the button that would open the door. "There are two others before you. Your time will be the beginning of next week."

Five days. Jesus, in five fucking days, he'd be dead.

Would Sera ever know? Would she care? If only he could see her again.

****

Sera gripped her head and collapsed onto the bathroom floor with a groan. The mug full of warm blood she tried to place on the counter smashed against the tiles near her hip, splashing her with the contents. The smell permeated the air and turned her stomach. What the hell was wrong? As the thought formed, her throat fought down a wave of bile.

Now she was really worried. Vampires did not throw up.

She barely made it to the toilet before she disproved that myth. Clutching the bowl, she got rid of every drop of blood she'd consumed after returning to her apartment. Mixed in was something she didn't recognize and would rather not contemplate, but she couldn't ignore that it was the strange purplely color of Valentino's blood.

Had she taken too much from him? Was vomiting a result of gorging? That would certainly explain why she'd never thrown up before. Then again, maybe she just wasn't used to fresh blood. Maybe this was like food poisoning or something and she'd feel fine in twenty-four hours.

Another wave of nausea rolled through her, and she lurched back over the toilet, but nothing came up this time. She heaved for several moments, then rested her head on the cool rim. If this didn't pass soon, she'd never be able to go into work. Mr. Henry would probably call in the FBI to investigate her reasons for calling off since she'd never done so before.

After several minutes passed without her nausea coming back, Sera attempted to get to her feet. Bad idea. The moment she straightened her legs, the room tilted and she fell back down. Her head bumped the rim of the toilet on the way to the floor, and she winced at the sharp pain. Something was definitely wrong.

If you need me, do not hesitate to call.

Constantine's words drifted into her head. Should she call him? And if she did, would he even know what was wrong with her? Could she risk not calling him? But wait a minute, she was vampire, and vampires didn't get sick. Though she should tell that to the foul mess in the toilet.

Yeah, she definitely needed to call. Too bad the phone was in her bedroom. But did she need a phone? As freaky as it was, Constantine was always present in her thoughts, so maybe if she just focused hard enough he'd realize she needed him. Worth a shot.

Sera closed her eyes and opened her mind. Constantine was there in an instant. If she weren't so desperate, she'd be bothered.

"What is it, my pet?"

I need you.

"Say no more." With that, the connection was severed and so was Sera's grasp on consciousness.

She came to in Constantine's arms. The familiarity of his embrace made her squirm, but he refused to loosen his hold on her. Instead, he stroked her hair off her face and cooed words of comfort, which made the whole situation worse.

"Let me go," she bit out, still struggling. They were on her couch. Well, it was better than the bed.

"Be still before you make yourself ill again, my pet."

Sera looked up into Constantine's face and scowled. Damn, why did he have to still be so handsome? His eyes were just as black, just as mesmerizing as they'd always been. His inky hair spilled around his face like fine silk, begging to be touched, and his features still managed to look god-like. Damn him.

"Have you missed me?" He flashed a wide, brilliant smile and trailed a finger down her nose. "I've missed you."

"I don't believe you."

He shrugged and adjusted his hold to allow her to sit by his side, but he did not release her. "Believe what you will." Before she could offer further protest, he went on. "Now tell me what I had to flush away in your bathroom? You aren't, by some strange happenstance, pregnant, are you?" He sounded truly horrified by the notion.

Sera's stomach flipped. "My God, could I be?"

Constantine rolled his eyes and shook his head. "No." His gaze settled on her face and became serious. "Would you wish to be?"

"Does that matter? You made sure I could never be a mother."

He let her go and got off the couch. "When I offered that final bite you were more than willing, my pet."

It was true, but it still pissed her off. Crossing her arms, she glared up at him through her bangs. As she did so, she noticed how immaculately attired he was. Had he been at a party when she called? Focusing on the expensive fit of his black slacks, she hoped there was some woman somewhere wondering why he'd had to leave in such a hurry. The thought almost brought a smile to her face.

"Still jealous, my pet?"

Sera lifted her gaze past Constantine's maroon shirt to meet his smug gaze. "Tell me why I got sick."

His disappointment over her not rising to the bait shown in his eyes. "I do not know."

Hmm. She changed tack. "Is it possible for fresh blood to make me sick?"

"No."

"Are you trying to be difficult?" she snapped.

"Not at all."

With an angry snarl, she shot off the couch, determined to stalk to her room and slam the door. She didn't get far before her knees buckled, and she fell into Constantine's expectant arms.

"You are still weak."

Sera gripped the front of Constantine's silk shirt and struggled to stand on her own. It was no use. She collapsed against him and laid her cheek on his chest. "What's wrong with me?"

"I told you, I do not know." His tone was gentle as he stroked a hand over her hair. "But I believe I should take you to the coven, after I feed you."

She knew what that meant. She shook her head against him. "No. I don't want your blood." It would only reaffirm the bond between them.

"You have no choice, my pet. It is a long trip, and I

want you there as soon as possible, which means traveling by day. In your present state, you will not be able to tolerate even the thought of sunlight."

Damnit, he was right.

"For once, do not be so stubborn."

She'd never been stubborn.

Constantine's chuckle increased her ire, and she gritted her teeth and slid her hand down his side to snatch his wrist. Fine, if he wanted her to feed, she'd feed. She lifted his hand, ripped the cuff of his shirt to expose his skin, then sank her fangs into his veins. She made no attempt to be gentle, but Constantine offered no complaints. He merely held her and allowed her to take what she needed.

Damn him.

Chapter Thirteen

It was really rather irritating how much better she felt with Constantine's blood running through her veins, but Sera would cut off her own head before she admitted that out loud. Not that she had to. Constantine hadn't stopped grinning like an idiot since she shoved his wrist away and licked her lips.

"Pack lightly," he called to her as she headed out of the living room. Did pack lightly mean she could leave him behind? "No, it does not, my pet."

Ugh!

Sera darted into her room, slammed the door, and froze. The air smelled of Valentino. Unable to help herself, she took a deep breath and held it in. She hated how things had ended between them, but it had to be for the better. He'd go on with his life, and she'd go on with hers. Doing so together just didn't make sense, especially if she was going to reinstate herself with a coven, and she knew that's what Constantine hoped for. He'd take her there, and leave her.

Just like he'd done in England.

So why are you agreeing to go?

"Because I don't have any damn choice," she snarled out loud. "I didn't have a choice centuries ago, and I don't have one now."

"It's for the best, Seraphina." Constantine's voice reached her through the door. She hated when he used her name almost more than when he called her "my pet."

She shot a hateful look toward the door. "Just leave

me alone, all right? I agreed to go, but you don't need to hover." Silence met her angry words, and she chose to believe that Constantine had headed back into the living room to give her some privacy.

She'd only managed to toss two pair of jeans into a duffel bag when she spotted Valentino's discarded bath towel on the floor near the bed. Instantly, the image of him standing in the doorway, damp from the shower and looking good enough to eat, filled her mind. Knowing she shouldn't, she dropped to her knees and gathered the towel onto her lap. In some places it was still damp, and the folds held the scent of her bath soap mixed with Valentino.

Sera lifted the red cotton to her nose and inhaled. If she could go back in time, she'd do things totally different. Valentino had obviously wished to talk on the ride over to Captive Fantasy, but her brittle wall of self-defense had kept him quiet. She'd been too afraid that he might convince her to give things a try. That he might say something that made sense, and then she'd have to admit her feelings toward him transcended what he could do for her in bed.

Terrified, and eager to be away from him, she'd peeled away from the curb the moment the door closed behind him. His shocked expression in her rear view mirror would haunt her forever. She buried her face in the towel. "I'm sorry."

Constantine opened her door without knocking and met her gaze over the edge of the towel. His eyes were sad. "Were you really falling in love with him?"

"It's none of your business." She tossed the towel back to the floor and stood up to finish packing.

"I fell in love with a mortal once."

She knew he wouldn't let it go. Pulling random shirts out of her closet, she ignored him.

"She was lovely and too innocent for me, but I couldn't resist. I believed she would accept what I was, and maybe long to join me. For a time, I think we were happy together."

Sera stared at the blouse in her hand as she twisted the white sleeve around her fingers. Was he talking about her? He had never loved her. He had used her desire to be loved against her until he had what he wanted from her, and then he'd turned his back.

"But then, like a fool, I turned her away when she failed to meet my exceedingly high expectations. I wanted her to be exactly like me. I wanted her to revel in what she had become, to crave blood as I did. To take it with absolute abandon, but she did not, and I refused to understand."

Sera threw the blouse into the duffle bag and rounded on Constantine. "Stop it! You never loved me. I was nothing but a toy to you. A *pet*."

"That is not true."

It had to be true, because it was a lot easier to hate him if she believed he also hated her. "I don't know why you're saying these things, anyway. I wasn't falling in love with Valentino, so you don't have to worry that I'll start to cry on your shoulder or something."

He didn't look convinced. "So what was going on between you two?"

Sera gestured toward the bed and hit Constantine where it would hurt the most. "Sex," she snapped. "Good, hot, kinky sex. The kind of sex I could never have with you."

He stalked toward her, making her regret the taunt. "Oh, you could have had any kind of sex with me you wanted." He took hold of her shoulders and yanked her against his chest. "But the little princess was afraid to let go. You were afraid to act like a whore, I believe you said. You believed finding sublime pleasure would send you to hell." He gave her a little shake. "Well, guess what, my *pet*?"

"Let me go. Now."

He didn't. "You can't get more damned than you already are. I tried to tell you that, but you wouldn't listen. Do you think drinking from a plastic bag makes you less of a monster?"

"Let me go." She refused to beg, but she knew he could sense her growing fear. Did it please him to know she was afraid?

"I've never wanted you to fear me," he said in a low tone. "From the first night on, I've only wanted you to crave me."

"The only thing I crave when in your presence is a way to escape."

He let her go so fast, she fell backwards onto the bed, squishing her duffel bag and cursing when the buckle pinched her butt through her leggings. Constantine glared at her, looking for all the world like he'd really love to strangle her, then surprised her by turning and stalking out of the room.

Sera collapsed onto her back with a loud sigh of relief. It was going to be a long trip to the coven, and she wasn't looking forward to it for one second.

That makes two of us, my pet.
****

It didn't take long for Valentino to grow restless. The sterile environment of the lab offered minimal entertainment, and the need to get the hell out of there consumed him until he simply tossed caution to the wind and leapt off the table. For a few moments he held onto the metal edge for balance, but then his muscles strengthened and he felt stable enough to head for the door. It opened before he reached it, and Dr. Reynolds strolled in, looking relatively unsurprised to see Valentino on his feet.

"Brilliance had to be sacrificed as well, it seems," he muttered under his breath as he circled around Valentino. "Were you going somewhere, CF19?"

"Can I at least wait out my demise in my room?"

The doctor seemed to consider his reply for an awfully long time. Finally, "I suppose there would be no harm. You aren't contagious, after all." His expression tightened before he went on. "Just see that you don't bite anyone."

Valentino fought the urge to growl. "I'll do my best."

Dr. Reynolds waved toward the door. "Go on, then. I'll pay you a visit later tonight to give you another injection."

Valentino wasted no time in escaping the lab. Naked, weak, and feeling like absolute shit, he climbed into the elevator and hit the button that would dump him on the main floor. The moment the steel box jerked into motion, he collapsed against the wall and closed his eyes against the fire in his veins. He refused to believe that Sera knew she was poisoning him with her bite. How could she, after all? She didn't even know he wasn't quite human.

God, how would she react to that? Maybe being a vampire would allow her to accept it more easily. Maybe he should have taken the time to tell her all about Captive Fantasy. She'd asked, after all. Doing so might have made a difference. What sort of difference, he didn't know.

The elevator doors slid open, and he shoved Sera from his thoughts as he caught sight of a blonde woman hovering in the hallway. Her tall, curvy body was barely covered by the tight, gold dress she wore, and she turned as the elevator made a clicking sound. Damn. Jennifer. Her brown eyes widened, then raked him from head to toe. Before he could utter a sound, she headed toward him and stepped inside. The doors shut behind her, and her coy smile grew.

"Fancy meeting you here," she purred.

Valentino managed a weak smile in return.

Jennifer stepped closer and dropped her gaze to his chest. "Do you always roam the halls naked? Not that I'm complaining." She looked up and winked. "It'll save time." She grabbed the hem of her dress as if to lift it to get down to business. Somehow he knew there wouldn't be anything underneath.

"I can't entertain you tonight, Jennifer."

Undeterred, she leaned into him, pressing his spine against the cold metal wall. "You gave me your word."

"I realize that, but that was before I got sick. I've been ordered not to work tonight."

She wasn't listening. Shifting her weight to one side, she walked her fingers down the center of his chest, clearly aiming to take matters into her own hand. Not that it would prove anything. The way he was feeling, not even Sera could coax a hard-on out of him.

Jennifer curled her fingers around his flaccid penis and began to stroke him from root to tip. It felt good, but nothing happened. She frowned at him and increased her efforts until he finally covered her hand to get her to stop. "I told you, I was sick."

"You don't look sick." She leaned back to look him up and down.

"It's food poisoning."

Her fingers flexed under his hand, and her frown deepened as she met his gaze. "Are you too sick to do *anything*?" She licked her lips just in case he missed her meaning.

The thought of using his mouth on her actually churned his stomach. "It would be best if I didn't." His reply had nothing to do with the poison in his veins and everything to do with wanting Sera's pussy to be the last one he remembered.

Anger flashed in Jennifer's eyes, and she shifted against him to straddle his thigh. "I don't like being told no, Valentino." Proving his earlier assumption correct, she rubbed her pubic hair against his skin. "I paid good money to get in here, and I expect you to perform."

He gripped her shoulders to hold her breasts away from his chest. "Look, Jennifer, I'm sorry to disappoint you, but unless you plan on getting off on my leg, I can't help you tonight." Releasing her, he reached out to open the doors again.

Jennifer wasn't ready to admit defeat. She followed him out into the hall and all the way to his bedroom door.

He could actually feel her gaze on his ass the whole time. "You know," she started as he shoved the door open. "I can't imagine prudish Sera enjoying you."

Valentino gripped the doorknob and looked over his shoulder. "I won't discuss her with you."

Jennifer arched a platinum brow. "I see. I would think it goes against the rules to fall for one of your clients."

"Good night, Jennifer." He stepped into his room, but she slid in after him before he could shut her out. Jesus Christ. Doing his best to pretend she wasn't there, he headed for his bed and the promise of a comfortable rest.

"Was she even able to orgasm with you?"

That got his attention, and he turned around to glare at her. "I cannot imagine Sera discussing such a thing with you."

Jennifer shrugged. "She didn't, but her best friend can't keep a secret under the influence of good wine."

Sera would be mortified.

"So did you give her one?" Jennifer pushed. "Did she scream and beg for more, or did she run away horrified by what she'd finally been able to do?"

Valentino had had enough. Moving toward Jennifer, he walked her back toward the door and caged her in with his hands braced above her shoulders. "Do you scream when you come?"

She blinked, and he heard her breath catch in her throat.

"I bet you do. In fact, I bet you do it so that your lover thinks you're for real."

She exhaled and shook her head, ready to voice a denial, but Valentino wouldn't let her.

"Everything about you seems fake, so I'd imagine your orgasms are as well."

Her eyes narrowed dangerously. "How dare you talk to me like that?"

"But it's true, isn't it? Did you come here tonight thinking to fool me as well? You would have failed, if that was the plan."

"I've never met a guy who can tell the difference," she spat. "You're all too wrapped up in your performance issues to pay close attention to us."

"I can tell the difference."

"Sure, you say that after you tell me we can't have sex tonight."

Despite the protesting muscles in his arms, he leaned closer to her, but stopped before their bodies touched. Again, her breath caught in her throat and she stared at him with giant eyes. "Do you want to know how I can tell?"

She nodded, and her gaze drifted toward his mouth.

"You want a kiss, don't you?"

She nodded again.

"Too fucking bad."

With a sharp gasp, she jerked her gaze to his. "Does Sera know what a jerk you are?"

"She has no reason to."

Jennifer pursed her lips and cocked her chin in the air. "I believe you were going to tell me what supreme wisdom allows you to sniff out a fake orgasm."

"It's really rather simple."

She arched a brow. "I doubt that."

"When a woman comes, there is a spontaneity to her convulsions that can't be faked. It's the rhythm of your pussy that gives you away, Jennifer."

Her face exploded with color, and she squirmed against the door. "You cannot possibly tell the difference." The ragged cadence of her breathing let Valentino know that his words had gotten under her skin. "You're lying just to irritate me."

"Am I?" He let his thighs brush hers. "You should know there are other things that give you away, as well."

"Oh really?"

Valentino nodded. "Really," he drawled. "For instance, the flush of your skin and the beat of your heart." He placed his palm over her racing heart and smiled. "Yes, just like that. It lets me know how aroused you are. You can't fake that."

"I'm fully clothed, irritated, and far from aroused."

"You even lie to yourself. Interesting." He took his hand away and braced it against the door again. "I can assure you, that if you and I were to have sex, you'd never be able to fake an orgasm." She opened her mouth, but he talked over her. "I'd be buried so deep inside, you wouldn't be able to think about clenching your muscles at the right time."

"I—"

"Your pussy would take over and strangle my cock when and how it wanted to, and you wouldn't be able to do a damn thing about it."

Her lips parted, her tongue peeked out, and she shuddered right before his eyes.

"Yes," he whispered with his lips hovering over hers. "Just like that." As she gasped for breath, he pushed away and turned toward the bed. "Now get the hell out of here, Jennifer."

The door hinges rattled under the force of her exit.

If things were different, her anger would be cause for concern, but he'd be dead in five days. Nothing had the power to concern him now.

As promised, Dr. Reynolds appeared a few hours later with a nasty looking syringe in his hand. Without permission, he poked the needle into the bend of Valentino's arm and shot him full of God only knew what. After issuing another order to remain calm, he left Valentino to drift into a drug induced slumber.

Sera came to him in his dreams. Her beauty made him moan and the satin bedsheets slithered over his thighs as he writhed under the intense pleasure of seeing her once more. If only he could touch her for real. Her lips feathered over the side of his neck, her teeth scraped his skin, and her sweet voice whispered in his ear, "I can save you." Her tongue flicked out before he felt her teeth again. "One bite and you need never fear death again. Do you want to be saved, Valentino? Do you?"

Valentino jerked awake and stared around his room. His heart beat so hard in his chest, the pain brought tears to his eyes. My God, was that the answer? If it was, he needed to find a way to get the hell out of here, and then he needed to convince Sera that making him a vampire would somehow benefit both of them. Though how, he had no idea. Clearly she didn't relish being a vampire, so why make another?

But first things first. He needed to get out of Captive Fantasy. And to do that, he needed help. One name instantly came to mind. Raphael.

It was time to test just how strong their friendship really was.

Chapter Fourteen

Halfway between San Francisco and Santa Fe, Sera wanted to roll down the window of her Mustang and jump out. She just couldn't bear Constantine's company anymore. His attempts to pretend the scene in her bedroom hadn't happened had moved beyond annoying, and she was ready to cover her ears and scream.

"How much longer?" She sounded like a petulant child, but didn't care. If she weren't so weak they could have been there by now, but oh no, Constantine had insisted on driving. She'd rather take her chances with teleportation and risk falling out of the sky.

He shot her a glance and a wicked grin. "I can think of something for you to do that will pass the time." He nodded toward his lap.

Sera rolled her eyes and glared out the tinted window. In addition to the tinting, she wore dark sunglasses to protect her from the waning sun. It had not escaped her notice that Constantine did not seem to require such protection. Yea, for him. No doubt it was all the fresh blood he'd been feasting ravenously on for centuries.

"I hope you lose the attitude before we arrive. I doubt the master will take kindly to it."

Sera shrugged. She didn't really care if the master liked her or not. Maybe he'd hate her so much he'd refuse to let her stay. She nearly jumped out of her skin when Constantine grabbed her hand.

"You need the coven's protection."

117

She turned away from the window to glare at his hand. "Stop touching me."

He actually did. With a sigh, he fixed his attention back on the road. "Sometimes you make me regret that night."

"What night?" The question was out before she could stop it.

"The night I turned you." He looked over. "Despite what you believe, I didn't regret it right away."

"No, you waited about a hundred years."

"Forget it." He turned away again. "There is obviously no talking to you."

Sera leaned her head back against the seat and closed her eyes. "Let's agree to just leave each other alone for the rest of this trip, okay?"

"Whatever," Constantine mumbled.

They drove on in a heavy, awkward silence, finally reaching Santa Fe as the sun threatened to rise on a new day. Constantine seemed to know exactly where he was going as he turned down street after street without a moment's hesitation. Sera watched the passing scenery through her sunglasses and decided the city was really quite beautiful. It was the sort of place she could imagine taking a honeymoon to.

"Such wistful thoughts will get you nowhere," Constantine remarked.

Sera ignored him.

"Here we are," he announced after a few strained moments had passed. He pulled off the road and stopped in front of a towering iron gate. He lowered his window to give his name to the security box, and then the gate groaned open. He shot her a look as he pulled through. "Just behave."

Sera scowled, then lost interest in Constantine as the coven house appeared at the end of the drive. Holy shit. Constructed of white adobe, it looked more like an old Spanish church than a house. It even had one of those arches at the peek of the fancy roof that housed a bell. Did it ring at sunset to summon all the good little vampires in for the day?

"Seraphina," Constantine warned in a low rumble.

She continued to pretend he wasn't at her side. Only a few windows in the vast mansion blazed with light, but the courtyard was full of cars. Matching cars, in fact.

Sera couldn't help but gawk at the long row of giant, black Hummers. The lone, black Mercedes sedan on the end seemed grossly out of place. "This is beautiful," she whispered.

"Yeah, wait until you go inside."

Feeling a tad overwhelmed and more than a little underdressed, Sera tried to hide her anxiety from Constantine as he parked her car behind a towering Hummer. Not sure what she should do, she waited for him to get out and open her door for her. He held out his hand as if she were disembarking from a carriage.

Sliding her hand into his, she hissed, "You could have told me to wear something else."

"You look fine."

There was nothing "fine" about her blue jeans and pink hoodie, and she knew it. "This is not what I want to be wearing when I meet the master."

He shrugged and curled her hand around his arm. "I'm telling you, it won't matter."

"Then why are you in a suit?"

"I've been in a suit since answering your cry for help. I, unlike you, did not have the benefit of packing for out trip."

Sera gave up. Nothing she said at this point would calm her nerves. As they approached the wooden front door, it opened, and Sera's anxiety nearly made her faint. What was wrong with her? She was a vampire too, for God's sake. She had every right to be here.

"Constantine, welcome." A glorious looking man with pale blond hair, startling blue eyes, and a killer smile appeared at the door to gesture them inside.

Sera tried really hard not to stare but figured

somebody this good looking would be used to such a reaction. Like Constantine, he was dressed in a suit, only his shirt was white instead of maroon, the collar was open a little further down his chest, and the hem was left untucked. Had he dressed in a hurry to answer the door? If so, did that mean there was a really disappointed—or worse pissed off—she-vampire somewhere upstairs?

The man's blue eyes drifted to her face, and his smile was all for her. "You must be Seraphina." He extended his hand and Constantine released her so she could accept it. "Welcome to *Villa Sangue.*"

"Thank you." She managed the weak response while shaking the man's hand. *Villa Sangue.* Or House of Blood, loosely translated. How lovely. Why not just name the place Devil's Den or Lair of the Vampire? Either would be just as obvious.

A twinkle gleamed in the man's blue eyes. "I'll see that you are shown to your room, so that you may rest after your journey." Mr. Gorgeous looked over his shoulder and motioned another man forward who must have been hovering in the shadows. "Show our guests upstairs and see that Seraphina has all that she requires."

"Yes, master."

Master? Sera looked at the blond god with new eyes, and his smile told her she was correct in her assumption. Her mouth fell open. After a moment, he shifted his gaze to Constantine. "Do join me in my study once you have settled Seraphina into her room."

Constantine nodded, and the master left them.

"Oh my God," Sera breathed. She watched the master vampire disappear down the hallway, and once he was out of sight, she turned on Constantine. "You could have told me who that was."

"It was more fun to watch you figure it out."

"Bastard," she hissed under her breath, then stalked away to follow their guide up the split, marble staircase. She trailed her hand along the fancy iron railing, thinking the house was too insane for words. She could hardly wait to see what the bedroom looked like.

Their guide halted midway down the second floor hallway and gestured toward a partially open door. "You will find all you need has been provided." With a bow, he left Sera and Constantine alone.

Sera shoved the door open a little further and gasped. The interior was extraordinary; all dark, paneled walls and rich, sumptuous fabrics of silver and black. The bed dominated the room, but her gaze slid by it to focus on what sat beside it. A man. A mortal man, if the racing heart and sharp aroma of blood was any indication. He smiled and got to his feet to show off over six feet of masculine perfection. Where the devil were his clothes?

Sera rounded on Constantine and caught him off guard before he could erase his amused expression. "What the hell is that?" She pointed over her shoulder.

"I think it's meant to be your midnight snack." His eyes twinkled as they rested on her face. "I believe I'll leave you to it."

Sera clasped Constantine's hand to prevent him from leaving her. "I can't drink from him," she said in a panic. "You know that."

With little effort, Constantine slid his hand free and patted her on the cheek. "Just pretend he's Valentino, and we both know you'll do fine." He left her without looking back.

"I can bleed into a cup, if you'd prefer that?" her naked "meal" kindly offered.

Sera closed her eyes and counted to ten. This was the reason she wanted to live separately from a coven. Certain behavior was just expected. Behavior she didn't wish to partake in. Behavior that actually made her palms sweat and her stomach twist into knots. If it was expected of her to partake in this "snack," would it be viewed as an insult if she refused?

"Mistress?"

Her eyes flew open, and she turned back to face the

room. "Don't you dare call me that," she snapped.

The man appeared startled, then nodded and clasped his hands behind his back. He looked like a cadet awaiting orders. But he was naked, impressively so, she noted. Nonetheless, given the tawny hair sprinkling his broad chest and covering his muscular thighs, she'd never be able to pretend he was Valentino. What was Constantine thinking to suggest such a ludicrous thing?

She met the man's expectant gaze. "I don't need you tonight, so you can go."

His frown accentuated the width of his mouth. "I was told to provide you with a meal, mis—ma'am."

Sera sighed and finally stepped into the room. She left the door open. "Fine, but I won't bite you."

"I offered to bleed into a cup."

She waved a hand and shot a weary gaze toward the bed. The sooner this was over, the better. "Do whatever, but don't do it in front of me."

With a nod, he headed toward a door tucked into the wall. Bathroom, maybe? He was only gone for a few moments, but it was long enough for her to kick off her shoes and stretch out on the really soft mattress. What heaven. The smell of blood pulled her attention to the side of the bed, eye level with her "snack's" package. While she stared, he grew hard.

"I'll fulfill any hunger you have," he offered.

Sera yanked her gaze away and sat up to reach for the plastic cup full of fresh blood. The strong smell coated the inside of her nose and coaxed saliva to the tip of her tongue. The first sip felt warm and satisfying sliding down her throat, and without too much hesitation, she drank the rest.

Whoever he was, he was yummy.

She handed the cup back with a smile. "Thank you, now you may leave."

He set the cup on the nightstand and crossed his arms. "What about sex?"

Were all the mortals here this blunt? She struggled

122

to keep her gaze from drifting downward. "I don't need sex." Not that she didn't want it, but just not from him.

Instead of doing what she hoped he'd do, which was leave, he uncrossed his arms and reached down to trail a finger across her shoulder. "You seem tense. I could give you a massage?" His other fingers joined the first, and he squeezed the tight muscle in the crook of her neck.

It felt good.

Sera almost sighed with pleasure. "It's okay, really. I think I just need to rest." Valentino's visit had preempted her normal routine, and the trip here had been agonizingly long and unbearable. She was beginning to feel the effects. Her "snack" kept rubbing her shoulder and finally she did moan and let her eyes drift shut. "Feels good," she mumbled.

"It'll feel better in a moment." That was all the warning offered before her hoodie was tugged up and over her head. His hands gripped her muscles again before she could protest the liberty he'd decided to take. "Just relax."

Sera managed to do just that until the mattress buckled under extra weight. She opened her eyes and discovered her "snack" kneeling on the bed next her hip. "No." She reached up and took his hands from her shoulders. "I told you I didn't need sex."

"I disagree, but it's not my place to force the issue." He stood back up, doing nothing to hide the hardened length of his penis from her. In fact, he looked mighty proud. "I'll leave you alone and take care of this," he waved toward his erection, "where it might be more welcome."

No doubt there were many such places inside this nest of vampires.

Sera nodded and reached for her hoodie. Her "snack" left the room while she struggled to pull the shirt back over her head. When she emerged, the room was blessedly empty. With a sigh, she lay down and stared up at the ceiling. Thoughts she didn't want intruded before she could succumb to sleep.

Had Valentino entertained Jennifer? Was he resting up now to do so again tonight? Or would it be a different woman entirely? Did some nights bring more than one? How many women would it take before he forgot her?

With a fierce growl, she rolled onto her side and buried her face in the pillow. None of this mattered. She didn't care what Valentino was doing, or with whom. For them it was over.

She punched the pillow. "Fuck." Why did her body have to crave him so damn much? And not just his blood. Oh no, her vagina wanted his cock. She wanted him hard and deep inside her. She wanted to feel the tip of him crashing into the upper reaches of her womb. She wanted...she wanted...she wanted to stop thinking about him!

Sera punched the pillow again, then rolled onto her back. All of a sudden her jeans were too confining, and she knew sleep would fail to come until she was more comfortable. She didn't know if her duffel bag was somewhere in the room, so she simply rolled off the bed, stripped naked, and then stretched back out on top of the cool satin comforter. Her body, already wound tighter than a damn violin string, reacted violently to the feel of the lush fabric.

Her back arched, her feet slid toward her ass, and to her horror, her knees parted. Oh God, she hadn't masturbated in years, but the urge to do so now was too strong to ignore. If she were at home, she might even seek out the dildo Becca had bought for her a few Christmases ago. The atrociously large penis had never left its box, nor had the desire to take it out ever arisen. Until now. If it were in her hand, she'd rub it between her legs and pretend it was Valentino.

Sera stifled a moan and twisted the comforter in her fingers. Maybe the feeling would pass if she ignored it? She needed to think of something non sexual. Jesus, what? Every time she closed her eyes, she conjured the image of Valentino standing in her bedroom door dressed in nothing but one of her bath towels. The image took on the dimension of a fuzzy dream, and she watched the towel drift to the floor.

He was aroused, and his eyes smoldered as he headed toward the bed.

"Is this what you want, Sera?" He gripped his penis and gave it a good long stroke.

Sera nodded, unable to find her voice. Her hips shifted on the bed, and she pressed her knees wider apart.

He halted at the foot of the bed, locked his gaze on hers and continued to idly stroke his erection. Up and down. Up and down. It was rather maddening to watch.

"You have to tell me what you want."

Oh God, she didn't want to play this game. She just wanted him to fuck her.

He smiled as if able to read her mind. Hell, it *was* a dream, maybe he could. In that case; she envisioned him crawling onto the mattress to claim her with his mouth, then his fingers, and finally his cock. Her moan shattered the silence of the room and nearly pulled her out of the fantasy.

A finger stroked between the folds of her sex and she drew in a sharp breath. "Yessss..." He continued to touch her, first with just one finger, then eventually with his entire hand. His palm felt hot despite the warm arousal spreading through her and she lifted her hips off the bed to press against the cup of his hand. His chuckle shivered down her spine and she arched higher.

"Inside," she begged.

Abruptly he shoved two fingers deep inside her, and she bit back a scream. "Yessss..." she hissed again. Oh yes. So good.

Trapped between her tight, vaginal muscles, his fingers danced and probed until the room filled with the loud sound of her gasps. If she came now, she feared the fantasy would end, and she wasn't ready to say goodbye to Valentino again.

"Slower," she whispered, and the pace of his fingers

obeyed.

In and out they moved, until she was dizzy with the feeling. The room tilted behind her tight eyelids and her skin pulled taut over her body. Oh no. In the hopes that some pain might stave off the building climax, she dug her fangs into her bottom lip, but the taste of blood only managed to shove her over the precipice.

The room filled with the tangy aroma of her cum as she convulsed on top of the bed and saturated the palm of her hand.

"Bloody hell, Seraphina, you've made me ejaculate inside my pants."

She ripped her hand from between her legs and shot a frenzied glance toward the sound of Constantine's voice. He stood in the doorway looking back at her. Despite the words, he didn't seem too upset. With a horrified cry, she fumbled around for the comforter and managed to slither between it and the cool sheets. Oh my God, that didn't just happen. She did not just masturbate in front of Constantine.

But clearly she had.

His smug expression told her he'd never let her forget it either. "No need to turn all bashful, it was really quite the show." He stepped inside and closed the door. "Next time, you should close the door, lest you entertain someone other than me. Wouldn't want one of the many mortals roaming about to get the wrong idea."

Sera pulled the comforter over her head. "Go away."

Constantine laughed in response, and she heard him coming closer to the bed. "We need to talk, Seraphina." His voice was suddenly very serious.

She peeked over the edge of the blanket. "It can wait."

He shook his head and sat on the edge of the bed. "No, I'm afraid it really can't." There was something hovering on the edge of his tone that forced her to sit up and give a little nod. "It's about Valentino."

Sera's lungs ceased up. "Wh-what about him?"

126

Before answering, Constantine took her hand and laced their fingers together. He lowered his gaze from hers and his whole demeanor turned really damn scary. "He's not exactly human."

What?

The word screamed in Sera's head, but her throat closed around it, leaving her to stare in mute shock at Constantine's profile.

He lifted his gaze and stroked the top of her hand. "The details are sketchy, but it seems he is some sort of experimental clone designed to provide heightened sexual pleasure. The blood in his veins is synthetic, but not the same as what you choose to put in your fridge. The master believes biting him might have put you at risk."

Sera shook her head, unable to move past the part about Valentino being a clone of some sort. He wasn't real? He wasn't *human*?

"To be safe, he suggested you undergo a full transfusion, and it only makes sense that I act as the donor."

Transfusion. Donor. The words broke through Sera's stunned disbelief one at a time. She blinked twice, then focused on Constantine's black eyes. "What did you say?"

He leaned toward her and brushed a kiss over her forehead. "It's a lot to take in, and you need to rest." He released her and placed her hand in her lap. "We'll talk this evening."

"Wait?" She called after him, but he merely tossed a tight grin over his shoulder before leaving her. For a long time she stayed frozen in place, staring at the door and trying to process the insanity of Constantine's words.

A clone? Not human?

This reeked of things a little too sci-fi for even a vampire to comprehend. How could Valentino not be human? He felt normal. He looked normal. Okay, maybe he looked a little better than normal, and he had even tasted better than normal. All right, damnit, he felt better than normal too, but that didn't mean he wasn't human.

Sera collapsed onto the pillow, no longer able to fight off the grasping embrace of sleep, and unwilling to ponder what Constantine had said a moment longer. Tonight, they would talk again, and of course he'd tell her she had misunderstood him.

Valentino was all human male. He had to be.

Chapter Fifteen

Raphael stared at Valentino as if he'd lost his mind. The reaction wasn't a surprise. "You're crazy if you actually think you can escape."

"I have to try." Valentino shoved the covers to his waist and sat up. Dizziness greeted the action, and he drew a deep breath and waited for it to pass. It must be almost time for another one of Dr. Reynolds' injections. "I thought I could count on you to help me."

Raphael raked a hand through his long blond hair and shook his head. "I'm your friend, Val, but I can't help you commit suicide."

"I'll be dead in a few days anyway."

There was no good way to dispute that, and they both knew it. Raphael scowled. "This is insane."

"I just need to get out and find Sera." There was no need to watch what he said to Raphael. Thanks to Valentino's inability to entertain clients, the doctor had ordered all the cameras and microphones in the room turned off.

"I think she'll be able to save me." He'd told Raphael about Sera being a vampire and about the dream he'd had where she had offered to make him one as well. To say that his friend had responded to both bits of information skeptically would be a gross understatement.

In fact, his disbelief was still stamped on his face. "You are risking a lot because of some loony dream. I don't like it."

Valentino rolled his eyes and shoved his hair off the

side of his neck. "You've seen the bites, you've heard Dr. Reynolds' theory, so you know I'm telling you the truth about her."

Raphael stared at the marks still visible but didn't comment. "If I agree to help you, what do you need me to do?"

Relief nearly made Valentino collapse onto the pillows. "Thank you."

Raphael shook his head. "I didn't say I was going to help yet."

A slight obstacle in Valentino's opinion. "We both know you will. Now listen," he went on before his friend could say more. "I'm thinking it would be easier to sneak out during hours of operation. Friday is the busiest night, so it would make sense to go for it then."

"That's the day before."

The words were chilling. Valentino nodded. "Yeah, the day before the end, you might say. If I fail, it's over." Silence followed the grim pronouncement.

Raphael's firm voice broke through the mounting tension. "Whatever you need, I'll do it."

A plan, albeit a rather wobbly one, was hatched. Raphael looked doubtful as he headed for the door. "What if Tabby doesn't come Friday night? You've ignored her twice, after all. Maybe she won't bother to try again?"

Valentino knew Tabby a lot better than Raphael. She'd come, and she'd gladly step right into his plan without even realizing what she was a part of. "I'll worry about Tabby; you concentrate on getting a healthy supply of whatever injection Dr. Reynolds has been giving me. I won't get too far without it, I'm afraid."

"I'll do my best."

Valentino prayed that Raphael's best would be good enough.

****

The next morning made Valentino realize he wouldn't need his escape plan to work. Why? Because he was dying.

130

He curled onto his side with a moan of raw agony. His insides were on fire. No, that wasn't severe enough. His insides were clawing their way out. The pain tearing through his abdomen brought tears to his eyes. What the hell was going on? On top of the battle waging through his lower half, his heart seemed as if it had to fight to beat. The pounding rhythm in his ears faltered more than once, and he held his breath, afraid it would never start up again. It did, but so slowly, he barely felt or heard it.

The door clicked open, and Dr. Reynolds' voice broke into Valentino's misery. "Good morning, CF19. It's about time for your—what the hell is wrong?"

Valentino shook his head and let another moan shudder through him. If this—whatever it was—went on for much longer, he'd beg the doctor to kill him today. Now.

Dr. Reynolds put a hand to his forehead. "You're like a block of ice." His touch drifted over the curve of Valentino's bare shoulder. "My God, your body temperature must be half what's normal. Did you ingest something?"

Again, Valentino merely shook his head. He pressed his fingers below his naval, but the churning pain didn't ease. It actually felt as if his stomach was shrinking. His heart faltered again, and he caught his breath. He waited.

"What is it?" Dr. Reynolds' demanded. "Tell me what you are feeling?"

"C-can't h-hear...h-heart."

The bed dipped as Dr. Reynolds' leaned closer. "What did you say?" Before Valentino could answer, the cold press of a stethoscope touched his chest. Only it wasn't as cold as it should be. In fact, it seemed hot. "My God," the doctor breathed.

Valentino managed to slit one eye open. He wished he hadn't when he saw the doctor's pinched expression. Their gazes met, and Valentino silently begged for some sort of explanation.

Dr. Reynolds pulled the stethoscope away and

reached for Valentino's wrist. He measured his pulse for a few moments, then eased him onto his back to poke at his abdomen. Valentino winced at the pain of each touch, surprised by the doctor's mumbled apology. The examination continued for several more minutes.

"I'll need to take blood," Dr. Reynolds announced. "As soon as possible."

Valentino forced his head off the pillow and his eyes to open. "Why?" The word was weak but at least he hadn't stuttered.

Dr. Reynolds looked disinclined to answer as he backed toward the door. "I'll be back."

"No!" Valentino nearly blacked out as he reared up in bed. "Tell me wh-what's wrong."

"I don't know for sure."

"But you h-have a theory."

Dr. Reynolds shoved his hands into the pockets of his lab coat and bowed his head. Was he afraid to see how Valentino would react to whatever bomb was about to drop? What could be worse than hearing you were to die in a few days? "I believe you are beginning to transform."

Transform? Into what? He couldn't force the questions out.

The doctor lifted his head and shook it sadly. "I was under the impression one had to ingest their blood to undergo a change, but I must be wrong."

Valentino fell back onto the pillow. It was all way too clear now. "I did," he said quietly.

"You did what?"

He answered without taking his eyes off the ceiling. "I swallowed her blood. She bit her lip. It bled. I kissed her. The taste...it was good." He closed his eyes and recalled the ecstasy of the moment. He'd do it again.

"You've damned yourself then, CF19, and there is nothing I can do to help you."

Strange to hear the doctor speak of damnation when he was responsible for stealing the souls and free will of so many.

"It's a hazard to the others to have you here, but clearly the gas chamber will not kill you now." The doctor actually sounded disappointed. Did he enjoy tossing men into the damn gas chamber? "You'll be eliminated another way."

Valentino jerked his head off the pillow. "H-how?" Jesus Christ, was the man going to put a stake through his heart?

"I've read decapitation is the only proven method of killing a vampire."

Somehow the stake sounded better. "I'm not a vampire."

"Yet," Dr. Reynolds added. "It is not the way I would like to end your existence, but I have no choice." He headed for the door and paused before leaving. "The door will be locked and no one will have permission to enter. Is there anything you'd like me to say to anyone?"

Valentino shook his head and lay back down. "No. Nothing. No one."

"Very well." The door clicked shut behind Dr. Reynolds, and the sound had a finality to it that froze the blood in Valentino's veins.

A great deal had changed since he'd hatched his plan with Raphael yesterday, but one thing remained very much the same. He needed to get out, and he needed Sera. Come hell or high water, he'd escape today and find her.

Chapter Sixteen

Sera woke up surrounded by the unfamiliar fragrance of another woman. She lifted her head and spotted a chestnut-haired stunner pacing the room. Dressed in a knee-length, black skirt and a white, V-neck sweater, the woman looked like some sort of sexy secretary. Maybe that's what she was? If so, why wasn't she somewhere else answering the coven phone or something? Only one way to find out.

"Who are you?" Sera didn't bother to be polite. It was rather annoying to have uninvited people strolling into her room. Though this guest was an improvement over Constantine.

The woman halted and turned toward the bed. Her green eyes shone even at a distance and her smile seemed open and honest. "Hello, I hope I didn't startle you?"

Sera shoved her hair out of her eyes and sat up with the blankets tucked under her arms. "No, but who are you?" Although a fellow vampire, the steady beat of the woman's heart let Sera know how young she was. Hmm. Had idle curiosity brought her here?

The woman approached the bed, her footsteps silent and graceful in spite of the skinny heels she wore. "My name is Sylvia, and I wanted to welcome you to the coven before my husband ordered you to spend the rest of the evening sequestered in his study." She held out a pale, elegant hand and smiled when Sera hesitated. "I won't bite."

Sera rolled her eyes and accepted the gesture. "It's

nice to meet you, but why would your husband want to spend the evening with me?"

Sylvia pulled her hand back and her smile faltered. "Oh, I assumed you would recognize my name."

Such an assumption did not bode well. "You're the mistress, aren't you?"

Sylvia nodded. "Yes, but that doesn't mean you have to jump out of bed to curtsy to me. I want us to be friends, not queen and subject."

Yeah? How would Master Vamp feel about that? And how the hell could someone so young be queen? She was under the impression that only the truly ancient could ever hold such a place of power. In fact, were there any other queens? If so, she'd never heard of any. Male vampires seemed to dominate in every country. Could America really be that different?

"Once you've spoken to your master, I'll gladly answer all of your questions."

Sera didn't appreciate Sylvia's ability to read her mind, but she held her tongue and nodded politely.

"Now then," Sylvia began, propping her hands on her slender hips. "I was informed that you brought a bag full of very inappropriate clothing with you. Is this true?"

Sera frowned and made a note to strangle Constantine when she saw him again. "I brought jeans and stuff."

The queen shook her head and clucked her tongue. Again she held out her hand. "Come with me and we'll see that you have everything you need before you are summoned."

Summoned sounded rather ominous. Sera slid out of bed, self-conscious to be naked in front of a stranger. She grabbed the comforter, but Sylvia chuckled and snatched it out of her hand.

"I brought you a robe." She lifted a long, black robe from the foot of the bed. Smiling, she held it open for Sera to slip into. "I hope you learn to like it here."

Sera knotted the belt and gave a little nod. "It'll take

some getting used to. I've been on my own for a really long time."

Sylvia cupped her cheeks and then leaned forward to kiss her forehead. "You are no longer alone, Seraphina. Never forget that." Her lips brushed against Sera's skin, causing a shiver of strange awareness.

Sera pulled away, feeling more than a little odd, and offered a shaky smile. "Thank you."

Sylvia returned the smile with an open, honest one and then led the way out of the room. "First you need to feed."

Oh no. Sera's mind conjured an image of her "snack" from the previous evening. Was he in the house somewhere, naked and waiting? Would Sylvia linger and demand to watch her bite the mortal? When she refused, would she be evicted?

Sylvia slowed her pace and reached back for Sera's hand. "We have blood in the kitchen." She winked and squeezed her fingers. "I prefer it to drinking from mortals, since I was one not too long ago."

"How long?" Sometimes curiosity just refused to wait.

"I was turned during the last blood ritual."

Although she didn't belong to a coven, Sera knew all about the ritual. It was a time for vampires to gather and revel in their true nature. Or so she assumed that was what it was all about. The books she'd read might have gotten it wrong. To the best of her knowledge, the last ritual would have been about six months ago. Wow. Sylvia *was* young.

"Age hardly matters anymore, my dear." Sylvia halted all together and pulled Sera close to whisper, "And I have the blood of kings running in my veins now. No one would be foolish enough to challenge my role here."

Sera took the words precisely the way they were intended, as a warning. Feeling as if she had just been put in her place, she followed Sylvia through the vast house. The halls were dark and twisting, and she hoped she wouldn't be expected to find her way back alone.

There was no doubt she'd end up lost. Finally, they reached the kitchen after passing through a large, elegant dining room. It hadn't escaped Sera's notice how empty the house was.

Where were the others?

"Most everyone can be found in the gathering room this time of day." Sylvia headed for the fridge. "Do you prefer it warm?" She looked over her shoulder and held up two bags.

Sera nodded. "Yes, please."

With a little grin, Sylvia slit the bags open, filled two large mugs, and popped both in the microwave. "My husband frowns on this habit of mine," Sylvia remarked without looking toward Sera. "But I don't care. I'll gladly drink *his* blood fresh from the veins," she glanced over and winked, "but I don't relish the thought of having a servant following me around."

"Doesn't that make him angry?"

The microwave dinged and Sylvia removed the drinks before answering. "It did in the beginning. I think he might have even regretted his decision to make me his queen." She handed Sera a warm mug and nodded encouragingly.

Sera sipped with pleasure.

"I assured him I would do what was required if and when the occasion arose, but I wouldn't live my life by his dictates simply because he was king." Sylvia paused to drink for a few moments. She lowered her mug and licked her lips. "Mmm...delicious. Yes?"

Sera nodded and lifted her mug again. Her synthetic blood didn't taste this good.

"It's not synthetic, dear."

She choked down her last swallow and stared at Sylvia. "It isn't?"

Sylvia plucked the empty mug from Sera's hand and set both in the sink. "No," she said over her shoulder. "The servants all donate so there is always a supply in case of an emergency."

"Oh." Sera had no idea what else to say to that. Though it explained why the blood had tasted more like her "snack" than the stuff at home. Speaking of... "Who was the man in my room last night?"

Sylvia didn't even pretend not to know. "Oh, that was Rick."

Rick. Such a normal sounding name. How on earth had he become a vampire's human servant?

"He doesn't belong to just one vampire, Sera. Rick is one of the mortals who serve the entire coven. I thought you might like him." Her expression turned sheepish. "I apologize if he was not to your taste."

"He was fine. Thank you." Heat rushed to Sera's cheeks and she looked away from Sylvia's probing stare, all the while attempting to block her memories of just how fine Rick really was. His blood had been delicious, his body glorious, and his offer to give more almost tempting enough to accept.

"Now that you've had breakfast, let's go find you something to wear." Sylvia swept by her on the way to the door, leaving Sera no choice but to follow in her wake. The woman certainly acted like a queen.

Outside the kitchen, Sera shuffled to a halt at the sight of the master making his way through the dining room. Tonight he was dressed in black jeans and a pale blue, dress shirt. Like last night, the shirt was untucked and partially unbuttoned, and he looked just as gorgeous. No wonder Sylvia willingly nipped into his veins. Who wouldn't?

Sera tried not to stare as the master reached his wife, cupped her face, and kissed her passionately. The display made more than just Sera's face grow hot. All over, she felt the tiny pinpricks of awareness Valentino had awakened from dormancy. Without his touch to relieve the ache, the feeling grew more annoying by the moment. The master finally pulled back from his wife and turned his startling smile upon Sera. Instinctively, she curtsied and did her best to shove her rising sexual awareness back into its cave. It didn't want to go.

The master shook his head and reached for her hand. "There is no need for that." He coaxed her to straighten and gave her fingers a slight squeeze before releasing her to gesture toward his wife. "Allow Sylvia to find you something to wear and then join Constantine and myself in my study. Sylvia will show you the way."

Sera nodded and fidgeted with the front of her robe. She was too aware of being naked underneath the black silk and the way her nipples pressed against the fabric, but the master didn't seem to notice. Should she be relieved or insulted?

"We have much to discuss, Seraphina," he said. His tone had hardened, as had his eyes.

"Yes, I know." He would wish to talk about Valentino. Everything Constantine had told her came rushing back, and with it, the raw emotions. Why on earth did she feel so betrayed? Why on earth hadn't Valentino confided in her? She was a vampire, for goodness sake, didn't he believe she'd understand? Did she understand? No, not really.

The realization made her frown, and she barely heard the master take leave of his wife. The touch of Sylvia's hand on her arm startled her from her musings, and she looked up, blinking. "Forgive me, I didn't hear you."

Sylvia merely smiled the sort of smile one would expect from a doting mother and led Sera from the room by the hand. "You'll be fine, my dear."

Sera wasn't so sure.

****

A little over an hour later, dressed in a borrowed, olive green, shirtdress and beige pumps, Sera walked into the master's study. She wanted to call Sylvia back as the woman slipped away, but she managed to fix her gaze straight ahead and wait for an invitation to sit. The master stood and motioned toward the chair next to Constantine's. It didn't escape her notice that he'd tucked in his shirt and tossed on a black jacket.

She glanced at Constantine on the way to her offered seat and saw that he wore a different suit than the one from last night. It was charcoal gray with a crisp white shirt underneath. Unfortunately, he looked incredibly dashing. She eased her gaze away and stepped around the chair.

"You don't look too bad yourself, my pet," Constantine commented as she sat down and crossed her legs. "Much better than jeans and a hoodie." He winked to let her know he was teasing.

Sera forced a tight grin and shifted on the smooth leather seat. Facing a firing squad held more appeal than having to answer whatever questions the master wished to voice. She peeked up through her lashes and met his stunning blue gaze. At that moment, she was very relieved not to be a mortal. Such eyes would easily mesmerize.

"Forgive me for having to put you through this," the master began, "but I must know everything about your association with the man Constantine has named Valentino. For some reason you've had a strong, nearly fatal reaction to his blood, and before we cleanse your system we need to know how much you ingested, how frequently, and how you felt afterward."

Fatal? Sera's brain refused to move on from that shocking word. Had she nearly died on her bathroom floor? She felt Constantine's gaze and looked over. His expression revealed all she needed to know, and her stomach crawled up toward her throat. She fixed her gaze back on the master. "I thought nothing could kill me?"

"Under normal circumstances, that assumption is completely accurate."

Sera laced her hands together and dug her nails into her palms. "In other words, his blood nearly killed me because he isn't human." Saying it out loud caused a burning wound to open in the vicinity of her heart. Damn. What was that all about? She'd gone to Captive Fantasy looking for an orgasm, not love. Why did things always have to become complicated?

"What exactly is he?" she asked, though part of her didn't want to know. Maybe he'd only been able to coax passion from her because of whatever he was? If so, that meant she really was broken and no mortal man could fix her. How was that for depressing?

The master shifted his attention to Constantine. "Would you like to tell her?"

"I want *you* to tell me," Sera said before Constantine could respond.

With a single nod, the master complied. "Most of what you will wish to know is in this file." He shoved a harmless looking manila folder across the desk. She didn't reach out to take it, but her eyes locked on it and refused to budge. "To summarize," he went on. "Valentino is an experimental clone designed to provide extraordinary sexual gratification."

Sera swallowed and pulled her gaze from the folder. "But if he's a clone, then he's more or less human." She couldn't hide the hope in her voice.

The master shook his head. "No." He dragged the folder back toward himself and lifted the cover to scan the top page. He spoke again without meeting her gaze. "Captive Fantasy is the brain child of Dr. Sven Reynolds." He glanced up. "The man used to practice medicine in Russia and discovered some combination of chemicals that, when manipulated, will recreate human DNA. You need only correctly mix the formula, incubate the result, and wait."

"Wait for what?" Dear God, had Valentino been *hatched*? It certainly sounded like it.

"You must wait for the mixture to show signs of life," Constantine answered.

Sera reluctantly looked at him. "Then what?" By now her nails were making her palms bleed, but the pain helped focus her.

"Then the mixture is injected into a female egg, and

once the egg is fertilized, it is placed into the woman's womb to develop as any normal child would."

Something in Constantine's tone made Sera's skin tingle with unease. "Where are these women?"

It was the master who replied. "We do not know what becomes of the women." There was a great deal of regret in his tone.

"I see." It seemed an appropriate response, but she actually saw nothing.

"How much of his blood did you take, Seraphina?"

She looked at her hands in her lap and mumbled, "I'm thinking, more than I should have."

Constantine reached out and covered her hands with one of his. She didn't bother to look at him. "You knew no better," he said. "And the blame for that falls solely on my shoulders."

Sera couldn't resist the urge to lift her eyes. Constantine's remorse was clearly etched on every plane of his face. Why did he have to start caring about her at the same time she was falling in love with some non-human freak of science? Why, why, why?

"I've always cared," he said softly. He released her hands with a lingering caress and turned to the master. "I've already offered to donate my blood for Sera's transfusion, and I think the sooner, the better."

"Will doing so put you in danger?" She had to know. She wasn't sure if it mattered or not, but she had to know.

Constantine flashed a cocky grin. "I'm strong enough to take it, though I hope there are a few mortals handy once the procedure is done." He winked and licked his lips like the true blood-sucking monster he was.

Sera rolled her eyes, thankful that he had helped dissolve her moment of weakness toward him. She looked toward the master, the question she needed to ask lodged in her throat. Swallowing shook it free. "Does it matter that he ingested some of my blood?"

All hell broke loose.

Chapter Seventeen

Constantine flew out of his chair so fast he was nothing more than a blur before he came to land in front of her. His hands gripped the leather armrests, his arms caged her in, and his eyes shone with black fury. "What did you say?"

Sera melted into the chair as far as she could go. It wasn't far enough. The master spoke before she could find her voice.

"Back off, Constantine. We'll get nothing out of her if you insist on frightening her." He appeared over Constantine's shoulder to flash Sera a sympathetic look, then he took a hold of Constantine's jacket and physically pulled him away from her. "I said, back off."

Constantine straightened and shot a dark look toward his master. "He took her blood. Do you have any idea what that means?"

Sera figured out of the three of them, the master was likely the only one who knew exactly what it meant. She dreaded the moment he would tell her. Without answering Constantine, he swung his attention back down to her. She shifted in the chair and forced herself not to look away from the probing eyes.

"I don't think he took a lot," she offered. Did it matter?

Wearing a look of open concern, the master knelt in front of her and reached out to cup her cheeks. The contact sent shockwaves through Sera. "The amount does not matter, Seraphina. You've given him your blood, and you have taken his. Doing so forged a bond that cannot be broken."

Sera glanced up at Constantine. "A bond like ours?"

"No," he all but growled before turning his back and stalking to the far side of the room.

"I don't understand." Sera shook her head within the master's grip and once more met his gaze. "I don't understand," she said again. Tears burned her eyes and clogged her throat. "What have I done?"

The master released her with a sigh and stood back up. "Sharing your blood with Valentino has made him your servant."

"You forget he's not human, master," Constantine said without moving. The rigid line of his back scared Sera more than any look he could ever think to toss her way. She'd seen this stance before. Once. Right before he pointed at the door and ordered her to get her pathetic person out of his sight.

She jumped as the master took hold of her hands. "You are safe here. Don't ever forget that."

Constantine whirled around. "Do not insinuate that I would hurt her."

The master glanced back at Constantine without releasing Sera's hands. "You failed to teach her what she needed to know to keep herself and others safe. In my opinion, the damage has already been done."

Constantine opened his mouth, then wisely snapped it shut. He bowed his head and his silky hair slid forward to hide his features. "What would you have me do, master?" The submissiveness shocked Sera.

"You'll be responsible for bringing Valentino to the coven."

Sera pulled her hands away and shot out of her chair. "What? You can't send Constantine after Valentino. He'll kill him." She met Constantine's gaze over the master's shoulder. "I'd never forgive you if you did."

"He won't touch a hair on his head," the master said softly. "If he does, he'll answer to me."

Constantine's features hardened, but he nodded curtly and started for the door. The master's voice halted him. "I'll have Fabian and Jamie go with you." He moved to his desk to push a button on the phone. "Lynnette, have Fabian and Jamie make preparations to leave. I want them to accompany Constantine to San Francisco."

"Yes, master."

The phone beeped and the master swung his gaze toward Constantine. "Time is of the essence. Now go."

Sera listened to the study door open and close and then dug her nails into her palms again. Being alone with the master was almost worse than facing Constantine's anger. Not sure what do to, she bit her tongue and blinked back tears.

"Please, Sera, sit back down." He waved toward her chair and offered a pleasant smile. Once she obeyed, he perched on the corner of his desk and rested his hands atop his thigh. "I should warn you, that I have no idea what effect your blood will have on Valentino."

Sera swallowed and unclenched her teeth. "But I gather you have some theories?"

The master nodded. "Yes, of course. Given that he isn't human, your blood might not affect him at all or..." he trailed off.

Sera shook her head. She didn't want to hear the rest.

"It might kill him," he concluded.

Bile surged up the back of Sera's throat, and no amount of swallowing would force it back down. Dizzy, she stumbled to her feet and gestured toward the door. "I want to go," she whispered. She wanted to go home, to leave the coven, but she knew that wouldn't be allowed.

The master rose and came toward her. While she struggled to remain on her feet, he gathered her in his arms and pressed her cheek to his chest. The rich, masculine scent of his skin surrounded her as completely as his arms. His lips brushed the top of her head. "You aren't well, Sera. It isn't safe for you to leave. I'm sorry."

A tear plopped onto her cheek and rolled toward the edge of her mouth. "If I killed him, I don't want to live." With every ounce of her being she meant those words.

The master stroked her hair, kissed the top of her head once more, then turned her toward the door. "Sylvia will be waiting outside, and she'll remain with you for as long as you'd like her to." He guided her across the room, and without warning, the door opened and the queen reached for her.

Sera pressed back into the master's chest. "I want to be alone."

Sylvia frowned and came forward with a little shake of her head. "You must come with me, my dear. We need to make sure all of the bad blood is out of your system before it makes you ill again."

No, Sera wanted to yell. If she went through with the cleansing or the transfusion, or whatever they were calling it, she'd lose Valentino. If he was dead, all she had was the blood in her veins. If it killed her, so be it. She shook her head and stepped out of the master's embrace. Surprisingly, he let her go. "I'd rather go to my room and wait for Constantine to return."

Sylvia glanced toward her husband, then back at Sera. "Very well." Her tone was heavy with disapproval, but she stepped aside and allowed Sera to leave the study. "I'll have fresh blood brought to you, and I expect you to drink all of it."

Sera glanced back and the look on her queen's face told her to simply nod and continue on her way. She reached the base of the towering staircase and the master's low voice slipped into her ear.

"She'll only get worse if his blood is allowed to fester within her."

"She'll be more amicable once Constantine returns with either news of Valentino's death or the man himself. We can leave her be until then."

Sera ran up the stairs before the master could respond to his queen's wisdom. God willing, Constantine would return with Valentino, whole and healthy. She refused to consider the any other option.

****

Valentino contemplated the locked door of his room before sweeping his gaze around the windowless walls. He'd been trying to come up with a way to escape for the entire day, and so far, nothing. At least he didn't feel as if he were dying anymore. His heartbeat was strong in his chest, and his unusually cold temperature had risen to something close to normal. All in all, he felt pretty damn good.

But that wouldn't help him get out of here and to Sera.

The thought of her coaxed his dick to life and he glanced down, relieved to discover all of him was back to normal. Maybe later he'd question the sudden reversal of his health, but right now he needed to concentrate on getting out. But how?

As if in answer to the silent question, the door flew open, and he stumbled back to avoid being knocked aside. Two men he'd never seen before filled the opening, neither looking too friendly or helpful. One had to be at least six-foot-five and about two hundred fifty pounds of pure muscle. He had short, dark hair and piercing green eyes. The other was only about two inches shorter and maybe ten pounds less intimidating. He had long brown hair and unfriendly gray eyes. Both were dressed in head to toe black leather and looked like the leaders of a bad ass biker gang.

Their arrival brought with it a heavy dose of unease.

A third man sliced between them to enter the room, and it was obvious he was the true leader. Valentino hated him on sight.

"Valentino, I presume?" The leader's black eyes raked over him then returned to his face with a look of disgust. "Do you ever wear clothes?"

Valentino frowned. "Do I know you?"

The leader motioned the other two forward. "Get him

dressed so we can get the fuck out of here."

The other two moved to obey, but Valentino threw up his hands in defense and skittered backwards. "Hold on a damn minute. Who the hell are you guys?"

The tall, green eyed beast brushed by him to yank open the closet door. He ripped a black t-shirt from a hanger and tossed it toward Valentino, who made no move to catch it. It hit him in the chest and fell to the floor. "Where are we going?" A pair of jeans followed and then boots, which he narrowly avoided being struck by.

"We're taking you to the coven."

Valentino swept his gaze back to the black-eyed leader. "The coven?" Vampire lived in covens, didn't they? Did that mean they were taking him to Sera?

"Save your questions until we're out of here." With that, the leader turned his back and stepped out of the room.

The giant with the gray eyes bent to scoop Valentino's clothes off the floor. "He's controlling the entire club, so you had best hurry before his powers weaken,"

More questions begged to be asked, but Valentino simply took the clothes and slid them on as quickly as possible. With his boots in hand, he followed the two men from the room and through the club. The leader stalked ahead of them, head high and shoulders rigid. The black trench he wore swung around his calves like an ominous cape. If asked to cast a movie about vampires, this guy would be at the top of Valentino's list.

Music thumped and bodies swayed around them, but despite the near-capacity crowd of women, not a single face turned in their direction as they headed for the exit. It was an unnerving display of the leader's power. Could Sera do such things?

Feeling as if he were being led into damnation, Valentino glanced back once to watch the door swing shut behind him. He didn't need to ask to know he'd never see Captive Fantasy again. Mixed emotions churned inside him at the realization. It was all he'd ever known, after all.

"Close your eyes," a voice ordered from behind him. Before he could turn to identify which of the three vampires had spoken, cruel fingers encircled his throat and squeezed. Lights exploded behind his lids, and his lungs struggled to send oxygen to his brain. "Relax," the voice whispered in his ear. "Let the blackness take you and when you awaken, you'll be among the coven."

Valentino gasped for breath a moment before the blackness closed in around him. Still clinging to consciousness, he felt the earth fall away from his feet and then he was floating. His last thought before oblivion claimed him was of Sera's clear eyes and lush smile. She called to him and lifted her hand to beckon him forward. Her fangs flashed behind her blood-red lips, then the vision faded away, as did the world.

Chapter Eighteen

Sera was tired of pacing. She headed for the bed and plopped down on the corner. The fresh blood Sylvia had supplied sat untouched on the nightstand. Her nerves would not allow her to drink, not that she was even thirsty. A faint sound drew her gaze to the door, and she stood back up with her heart in her throat. Could Constantine have returned so soon?

Someone scratched at the wood, and she called out an order to enter. The knob turned, the door opened, and Rick strolled in.

Sera barely suppressed a moan as she sat back down on the bed. "Go away."

At least he wasn't naked, but his tight, blue jeans did little to hide his body. He ignored her and moved closer to the bed. She glanced up and noticed drops of water dotting his bare chest. Looking past the thick column of his throat, she saw the tips of his hair were wet as well. The rich fragrance of shampoo let her know he'd recently gotten out of the shower.

Being faced with a squeaky clean, gorgeous mortal didn't make her any thirstier or lessen her nerves one bit. "Go away," she said again.

Rick chuckled and dropped to his haunches in front of her. His sea-green eyes twinkled as he gazed up at her. "You haven't touched the blood the queen supplied. She feared you wouldn't."

"And you're here to force me to drink?" Sera shifted her knees away from Rick's chest, but he was too broad and escape was futile. The heat from his body warmed her legs.

"I can't force you to do anything, I told you that last night, but what's over there," he nodded toward the carafe on the nightstand, "will have gone bad by now. I'm here to supply you with fresh blood."

Sera glanced at his neck again. It was a nice neck; thick, corded, smooth. Not as nice as Valentino's. Her mouth watered at the comparison, and her fangs slid down. Clearly Rick was accustomed to the look of a hungry vampire, because he smiled and shifted closer. He even arched his head back like a good little meal.

"Bite me, mistress."

Sera licked her lips. "I told you not to call me that."

His smile grew as he brushed a few strands of wet hair off the side of his neck. The gesture made her teeth hurt. Damn. "Bite me," he said again.

With her fangs hooked over her bottom lip, Sera shook her head and snarled, "No."

Rick lifted his head with a sigh and reached up to cup the back of her neck. "I was told to make sure you drink, mistress. Orders are orders." He pulled her face down and arched his head back again. Being mortal, he shouldn't have possessed the strength necessary to force her mouth to his throat, but he did, and the moment her fangs touched flesh, bloodlust roared to life. "My blood is yours, take it."

Her nostrils flared as she caught the rich scent of what her body craved. A drop of drool fell from the corner of her mouth to moisten his skin and she knew she was lost. "I despise you for making me do this," she ground out before widening her jaw and sinking her teeth deep into his artery.

While Rick's blood filled her mouth, he tugged her off the bed and onto his thighs. He maintained his grip at the back of her neck with one hand, leaving the other free to roam her body. He cupped her breast through the shirtdress and her traitorous nipple hardened in response. Why did sex and feeding have to go hand in hand? Her dress rode up until she was able to straddle Rick's lap and feel the hard line of his erection against her crotch. He mumbled something under his breath that made his blood flow faster and shifted under her to increase the contact of their bodies.

The slide of his blood down her throat might be enjoyable, but she refused to have sex with him. She pulled free of his neck before things could get out of control and leaned back to look him in the eyes. "You've done what you were ordered to do, now go."

His hands dropped to her waist, and he moved her up the length of his erection. The contact forced a moan past her lips. Rick smiled and did it again. "We both want more."

Sera shook her head even as the aroma of her own arousal filled the air. This wasn't the body she wanted to ride. No matter how good Rick felt wedged between her legs, she wanted another. "Let me go."

Rick's eyes narrowed. "Is that an order, mistress?"

"Yes," she said sharply.

His hands went slack at her waist, and she scooted off him to get to her feet. Disappointment had taken much of the sparkle from his gaze. "You're never going to let me fuck you, are you?"

Sera shook her head and smoothed her dress over her thighs while trying to ignore the wound on the side of Rick's neck. She hadn't licked it closed and fresh blood called to her. She turned away, willing her fangs back up into her gums.

"Hey?" Rick's hand closed around her leg, just below the hem of her dress. "What is it with you?" His fingers stroked upward toward her thigh, and she shifted away lest he feel the heat of her denied desire.

"Take your hands off me."

He didn't. In fact, he touched her with both hands; sliding them up the backs of her legs and taking the dress along. "I've told you before, you need to relax." His hands moved around to the front of her thighs, and Sera reached down to cover them before he could make his way to her crotch.

She glared over her shoulder. "Don't make me hurt you."

"At least that would be something."

"I doubt you are starved for companionship."

"Maybe I'm bored with the other female vamps? Maybe I want to see what you can do for me?"

With a little shake of her head, she stepped away. "Sorry, I'm really not interested.

Whatever Rick might have said was lost when the door crashed open.

****

Valentino tore out of the vampire's strong grip the moment he was inside Sera's room. The guy attempted to take hold of him again, but he stepped out of range at the last moment. "Sera?"

She turned, and the half naked, blond kneeling behind her nearly toppled over. Her eyes widened, and her lips parted in silent surprise. She looked beautiful, and he ached to hold her.

"I brought you a gift, my pet," the leader snarled from behind him. He shoved Valentino further into the room then stepped up to his side. "So, how does he look? I personally think he's a little scrawny, but I'm not the one who has to fuck him, am I? Oh wait, given our bond, I am." His tone was sinister, and Sera's eyes narrowed as they slid his way.

"Shut up, Constantine."

There was no humor in Constantine's laugh. "I'll let you two play for awhile while I inform the master that the little clone is turning into a vampire. I bet he's not expecting that news."

Sera gaped as the vampire leader snapped his fingers toward the guy on the floor. "Get off your knees, Rick. No matter how much you beg, you won't get in her pants." His black eyes settled on Valentino. "Especially now."

153

Valentino stepped aside, and the door closed behind Rick and Constantine. Alone with Sera, he stared at her for a few moments then started across the room. She lifted her hand to her throat and took a step back. He stopped.

"Is it true?"

He decided not to assume he knew what she was asking. "Is what true? The part about being a clone or a vampire?"

She waved her hand toward him. "Both, either."

He nodded and started toward her again. "Yes, I'm a scientifically created sex toy." She flinched at that and took a step back for every one he took forward. "The vampire bit, I don't know if it's true, but it might be."

"But how?" She continued to retreat until finally her back was to the wall. "It takes a great deal to turn a mortal...I think."

"But I didn't start as a normal mortal."

Sera shook her head and fisted her hands at her sides. "You could have told me."

Valentino paused. "Would you have listened?" When she nodded and dragged her bottom lip into her mouth, he wanted to drop to his knees and tell her he loved her.

Her watery gaze met his. "I don't think it's possible for you to become a vampire."

Valentino didn't care. For the past few days he'd been waiting to die and trying not to think of never seeing Sera again. But here he was and here she was, and he'd be damned if they wasted another second chatting about whether or not he was turning into a vampire. "We'll talk later, Sera."

She shook her head and lifted her hands to hold him off. "No. I need to know what's going on with you. I was told my blood could kill you."

"Well, it didn't." He pressed closer, smashing her hands between their bodies. "If you shut up, you'll soon discover just how healthy I am." He dipped his head and kissed her parted lips before she could utter another word. God, she tasted good.

The dress she had on buttoned all the way down the front and was laughably easy to rip open. She gasped into his mouth then moaned when he slid his tongue toward the back of her throat. Without the rules of Captive Fantasy hanging over his head he could take her anyway he wanted, without having to wait for her to ask, and he wanted her right here. Right now.

She squirmed against him, and he ended the kiss to look into her eyes. She licked her lips and rested her head back against the wall. A small smile flirted at the corners of her mouth. "Hi," she whispered. "I missed you." She reached up to stroke his cheek and then dragged a finger toward his lips. "I missed you a lot."

"Oh God, Sera." He slammed his mouth back down on hers while his hands clawed at the lace of her bra. It shredded under his fingers, exposing her breasts to his touch. He squeezed her nipples, and she bit into his tongue. Blood filled his mouth, and he pulled free of her teeth in order to swallow.

"Careful, baby," he whispered against her mouth.

She moaned and reached up to fist her hands in his hair. Pulling his head back with one good yank, she aimed for his neck and sank her teeth deep into his flesh. Another moan wracked her body, followed by a purr of pleasure.

Valentino decided to let her drink.

Blindly, he clutched her hips and ripped her panties away from her body. She lifted a leg to his waist and wiggled against him as he fumbled between them to unhook his jeans. Eventually he managed to work his cock free, and he slicked it through her wet folds until she bit harder and moaned loudly. "You want it?"

She nodded against his neck and wiggled some more.

Sliding his hands under her ass, he lifted her off the floor. Instinctively, she curled around him, and his cock found her hole. He thrust forward, but she was too tight and the angle was all wrong. "Damnit."

"Mmm..." she mumbled against his neck, then eased her teeth free. "What's wrong?" She sounded breathless and sexy.

He met her gaze and watched her lick his blood from her lips. His cock jumped, making her gasp. "If you want it all, we need to move."

Frowning, she dug her nails into his shoulders and squirmed up the wall. She pulled him closer. "Just do it," she begged. "I don't care if it hurts."

"I do." Gripping her ass, he stepped back. She squeaked and wrapped her arms around his neck. "Shh, I'm only taking you to the bed." As he walked, his cock slid further inside her, and she dropped her forehead onto his shoulder with a sigh that ruffled the tips of his hair and tickled the wound on his neck. He halted halfway to the bed. "Feel good?"

She nodded without lifting her head.

With his feet braced apart, he clasped her ass tighter and lifted her slightly before easing her back down. He slid nearly the entire way inside before her sweet body closed around him and stopped him from going deeper. "Relax, baby."

She did, but only until he attempted to move. The moment he shifted his hips, her muscles tightened. "Sorry," she said in a rush.

He chuckled and moved toward the bed again. Instead of laying her down, he set her on her feet, and she blinked in surprise while he peeled the ruined dress and underwear off her body. After kicking off her heels, she sank down onto the edge of the bed to stare up at him. Her hungry expression demanded to be fed, so he stepped back and slowly eased his t-shirt up and over his head. If she wanted a show, he'd gladly give her one.

He threw the shirt aside and watched her gaze drift down his body. His cock still strained from his gaping fly, and it caught her attention. Clearly, she wanted the jeans gone. Well, who was he to stop her? "Why don't you take them off?"

Her gaze flew to his face. "Take what off?"

He fought a smile at the blush creeping into her cheeks. "My jeans."

The blush deepened, and she shook her head. "No. It'll be easier if you do it."

"But I want you to."

"Oh..." Her gaze lowered again, and her tongue poked out between her lips.

"God, Sera. Either do it or don't, but the look on your face is too much to bear."

She peeked up through her lashes and then shocked the hell out of him by dropping to her knees. Still looking into his eyes, she placed her hands on his thighs and licked her lips. "I've never done this before."

"Never?" He shouldn't really be surprised, given how uncomfortable she was with all things sexual. "You don't have to do it now." It killed him to say that.

She lowered her gaze and moved her hands up his thighs. "I think I want to."

Tension like he'd never experienced before tightened every muscle in his body as Valentino waited for the touch of Sera's hands or mouth. Either was likely to make him explode. He closed his eyes, unable to tolerate the sight of her kneeling before him. "You're killing me, Sera."

"It doesn't look like it." Her breath blew over his cock, making him even harder. "You look just fine to me." With that, she wrapped her fingers around him and stroked upward.

Chapter Nineteen

Sera felt Valentino shudder in response to her touch and it gave her the confidence she needed to stroke him again. This time, the shudder was accompanied by a low, sexy growl. She swept her gaze up his body toward his face. His eyes were shut, his chin nearly rested on his chest, and his hair eclipsed his features. She could just make out the tight line of his jaw. He opened his eyes to look at her through the fall of his hair.

"What do I do now?" She really didn't know. Constantine had never demanded oral sex from her, at the time she'd been relieved. Then she had discovered why. There seemed to be no shortage of women willing to do anything he asked of them. He didn't need Sera on her knees or anywhere at all, for that matter.

Valentino cupped her cheek and tipped her face up. "What are you thinking about?"

Sera shook the thoughts of Constantine away. She wouldn't let him ruin this. "Tell me what to do."

Valentino's gaze narrowed, but he didn't press her. "You can start by taking off my jeans."

Heat flooded Sera's face. "Oh, okay."

She released his cock and snared the waist of his jeans to shimmy the denim over his hips and down his thighs. He took over once they reached his knees and stepped back to strip them the rest of the way off. Naked, he moved in front of her again and took hold of his erection to slide it across her lips. She flicked her tongue out to taste the tip and gripped his thighs.

"Now, be a good little vampire and don't bite."

Sera glanced up and smiled wide enough to flash the tips of her fangs. "Are you afraid?"

He gave a nervous laugh. "Maybe a little."

She flicked her tongue out again, and he slid his hand down so she could lick more than just the tip. "I've managed to resist biting for a very long time. I think you'll be fine." The taste of him blanketed her tongue and made her scoot closer. She wanted him trapped between her lips.

Valentino's voice halted her as she opened her mouth. "You don't do so good when you're with me, and I have the marks to prove it."

Sera pulled back and snapped her mouth shut. Getting to her feet, she shook her head. "I'm sorry. You're right. This isn't a good idea."

"Just a damn minute!" Valentino took hold of her as she tried to turn away. He twisted her back around to face him and gave her a little shake. "So, that's it? I tease you about biting and you decide *nothing* should happen?"

"Maybe nothing should," she countered. "We aren't good for each other."

"What!"

Sera slid out of his grasp and covered her ears. "Stop yelling at me." She sat down on the bed, then jumped back up. The bed wasn't safe. "I said goodbye to you for a reason, Valentino. We weren't supposed to see each other again."

"What the hell are you talking about?"

Now it was Sera's turn to yell. "This!" She gestured between the two of them. "Us! We aren't good for each other. When I'm with you, I act exactly the way I never wanted to and you...you..." She huffed and turned her back on him.

"I what?" He gripped her shoulders from behind and leaned close to her cheek. "I what?"

Sera shivered. "Don't do that."

"Do what?"

She rolled her shoulders to try and escape his touch, but it didn't work.

"Don't do what?" he asked again.

"Stop purring in my ear."

"Ah. Like this? Mmmm..." His entire body vibrated with the sound, making her shiver again.

"Yes," she bit out. "Like that."

"But you like it. In fact," he hesitated and turned her around to face him. "You like everything I do, which leads me to believe we're very good for each other."

"No." Sera shook her head and braced her hands on Valentino's chest. Touching him wasn't any safer than sitting on the bed, but she didn't take her hands away. "I've ruined your life. How can you say I'm good for you, when I accidentally turned you into a vampire?"

"I don't think I'm a full fledged vampire yet." He snapped his teeth together. "No fangs."

"Ugh!" Sera shoved him back with enough force to make him lose his grip on her. "You are impossible."

He chuckled and reached for her again. "No, just incredibly thrilled to see you again, not to mention extremely horny."

Sera rolled her eyes and let Valentino gather her into his arms. "I can't win with you, can I?"

He put his mouth to her ear. "Oh yes you can." He walked her around until she faced the bed. "You looked good on your knees, by the way," he said softly.

Sera caught her breath and stared down at the silver and black comforter. "What are you going to do?"

Before he answered, he shifted his mouth to lick the side of her neck. "Maybe someday I *will* be able to sink my teeth into you? I know you'd like that."

"Valentino," she warned, though the thought made her hot all over.

He chuckled in her ear and nipped at the lobe. "So how 'bout you crawl onto your hands and knees like a good little girl?"

"Why should I?" Despite the challenge, excitement

coursed through her. She knew what he wanted to do to her, and it had been a really long time since she'd had sex in that position. The last time had ended with her nearly biting her lover's hand, so she'd avoided it from that point on.

"I thought you trusted me?" He sounded hurt.

Sera glanced over her shoulder. "I do."

Valentino smiled and slid a thigh between her legs. "Then get on your hands and knees."

How on earth could she resist? She crawled onto the bed and began to make her way up toward the pillows, assuming Valentino would need room to kneel behind her. She got halfway before he gripped her hips and hauled her back toward the edge. "Where you going?"

Sera looked over her shoulder but couldn't speak as Valentino positioned himself behind her. He met her gaze and blew her a kiss right before he nudged the fat head of his cock between her legs. Her muscles closed around him, but he fought past the tight grip and claimed her fully after only two thrusts. Flashes of light exploded behind her eyes, and she squeezed them shut and dropped her forehead to the cool comforter. "Oh man..."

Valentino's fingers flexed on her hips as he worked his cock even deeper. "Mmm," he hummed. "You were made to take it like this."

Sera moaned into the blanket. It was true. This position made having an orgasm seem possible. It also made her feel like an animal, and animals bite. She clenched her teeth together and ignored the growing impulse. At least she couldn't get to any part of Valentino's body. But she could smell him. And she need only swallow to recall what he tasted like. Oh dear.

"Feel good?" He shoved deeper, making it impossible for her to answer. His self-assured chuckle told her he knew how damn good it felt.

The sheer size of him was enough to make her climax, but even without that, he had skill. He pumped against her ass while pulling her back at the same time.

The head of his cock rubbed the furthest reaches of her womb until she burned with the need to come. But needing to come wasn't enough to push her over the edge. She lifted her head to tell Valentino what she wanted, but he already seemed to know.

Shaking his hair out of his face, he met her gaze over her shoulder, and then shifted her hips higher against his pelvis. Doing so drove him in at a much different angle, so that with each powerful thrust, his balls brushed the swollen head of her clit. It was unlike anything she'd ever felt before, and exactly what her body craved. She tightened around him in a rapid series of contractions that encouraged him to thrust a little faster.

"Val..." she breathed before burying her face in the comforter. If she screamed, the whole house would hear her. She'd rather run naked through the halls.

"Don't you dare hide." Valentino trailed a hand up the center of her back to take hold of her nape. He pulled her face free of the blanket then twisted his fingers in her hair. "I want to hear you scream."

"No." Sera tried to shake her head, but Valentino's grip was too strong. She bit her lip, tasted blood, and squeezed her eyes shut as her orgasm crashed down around her. The scream was a muffled pain in the back of her throat.

The friction of Valentino's thrusts became more intense, then halted altogether as he dug his fingers into her hip, buried himself as deep as he would go, and let go inside her with enough force to rock her forward. She caught her breath and had to fight not to scream all over again.

Eventually the madness lessened, allowing her to regain her hold on reality. She glanced over her shoulder and clashed with his milk chocolate gaze. "See?" he said, though his voice was nothing more than a breathy whisper. "You won that round?"

"By not screaming?" She noticed the trembling in her own voice.

He nodded and withdrew from her to roll her onto her back. Taking advantage of the slippery comforter, he pushed her up toward the pillows and stretched out on top of her. His skin was damp with sweat, making their bodies stick together in places, not that she minded.

With his lips lightly pressed to hers and his slick cock nestled against her throbbing core, he whispered, "But I plan on winning the next round."

Sera turned away from his kiss. "I can't do it again."

He brushed his lips down the side of her neck. "Why not?" He moved off of her and captured a nipple in his teeth.

Sera buried a hand in his hair and tried to get him to stop. "Please, I can't do it again."

He lifted his head and aimed for her mouth again. He kissed her before she could turn away. "Did I hurt you?"

Sera shook her head, and then arched back to let Valentino kiss the underside of her chin. His hair swept over her collarbone as he licked a path to the hollow of her throat then back up again. The gesture made her shiver.

"You need blood, don't you?" He nipped her neck with his teeth. "Take whatever you need."

"No." Tearing into his neck had been enough for one night. She didn't want to lose control again.

He braced his weight on his hands and stared down into her face. "Stop being stubborn, Sera. I want to have sex with you again and you need blood in order to enjoy it. Right?"

"Yes," she hissed.

"So bite me. What's the big deal?"

"The big deal, as you say," Constantine's voice rang out from somewhere in the room, "is that your blood nearly killed her."

Sera shoved Valentino off her and sat up to glare toward their unwelcome visitor. "What do you think you're doing in here?"

Constantine flicked his gaze toward Valentino. "Leave us."

Valentino snorted. "Not on your life."

Anger tightened Constantine's features. He resettled his gaze on Sera. "Finding you naked is becoming a pleasant habit, my pet."

Sera reached for Valentino as he moved toward the edge of the bed. He glared at her, but she kept her fingers around his arm. "He wants to get a rise out of you. Just ignore him."

"Yes, just ignore me, Valentino." Constantine strolled all the way into the room and sat down in one of the two chairs arranged in front of a large fireplace. "Just pretend I'm not here and go about your business." He glanced toward the bed. "I gather you were trying to convince Seraphina to bite you?" He shook his head. "Not a wise thing to do, but the choice is yours."

Valentino's bicep flexed under Sera's fingers. "You said my blood nearly killed her. Is that true?"

"Why don't you answer him, my pet?" With a wave of his hand, Constantine focused his gaze on the dormant fireplace.

Sera met Valentino's concerned look and nodded.

"Jesus." He ripped free of her now limp fingers and bolted off the bed. "Why the hell didn't you say something?"

Sera twisted the comforter in her hands, then yanked it out from under her to pull it over her naked body. She looked away from Valentino and the accusation in his eyes. "I feel okay now."

"But you took more."

Sera swept her gaze toward Constantine and found him staring back at her, one eyebrow raised. "Is that true?" he asked.

"Stay the fuck out of this!" Valentino snapped.

Constantine got to his feet. "I can't do that. Would you like to know why?" He went on before Valentino could respond. "I made her," he pointed at Sera, "which means if you kill her, I'll have to kill you. No one gets away with hurting what is mine."

"She doesn't belong to you."

Constantine's chuckle raised goosebumps on Sera's skin. "Oh, yes she does."

"If that's true," Valentino commented, "then you've treated her like shit for way too long."

Sera whipped her head around to look at Valentino, but his gaze was fixed on Constantine. She'd never seen him so angry. In fact, his expression was rather chilling.

"How I treat her is none of your business."

Valentino's eyes darkened. "You're wrong."

"Stop, both of you." Sera looked from one angry face to the other and thought of two alpha wolves fighting for territory. "Constantine, go away and let me talk to Valentino."

He looked ready to deny her that one little request, but gave a curt nod and headed for the door. He took a moment to glance back. "If you did take more of his blood, you'll need to be cleansed sooner rather than later. Regardless of what *he* claims to know about us, I do not relish the thought of losing you." With that, he yanked the door open and stalked out.

"What the hell does he mean by cleansing?" Valentino demanded the moment they were alone.

Sera fell onto the pillows and pulled the comforter over her head. Maybe it would be easier to just let Valentino's blood have its evil way with her? Maybe she just wasn't cut out to be immortal?

The comforter was ripped away, and Valentino's face appeared above her. "I want answers, Sera."

She sighed. "Then get dressed, because I can't think straight when you're naked."

"Obviously," he mumbled under his breath.

Sera bit back a retort and watched Valentino step into his jeans. He didn't bother to retrieve his shirt, nor did he button the top of his fly. Well, it was better than naked. Not by much, but when he returned to the bed and sat down, she realized she'd have to find a way to ignore the bare expanse of his chest and the tantalizing ripples of his abdomen.

"Now start talking," he ordered.

Chapter Twenty

Valentino listened as Sera told him how sick his blood had made her, how she'd mentally called out to Constantine for help, and how they'd ultimately ended up within the coven. She failed to tell him who the man kneeling at her feet when he arrived had been, and the need to know couldn't be ignored. He asked as soon as she fell silent.

"Who was the guy in here with you?"

She blinked, then frowned. "Rick?"

Valentino shrugged. "You tell me."

She waved her hand and shook her head. "He's no one."

Yeah, right. "Sera, he was half naked, on his knees, and about to plant his face in your ass. He's definitely *someone*."

Her eyebrows flew up. "Are you jealous?"

"Just tell me who he is."

After a little sigh, she gave in. "His name is Rick, and he's one of the mortals who serve the coven."

"In what capacity?" As if he needed to ask.

"Blood and sex," she answered, looking him straight in the eyes.

Valentino ground his teeth together as jealousy snaked through his veins. "I see. And what did he do for you?"

"You *are* jealous." She sounded pleased.

He was, and it irritated the hell out of him. "What right do I have to be jealous? Consider what I do for a living."

Her eyes widened before sliding away to focus elsewhere. "Yeah," she said softly. "If anyone should be consumed with jealousy, it's me."

Damn, he was an idiot. He reached for her, and she stiffened under his hands. "I'm sorry. That part of my life is over now, and I swear I'll never bring it up again."

She shook her head, still not looking at him. "Ignoring it won't make it go away." She peeked through her lashes. "We met at Captive Fantasy. Every time I look at you, I'll be reminded of what you did there, and with whom."

"I never slept with Jennifer, if that's what you're hinting at."

Her head snapped up. "I don't care if you did or not."

"That's good to know." Two could play the I don't give a shit about you game. He met her livid expression. "But the truth is, I didn't. My reaction to your blood prevented me from working. Jennifer wasn't happy when I turned her down."

"I imagine," Sera mumbled. "So, you did get sick?" Anger gave way to real concern.

Valentino nodded and adjusted his hold on her so he could move closer. She allowed it without too much resistance. "I was very sick. Dying, according to Dr. Reynolds. Seems the only thing my blood is susceptible to is you." He flicked the tip of her nose and smiled. "The good doctor assumed San Francisco would be free of vampires."

"There are actually quite a few. Not that I'm friends with them or anything, but it's always good to know how many predators live in one area."

Her words bugged him. "You aren't a predator." She shrugged and he gathered her against his chest. "In fact, you are most non predatory creature I've ever encountered."

"I don't believe that," she said against his skin. "Do a lot of women rip holes in your throat or take your blood without asking?"

"You didn't take anything I didn't want to give." He gripped her shoulders and pushed her back to see her face. "Had I known it would make you sick, I would have stopped you from biting me. You should have told me before things got out of hand in here."

"I know." She lowered her gaze and traced her fingers across his chest. "I'll need to have a transfusion to rid my body of your blood." She looked up and her hand stilled between his pecs. "I wasn't going to let them do it if you were dead. I didn't want to lose the only connection I had with you, even if it killed me."

Something squeezed at his heart and trapped the breath in his throat. Unable to speak, he dipped his head down and captured her mouth. She sighed as he kissed her and worked her hand up his chest and around to the back of his neck.

After a few moments, he ended the kiss. "What happens now?"

She put both arms around his neck and snuggled closer. "I need to get this transfusion done, but I'm not looking forward to it."

Valentino pulled Sera onto his lap and the comforter fell away. He cursed his jeans. "Will it put you in any danger?"

She shook her head under his chin. "No, but I don't want anymore of Constantine's blood."

Nor did he want her to have any. "Is there no one else?"

"He said he is the one who makes the most sense, and he's right." She looked up. "He doesn't own me, regardless of what he said to you."

He cupped her face and traced her lips with his thumb. "Someday, will you tell me the history between you two?"

"You won't like what you hear."

He kissed her forehead, then tilted her face down to kiss the top of her head. "As long as it's all in the past, I'll be fine."

"So, you are jealous?"

He wrapped his arms around her and hugged her tight enough to prevent her from looking up at him. "I like believing I'm the only guy who does it for you, if that's all right?"

"You are," she murmured against his throat.

"Good. That's exactly what I want to hear." He loosened his grip and reached for her waist. "You know what else I want to hear?"

Her hair brushed his chin as she shook her head.

Valentino gripped Sera's waist, lifted her from his lap, and laid her down on the bed. She stretched like a happy kitten before reaching out to clasp his upper arms. He pried her hands off one at a time and pinned them above her head. "I want to hear you beg," he finally told her.

She licked her lips as a faint blush stole into her cheeks. "What should I beg for?"

"Whatever you want."

"Anything?"

Valentino nodded. His cock pressed eagerly against the tight fly of his jeans as Sera's expression turned pensive. Hopefully she'd figure out what she wanted really damn quick.

"You know I'm not any good at telling you what I want."

He lowered his face to brush her lips. "Do we need to resort to yes's and no's again?"

She nodded and arched up to chase his lips as he pulled away. "Kiss me," she whispered.

"See, that wasn't so hard, was it?" He took her open mouth in a kiss that knocked their teeth together. She giggled quietly and pulled back, but he only followed to claim her again. She surrendered to the deep thrust of his tongue and raked her nails down his back.

A light knock on the door prevented the kiss from escalating into something more and Valentino shot a glare over his shoulder. "Who is it?"

Whoever it was clearly took the question as an invitation to enter because the door swung open and a stunning redhead walked into the room. Her lithe curves were barely hidden under a semi-sheer, black, t-shirt dress, and her long legs were bare all the way to her toes. She stopped abruptly, and her pink lips parted in surprise. "Oh, I'm sorry." The unabashed interest on her face said otherwise, as did the fact that she made no move to turn around and leave.

Valentino rolled off Sera at the same time he pulled the comforter over her. She flashed him a grateful look before he stood up to confront their latest visitor. "Can I help you?"

The redhead's gaze took a leisurely stroll up and down his body before settling on Sera. "Are you Seraphina?"

"Yes."

"The master says it's time, and he sent me to fetch you."

Valentino looked back at Sera to find her paler than usual. "I'll go with you."

"No, you won't," the redhead countered. She smiled when he looked at her, but the expression looked more deadly than friendly. "Sorry, but this is vampire business. No mortals allowed." She let her gaze walk all over him again. "No matter how delicious they might look." She took a step closer.

"He's mine," Sera said from the bed.

Valentino arched a brow at the surprising level of possessiveness in her tone. He didn't know she had it in her.

The redhead chuckled. "I suggest you mark him very well then, my dear, or you might discover he's wandered off when you weren't looking."

"I'm perfectly happy where I am, thank you," he assured the troublemaker.

The redhead lifted one shoulder in a lazy shrug and

shot Sera another look. "Do hurry or the master will be most unhappy." She headed out the door, but left it open behind her.

Valentino didn't know what to say as Sera tossed the comforter off and slowly crawled out of bed. Her hands shook as she reached for the black silk robe crumpled at her feet. She pulled it on and belted it without looking at him.

"I'll be right here when it's over." What else could he say? She was on her way to undergo some vampire cleansing ritual that clearly frightened her and he was the reason for it. Should he apologize?

She finally looked up and without a word, closed the distance between them to throw herself into his arms. She buried her face in the hollow of his throat. "I don't blame you."

Before he could ask how the hell she'd known what he was thinking, she darted away from him and hurried out of the room without a backward glance. He took a step to follow and the redhead reappeared. She shook her head and closed the door.

The sound of a key turning infuriated him.

He'd spent his whole life as a captive. Damn if he'd be one now. Not here.

After locating his boots and pulling them on, Valentino stalked toward the door, stopped a few strides away, and gave the solid wood a good kick. To his surprise, it splintered and the latch popped. His triumph was short lived.

He stepped into the hall and came face to face with the green-eyed beast who had broken him out of Captive Fantasy.

"I was told to make sure you stay put." The hulking vampire shoved Valentino back toward the room. "I suggest you stay put of your own free will."

Considering how unhappy Sera would be if she returned to find him beaten and battered, Valentino admitted defeat and glowered at the broad back of his jailer.

****

Sera eventually discovered her guide's name was Nadia, but that bit of personal information did nothing to put her at ease as she followed the woman into the deepest bowels of the mansion. The air grew cold and thick with moisture the further they went, until finally, Nadia led her into a vast stone chamber. What lay inside was far from inviting.

About a dozen vampires turned their gazes toward Sera. She recognized no one save the master, his wife, and Constantine, but even those faces weren't comforting. The master barked at Nadia to leave, and she slipped out, leaving the queen and Sera as the only females among the group of ominous looking males. Perhaps if everyone weren't in black Sera wouldn't feel so threatened. Though, even if dressed in pink, a dozen somber looking vampires would be scary.

She gripped the front of her robe, wishing she'd taken the time to actually get dressed. It only heightened her unease to know a thin layer of silk was all that prevented her from being naked and vulnerable.

The master moved forward and reached for her hand. He'd replaced his more casual attire with an exquisite suit of black silk. The fabric whispered as he moved. He didn't flash a brilliant smile, and his eyes looked straight through her. His power could not be ignored or denied. It caressed her skin like a ghostly touch.

"Come." He clutched her fingers and guided her deeper into the chamber. "We've put this off long enough, and now Constantine tells me you've taken more of the clone's blood."

"His name is Valentino."

A collective gasp echoed around the room, and Sera swallowed uncomfortably. Maybe speaking out wasn't such a good idea here.

The master merely nodded and led her across the cold stone floor toward the other coven members. Placed within the semi-circle of vampires was a fainting couch upholstered in deep, rich, plum-colored velvet. Black wooden legs, carved to resemble paws, supported the decadent piece of furniture. Torches flickered around the room, giving the whole scene a surreal atmosphere.

Constantine separated from the others, and the master motioned him forward. "The sooner this is done, the better." He coaxed Sera toward Constantine, joined their hands, then faded away into the shadows.

Sera met Constantine's gaze and saw lust burning in his eyes. Oh dear. "What exactly is going to happen?" Her whisper sounded too loud as it bounced off the stone walls. She flinched.

Constantine shook his head and reached out to cup her cheek. "No talking, my pet." Sliding his hand into her hair, he gripped the back of her head and swooped down to capture her mouth in a feral kiss. His fangs scraped over her lips, and his tongue plunged inside, taking advantage of her gasp of outrage.

Sera struggled, but it was no use. Constantine's grip could not be broken, and she only managed to dislodge the silky robe from her shoulder. The front gaped open above the belt, and she felt the cool brush of his shirt against her bare breasts. The contact ignited a maelstrom of fear. Whatever was about to happen in this strange chamber, she no longer wanted to be a part of it.

Constantine lifted his mouth and pinned her with a dark glare. "You will do this, my pet. Your foolishness has put you at risk, and I meant what I said about not wishing to lose you."

She wanted to shove him away and wipe the taste of him from her lips, but his embrace locked her in place. "I'm not yours," she said in a low hush. "I don't think I ever really was."

He shifted his hold to her shoulders and hauled her onto her tiptoes. "You can play with your science project if he makes you happy, but remember you will always be mine. No matter where you go, who you fuck, or what blood runs in your veins. You are mine." He shook her to stress his point. "Do you understand?"

"You're hurting me," Sera whispered.

Constantine spun her around and shoved her toward one of the fainting couches. "Let's get this started." His voice was now loud enough for all to hear.

Sera tripped on the hem of her robe, and with a quiet curse, she gathered the material in her fist and held it above her ankles. With Constantine breathing down her neck, she had no choice but to take a seat on the couch and await whatever torment he had in store for her. One thing was certain, however; she was bound to despise him even more when this was all over.

Paralyzing fear gripped Sera as three vampires came toward her. Two held her, while the other effortlessly removed the robe from her body. Naked, shaking, and more scared than she'd ever been, she watched Constantine peel the clothes from his own body. One piece at a time. He didn't seem to be in too great a rush, and she suspected he was attempting to put on a show for her.

She wasn't interested.

Once naked, he knelt before her and with a flick of his wrist, sent the other vampires away. He laid his hands on her thighs and slowly pried her stiff legs apart. "You might enjoy this, if you can force yourself to relax."

Sera licked her lips and dropped her gaze to Constantine's fingers. "I'm not one for an audience."

"They are necessary to insure the cleansing is done properly."

She lifted her eyes to his. "I refuse to have sex with you. If it's part of the ritual, you'll have to rape me."

His face hardened before he released her to stand up. "You'd like that, wouldn't you? You'd like to have something to hold over me for the rest of eternity. Well, sorry to disappoint you, my pet. I don't intend to rape you."

Relief washed away much of the fear. "Then why must we be naked?"

"Get on with it, Constantine," the master suddenly barked out.

Constantine flinched and once more dropped to his knees. He took hold of Sera's left wrist and carried it to his mouth. With his fangs brushing her delicate skin, he said, "I assume we're naked so that the blood is easier to clean away." Not allowing her to respond, he closed his eyes and sank his teeth into her veins.

Sera sucked in a sharp breath and clawed at the velvet fabric of the couch. Her body grew overly warm, then icy cold as her blood surged toward Constantine's mouth. To her surprise, he pulled away without swallowing a single drop, then turned her wrist downward to let the blood flow onto the floor. It didn't take long for her vision to blur and the room to begin to spin.

"Lie down," Constantine commanded.

She hesitated, caught in some sort of limbo.

With a quiet growl, he eased her onto her back. "Once you've bled out I'll feed you." He brushed some hair off her forehead as she tried to focus on his eyes. "Promise me you'll drink when I put my wrist to your lips."

Sera thought about shaking her head. She didn't want anymore of Constantine's blood. Ever.

"You will drink, my love, or you'll die. No one in this room will move forward to save you if that is the choice you make."

Those horrible words, along with the disturbing sound of her blood dripping onto the floor, followed her into oblivion.

Chapter Twenty-one

Valentino clutched at his chest as a blinding pain sent him to his knees. The same agony that had ripped through him his last morning at Captive Fantasy once more held him prisoner. He couldn't feel the beat of his heart under his hand, nor could he stop the rattling of his teeth as a chill worked its way through his body.

He knew he was dying.

Only question was, would he wake up a vampire, or was this really it?

Another pain tore through his chest, making him double over with a sharp gasp. The guard's footsteps were atrociously loud as he stepped into the room, demanding to know what was wrong. Valentino couldn't speak if his life depended on it. He shook his head and tried to breathe through another stabbing pain.

The guard grabbed a fistful of hair and yanked his head back. "What the fuck is wrong?" he demanded again.

"D-dying," Valentino forced out. He squeezed his eyes shut, and the color red exploded behind his lids. It brought to mind blood. Warm, fresh blood. His gums began to ache, and he clenched his teeth together to ward off the uncomfortable sensation. It didn't work. He nearly screamed when he felt his fangs rip through.

The guard released him and stepped back. "Jesus, you're changing."

Valentino leaned over his knees to press his forehead to the floor. The smell of polished wood burned the inside of his nose, and he feared his eardrums would shatter as

177

the guard raced out of the room with loud, angry strides. He'd never survive this...this...whatever this was. He wasn't even sure he wanted to survive it.

The chill worsened until his bones rattled, and his teeth knocked together. His new fangs dug into the inside of his bottom lip, ripping at the tender skin and filling his mouth with the taste of blood. Rolling onto his side, he swept his tongue along the bleeding wound and swallowed, but it wasn't what he wanted. He thought about the sweet, metallic taste of Sera's blood and groaned out loud as a hunger he'd never imagined possible ripped through him.

"Feed him before he loses control." The guard's voice penetrated the growing haze in Valentino's mind, and it was followed by the soft, melodic sound of a woman whispering, "Yes, all right."

Fabric rustled, the air stirred around him, and he pried his eyes open to find a delicate, blonde beauty kneeling before him. She smiled and began to unbutton the pale yellow blouse she wore. Just as her beige bra began to show, she grabbed the collar to expose her upper chest. "Are you able to bite me?"

Valentino focused on the steady pulse at the hollow of her throat. Her veins showed through the tight stretch of her skin, and he tracked one down toward her right breast. He licked his lips and found the strength to get to his hands and knees. He crawled toward her, watching her face through the curtain of his hair, then stopped as her gaze swung to his.

She smiled at his hesitation and scooted closer then arched her head back. It's okay, this is what I do."

She smelled like wildflowers and blood. Jesus, he could actually smell her blood. He nuzzled his face into the warm crook of her neck, unsure of what to do. His fangs throbbed, but it seemed cruel to just sink them in. He recalled the lash of Sera's tongue, and licked the skin of the woman's neck. She laughed softly and braced her hands on his shoulders. Through the hunger, concern for her well being whispered in his ear and he pulled back. "I don't want to hurt you." It felt weird to form words around his fangs.

"You won't." Her fingers flexed, urging him closer.

Still on his hands and knees, Valentino inhaled the lovely fragrance of the woman before him, closed his eyes, and sank his new fangs into her willing neck. Blood filled his mouth as her skin tore.

"Yes," she breathed.

He deepened his bite and crawled closer. Her hand left his shoulder to swipe his trailing hair back from his face, and she held it in place to keep it away from his mouth. He'd thank her later.

Right now he just wanted more blood.

"I'll leave you two alone," the guard said, then left with a shuffle of footsteps followed by the door clicking shut.

In the silence, Valentino reveled in the strong rhythm of the woman's pulse against his mouth. It beat in time to the flow of her blood, mesmerizing him. He jumped when her voice sliced through the moment.

"I'll let you know when to stop."

He nodded as best he could, but stopping was the last thing on his mind. The more blood he took, the more he craved. The woman offered no resistance as he continued to feed. Her hand stayed in his hair while the other lightly clasped his shoulder. She sighed softly when he adjusted his bite, and her body shuddered as if experiencing great pleasure. Thanks to Sera, he knew how damn good it felt.

The thought of Sera had the power to pull his focus from his actions. He slid his fangs free from the woman's neck, and she blinked at him in confusion. "Why did you stop?"

Valentino stared at the wound on her neck. It dripped bright red blood against her pale skin. The hunger came roaring back, and he clutched his gut and met the woman's eyes. "Your blood isn't working." No matter how good it smelled or how it tasted, he craved something more.

She frowned and buried both hands in his hair. "You didn't take enough." She arched her head back, and her fingers tugged at his hair. "Come, take more."

He stared at her neck, licked his lips, but then shook his head. "No. I need to find Sera."

The woman's hands drifted from his hair, and it fell over his eyes. She studied his face while fumbling with the buttons of her blouse. "I've done something to displease you, haven't I?"

Valentino shook his head and sat back on his heels. He could feel the warmth of her blood in his veins, but the hunger remained. He needed Sera. "I appreciate what you did."

The woman dropped her gaze. "It's what I do." They were the same words she'd said earlier. "Would you mind licking the wound so it stops bleeding?"

The question startled him. He shifted his gaze to her neck and reached out to catch a drop of blood before it could stain the collar of her blouse. She smiled as he leaned toward her to swipe his tongue over her skin.

"Thank you," she said softly.

He pulled back and got to his feet, offering his hand to help her up. The room swayed slightly as she accepted and met his gaze. "You were very gentle. More so than many who have been feeding for centuries. I thank you for that."

Valentino lifted her hand to his lips. She caught her breath and her cheeks turned bright red. "You were delicious."

The color in her cheeks intensified and she giggled softly. She slid her hand free and hurried toward the door. Before leaving, she hesitated and looked back. "You'll need someone to supply blood if you stay with the coven." She flashed a very interested grin.

Valentino raked his fingers through his hair and offered a brief nod. He wasn't quite ready to commit to anything.

"Well, my name is Stephanie. If you ever need me, just have someone call for me."

"Thank you." He watched her walk away and prayed he hadn't just formed some unbreakable vampire/mortal bond by taking her blood. He'd worry about that later, though. First things first. For some reason, feeding from Stephanie hadn't satisfied his hunger, and he needed to know why. God willing, Sera could answer his questions. Looking around the room, he spotted his t-shirt, went to fetch it, and pulled it on. He headed for the door, convinced that being a vampire would afford him some freedom now.

The green-eyed giant clearly saw things a bit differently. He stepped in Valentino's path and crossed his arms over his broad chest. "Where do you think you're going, freshy?"

Valentino shoved past the guy with ease. Yet another thing to contemplate later. He hurried toward the steps, aware of the heavy footsteps following close behind. At the bottom, the guard grabbed his arm and spun him around. Valentino snarled and ripped free. "I'm going to find her whether you try to stop me or not."

The guard fisted his hands at his sides, looking for all the world like he wanted to sling Valentino over his shoulder and carry him back to his room. Thankfully, he didn't. "You can't go to her during the ritual, you stubborn bastard."

"Does that mean you're trying to stop me?"

The guard shook his head. "No. I should, but I won't. But it'll be my ass if you're caught blindly roaming around, so follow me." He brushed past Valentino, then glanced back. "Coming?"

With a nod, Valentino followed.

The guard led him into the very bowels of the house, where the walls were made of thick stone and glowed with the light of ancient torches. The floor was a dangerous, uneven path and the ceiling barely high enough to walk under. All in all, a pretty eerie place.

The smell of blood permeated the air and grew stronger as they neared an arched doorway. Valentino's fangs stirred and threatened to lengthen. Sheer force of will prevented that from happening. What his body craved and what Stephanie had failed to provide was just up ahead. He could smell it, and as it coated his tongue and burned his nostrils, one name whispered in his ear. Sera.

The guard hung back as Valentino approached the doorway. "You go in alone." With that, he turned and headed back the way they came.

Valentino stepped inside and froze. His heart, or whatever remained in his chest, seized as he took in the horrid scene being played out in the center of the vast chamber.

Sera knelt naked before Constantine with her hands gripping his bare hips and her mouth fused to the flesh of his left thigh. Spread around her was a pool of dark blood. Valentino knew without moving closer who the blood belonged to. He could taste it in his mouth. He wanted to throw his head back and scream at the loss, but his gaze shifted to Constantine and anger boiled to the surface.

The man stared at Sera with an undisguised look of pure lust. The fingers of one hand twisted in her hair, and the other hand rested on her shoulder. Sera's eyes were closed, and her pale profile was smeared with blood. Constantine's blood.

Valentino's stomach turned and rage propelled him forward. His boots made enough noise on the rough stone floor to draw the attention of everyone but Sera. Constantine lifted his head with a dark, dangerous look in his eyes, but Valentino refused to let the unspoken threat stop him.

He stalked forward, took hold of Sera's nape, and hauled her to her feet. Constantine reached for her, but Valentino stepped between them. An unfriendly snarl answered the action, but he ignored it. The lower half of

Sera's face was covered in wet blood, and she did nothing to wipe it away as she stared up at him in confusion.

The sight disgusted him, and he made the mistake of letting her go in order to tear off his t-shirt. Once free, Sera darted away and hid behind Constantine. She peered around his shoulder and looked at Valentino as if he was the devil come to steal her soul.

What the hell had happened down here?

"Sera?" He kept his voice low and calm. "Here, baby, wipe your face." He held out the shirt, but she only ducked further behind the shield of Constantine's naked body. Damn. He lowered his arm and glared at the vampire. Constantine smirked, and Valentino's rage escalated. "What did you do to her?" It was hard to voice the question when all he wanted to do was rip the guy apart.

"I did what was necessary to save her from her own foolishness."

"Meaning?" The other vampires in the room stirred, and Valentino figured he was one wrong word from sending them into a frenzy. He'd have to tread carefully because he doubted their loyalty would lie with him.

Constantine's smirk turned into a smile. "Meaning, Seraphina is all mine." He spread his arms, and Valentino noticed the bite marks scattered about his chest. "She enjoyed it, I assure you."

Valentino took a step forward, but an unfamiliar voice stopped him from lunging at Constantine. "I suggest you keep your temper in check, Valentino."

Valentino turned to meet the startling blue gaze of another vampire. The man was tall, blond and undeniably powerful. His aura crackled around him like some sort of shield, proclaiming him the master of everyone within this chamber. Valentino didn't feel like playing minion. "What did this bastard do to Sera?"

The master's frown spoke volumes. He gestured toward the door with the elegant sweep of a silk clad arm. "Come with me, and I'll answer all your questions. This is neither the time nor the place for such a discussion."

"No." Valentino looked toward Sera, who continued to cower behind her goddamn maker. "I won't leave her alone with him for another moment." He focused on the master. "Tell me what I want to know right here, right now."

The blue eyes darkened to an unusual shade of indigo and narrowed in obvious dislike. An uncomfortable sensation crept over Valentino's skin, but he mentally pushed it away. Was the man attempting to control him?

"Constantine did as he was ordered to do." Irritation oozed from the master's tone. "In order to cleanse Sera of your deadly blood, he needed to drain her body and replace what she lost. Doing so has reaffirmed their attachment to one another and momentarily interfered with her memories."

"Interfered with her memories?" Jesus Christ. Valentino whipped around and caught Sera's eye as she pretended not to stare at him. "You don't know who I am?" His heart shattered as she shook her head and leaned into Constantine's side. The vampire wrapped his arm around her and pulled her to his chest.

There was no mistaking the triumphant gleam in the bastard's coal black eyes.

Chapter Twenty-two

The haze in Sera's brain started to thin as she snuggled against Constantine and stared at the man before her. Did she know him? No matter how deeply she probed, no memory stood up to be acknowledged. There was nothing familiar about the tousled dark hair, seductively handsome features, or even the toned, golden body. Surely she'd remember such a man? But she didn't, and the fact that he clearly knew her made her head ache.

"Shh," Constantine whispered, stroking a hand up and down her back. "Don't distress yourself trying to remember something unimportant." His words brought a hateful look to the stranger's eyes, but the gaze softened as it rested on her.

When he spoke, his voice did strange things to her mind and body. "If the memory lapse is temporary, I'll do everything in my power to help you remember." He moved toward her and once more offered his black t-shirt. "Take it and wipe your face. Looking like a monster doesn't suit you." The words, or maybe it was just the voice, tried to work through the fog in her mind.

Sera pulled away from Constantine and reached up to touch her chin. Her fingers came away sticky with blood. She glared at Constantine and snatched the offered t-shirt.

"Thank you." She was careful not to meet the man's chocolaty eyes, but she didn't miss the slight quirk of his full lips. Balling the shirt up, she licked a corner, then swiped the blood from her face. She longed to drag the soft cotton over the rest of her body as well. She could feel blood drying on her knees but didn't dare glance down. If she did look like a monster, she'd rather not see it.

When she felt clean, she held the soiled shirt to her chest, startled by the urge to carry it to her nose. Would a smell trigger a memory?

Constantine tore the shirt from her grasp before she could move a single muscle. He tossed it over his shoulder toward the other coven members, never taking his angry gaze off of her. "This man, and whatever he claims to mean to you, no longer matters. What happened here tonight has strengthened the bond you and I share, and nothing will break it."

"We'll see about that," the stranger challenged.

Sera looked over and straight into his eyes. He held her gaze and nodded once. Doing so forced a clump of hair to fall over his forehead. The tips brushed his cheekbone and teased the edge of his mouth. She stared and felt...something. She took a step, but Constantine caught her arm and yanked her back.

"Get him out of here."

She could only watch as the master's nod brought two vampires forward. They took hold of the stranger's arms and hauled him roughly toward the door. Not once did he break eye contact with her.

"I'll make you remember, Sera." The sound of her name poured over her. "No matter what he did to you, your body won't be able to deny what it knows."

Constantine's grip tightened on her arm. "You'll keep your distance from her."

Deep brown eyes continued to hold her gaze, as if Constantine hadn't spoken at all. "I know you, Sera. I know what you crave. What you long for."

Each time he said her name, a tiny spark tried to light itself in her brain. She tried to think of a way to hold the velvet smoothness of his voice around her. It was like a warm, tempting blanket on a cold day.

"Sera, you have to remember." Desperation replaced

the honeyed warmth of his tone. His eyes pleaded with her as he fought the men holding him. "Sera, please."

Suddenly she was very afraid to have him leave her. The pinch of Constantine's fingers made her squeal in pain and was enough to force her to look away from the stranger. She glared at Constantine, but he had eyes only for his new enemy.

"Come near her, and you'll both suffer." Only a fool would ignore the tone vibrating around those words. It made Sera's skin crawl.

The stranger was forced from the room before he could do more than fire off a warning glare of his own. His absence hit Sera like a sharp slap.

She ripped her arm free and stepped away from Constantine. He made no attempt to halt her as she retrieved her robe and shrugged into it. She held the sides together over the cinched belt and turned a livid expression on Constantine. "What did you do to me?"

His features tightened. "We'll discuss this later. In private."

Sera shook her head. She didn't care if the whole damn coven was privy to this conversation. She wanted answers. "Did you wipe my memories of him away intentionally?"

Constantine's angry scowl was answer enough. He raked a hand through his silky black hair and stepped toward her. "I did what I had to do."

Sera turned away from the look in his black eyes and headed for the door. No one tried to stop her, but Constantine's voice called out to her. "I meant what I said, my pet."

She stopped and looked back. All eyes, the master's included, were fixed on Constantine. He was quite the sight, standing naked and regal in the center of the glowing chamber. He might have erased memories of who the stranger was to her, but she had no problem recalling how ugly Constantine could be. How cruel. She hated him all over again for what he'd done to her in here.

His gaze narrowed. "If he goes anywhere near you, I'll make him pay, and you'll watch."

Feeling sick and helpless, Sera bolted from the chamber with her robe gathered over her knees to avoid tripping on the hem. She needed to be alone with her thoughts, her feelings, and all the doubts swirling in her brain. She refused to believe that Constantine's trickery couldn't be undone. But how, and did she dare risk a man's life just to jar her memories?

A sob caught in her throat and tears blinded her eyes as she raced down the dark, twisting hallways. God willing, she'd find her bedroom without getting lost.

"Mistress?"

Sera screeched to a halt and swallowed a scream as Rick materialized in front of her. The sudden shock of his appearance made her head spin.

He gripped her arms as she swayed dangerously. "Are you all right?"

Before she could answer, he scooped her up and cradled her against his chest. For the time being, he was the lesser of the evils, so she snuggled into his warm body and allowed him to carry her to her room. Once there, he strode to the bed and laid her down on the cool satin. He brushed her hair from her forehead, and his full lips pulled down in a frown.

"You aren't well, are you?" There was real concern in his voice.

Sera shook her head against the pillow and closed her eyes. She just needed to rest. Without warning, the smell of blood called to her. She didn't need to open her eyes to know Rick had opened a wound somewhere on his body. He meant to feed her, and she doubted she possessed the strength to resist.

"Take it, mistress." He brushed his skin across her lips, teasing her with warm, enticing blood.

"No." Whispering the word was her downfall. Her lips opened and closed around his skin, and her fangs slid into his vein. His blood flowed past her tongue, erasing the foul taste of Constantine. That alone made feeding like an animal almost tolerable.

Rick sat on the bed, close to her thigh, and pressed his skin tighter to her mouth. She wanted to pull away. She didn't want to take his blood like this, but she was too exhausted to fight it. The whole evening had been a nightmare, and this seemed a fitting end.

****

After the infuriating confrontation in the chamber, Valentino had been escorted to a small room buried under the rafters of the mansion, and left to stew. When an invitation arrived asking that he join the evening's "gathering," he was more than a little shocked. Not sure if it was a trap or an attempt to make peace, he accepted, thinking it would be an opportunity to see Sera if nothing else.

Stephanie arrived at his door a short time later with a bundle of clothing in her arms and a radiant smile on her face. "The master ordered me to be at your side tonight."

Ignoring the comment, Valentino took the bundle as she held it out to him. "What is this?"

"You can't join the gathering looking like that." She gestured at his jeans and bare chest. "I managed to pilfer something that should fit you."

"Thanks." He turned his back and tossed the clothing on the narrow bed. He could feel Stephanie watching him from the doorway. "You can go."

"I was ordered to be at your side."

He glanced back. "And if you're not?"

She stepped into the room and closed the door to lean against it. "I'd rather not find out."

Yeah, he couldn't blame her. "Fine, but turn around while I change." This wasn't Captive Fantasy, and he wasn't being paid to make Stephanie happy. She huffed, but did as he said. Quickly, he stepped out of his boots, peeled off his jeans and changed. "All right."

Stephanie turned around and ran her eyes over him

with a look he knew all too well. "I chose well, it seems." She looked him in the eye. "The boots will ruin it."

"Okay then, barefoot it is." Valentino dropped his boots and gestured toward the door. "Let's get this over with."

Stephanie coiled her hand around his arm and led the way out of the room. She chattered happily, but Valentino remained silent. As they made their way down the long staircase, he heard voices drifting from one of the rooms off the foyer. Stephanie pulled him toward a tall, arched doorway and the conversation ceased.

Uncomfortable with the undivided attention of so many vampires, he scanned the large room and located the master lounging against the far wall. The silk suit had been replaced by a pair of casual black slacks and a white open-collar shirt. A beautiful woman with rich chestnut hair stood at the master's side with her hand resting on his arm. Both of them stared along with everyone else. Valentino nodded, and after a brief hesitation, the master returned the gesture. On cue, conversation once more came alive.

"Over here." Stephanie pulled him toward a vacant oversized chair. She pushed him into it and curled at his side like a happy cat. He had no choice but to sling an arm across her shoulders.

"I'll be the envy of every mortal here now." She tucked her black skirt around her legs, but the long slit in front fell open to reveal a lot of skin.

It was a fetching sight, but Valentino didn't stare for long. Yes, Stephanie was lovely. In fact, with her pale blonde hair, light blue eyes and fresh complexion, she was the all American beauty. She'd make some guy really happy, just not him.

She pinched his arm. "Did you hear me?"

He nodded. "Why is everyone going to envy you?"

She flashed a coy grin and undid a button on his black, silk shirt. He let the action go, not wanting to draw a lot of attention in his direction. "Because, silly, everyone wants you." She worked several more buttons loose, then slid her hand inside. She spread her fingers wide, grazing his nipple in the process. She pressed closer and sighed. "You aren't cold like the others."

No, he wasn't, and he had his own theories as to why that was. Clearly he was a vampire with fangs and all, but exactly what sort of vampire, he didn't know. He wasn't even sure if he was part of the undead or not, and he wasn't too keen on asking anyone about it. Why expose a vulnerability?

Stephanie worked her hand down his chest to walk her fingers across the ripples of his abdomen. She wiggled even closer and freed the last two buttons on his shirt. "Are you hungry?"

Valentino ignored the question since Stephanie couldn't give him what he wanted. His gaze moved toward the door and he inhaled sharply. Sera hovered just outside the room with Constantine glowering behind her. The vampire said something only she could hear, and then the two of them walked into the room, hand in hand. How touching. He fisted his hand in his lap and continued to stare.

Not once did Sera glance in his direction, but her rigid posture let him know she was aware of his presence. Constantine caught his eye and tossed him a "don't forget I'd like you dead" look. Valentino nodded and grinned.

The feeling was mutual, after all.

"Hey," Stephanie grumbled. "It isn't polite to ignore me." Her hand drifted past the waist of his drawstring pants. The entire outfit was silk, and he might as well be naked. The heat of her hand touched him through the thin fabric, but he caught her fingers before she could do so in reality.

He tore his attention from Sera's rigid form to meet Stephanie's disappointed expression. "Sorry, that's off limits." He set her hand back on his chest, and her frown deepened.

"But I want you to make me your servant?" She sat

191

up and leaned away from him. "Doing so permits you to take my blood *and* my body."

He hated to dash Stephanie's hopes, but Sera's body was the only one he wanted, and he suspected her blood was what he needed as well. He planned to do whatever necessary to get her back.

In the hopes of lessening the sting of his rejection, he cupped the side of Stephanie's face and feathered his thumb across the apple of her cheek. "I don't need your body or your blood." He pressed his finger to her lips to stop her protest. "But I do need you to do something for me."

She nodded, an eager look seeping into her eyes.

"Is there any way you can distract Constantine away from Sera?"

The eagerness drained from her face and she pulled away from him. "No. And even if I could, I wouldn't."

Not what he wanted to hear. He removed his hands from her face. "Why?"

Stephanie lowered her gaze and trailed her hand down the center of his body. She snared the string at his waist and coiled it around her finger. "You really shouldn't upset Constantine."

Valentino covered her hand to stop her from tugging at the string, and waited for her attention to drift to his face. "Tell me what I need to know about him. Please."

"He hasn't been with the coven for very long, but long enough to earn a reputation. He isn't one to cross." Concern bled into her eyes. "He will kill you if you go near her."

"You say that as if it's already happened."

Stephanie's fingers flexed under his hand, and he released her. She immediately began to toy with the string again, but her thoughts seemed far away. "I was friends with the first mortal he chose from this coven, and she was very devastated when he turned away from her to choose another."

"Tell me what happened."

Her fingers slid down the length of the string and brushed over his lap. He wasn't sure if it was innocent, so he grabbed her hand and placed it on his stomach. She glanced up and he shook his head. "Behave."

"Sorry." Her eyes let him know the gesture had been intentional.

"What happened with your friend?"

"She was stupid enough to let another vampire bite her, is what happened." Stephanie's gaze darted away, and Valentino followed her line of vision to Constantine and Sera. "Constantine discovered the two of them together and he freaked."

Valentino cupped Stephanie's chin to bring her gaze back to his face. "Forget I asked."

"No. You need to know what he's capable of."

He slid his fingers up to her lips and shook his head. "No. Knowing what he's done in the past won't stop me from trying to get Sera from him."

Stephanie's eyes glistened and she ducked her head and sniffed softly.

"Hey?" Valentino tilted her face back up. "Why do you care what happens to me?"

She sniffed again and blinked against the moisture in her eyes. "You've been kind to me." She shrugged and tried to look away, but he wouldn't release her chin. "I would just hate to see him win, and you obviously adore her."

That was an understatement.

Valentino's gaze drifted toward Sera. She looked stunning, despite her rigid posture. She sat next to Constantine on a sofa upholstered in deep maroon velvet. The color highlighted the pale perfection of her bare legs under the short hem of her charcoal gray skirt. A plum colored blouse turned her eyes a clearer blue and made her hair seem somehow darker than black. He wanted to stalk across the room and rip her away from Constantine's side.

She belonged with him, damnit.

"He won't give her up."

Valentino tore his gaze away to look at Stephanie. "I have to try."

She didn't look too happy with his reply but snuggled back against his side and once more trailed her hand toward his pants. "Well, if you fail and manage to survive, my offer stands."

Failing wasn't an option.

Once more, he settled his focus on Sera, watching her profile closely. Her features were drawn tight with some suppressed emotion. Anger? Jealousy? He didn't know. With slow, cautious movements, she shifted to cross her legs. Doing so drew Constantine's attention along with just about every other male in the room. Valentino was no exception. He stared at the pale expanse of thigh and his body stirred to life.

"Mmm...is this for me?" Stephanie's voice purred in his ear, reminding him of her presence. "If so, I'm in for a good time." She squeezed his erection lightly and moaned.

Valentino reached down without taking his eyes off Sera. He covered Stephanie's hand, with the intent to move it away, just as Sera's gaze landed on them. Her eyes drifted down his body and widened when they reached his lap. Her mouth opened and then closed so she could drag her bottom lip between her teeth. The sight shot fresh blood to his groin. Unfortunately, Stephanie still had her greedy hand wrapped around his cock.

She cooed and rubbed her breasts against his arm. "If you ask nicely, I'll let her watch." She stroked him through the silk, and Sera finally jerked her gaze up and away.

"Damnit," Valentino snarled, pulling Stephanie's hand away and pushing it into her own lap. "I've had enough socializing." He got to his feet and Sera visibly stiffened. Was she afraid he'd approach her? What would her reaction be if he did? There was no need to speculate about what Constantine would do. Even now, the vampire was glaring at him.

Stephanie hurried out of the chair and wrapped her hands around his arm. "I'm sorry." She pulled at him until he looked at her. "I'm sorry," she said again. "I was only teasing. Please don't be angry."

"I'm not." Well, he was, but not at Stephanie. He forced a partial smile and laid his hand against her cheek. "I just need to get out of here."

"You need blood, don't you?"

Not hers, but it worked as an excuse to get the hell out of here.

Stephanie led him toward the door. "I'll give you as much as you want, but you won't want to feed in front of her."

No, he didn't. He glanced back and found Sera's steady gaze fixed on him. He halted, forcing Stephanie to stumble at his side. She huffed, but he ignored her. What he felt for Sera had to be written all over his face. But could she see it? Did it stir anything at all within her?

Disappointment burned through him when Sera looked away. Constantine reached for her hand, but she avoided his touch by crossing her arms. Valentino received a dark look as a result, and he took a step, more than ready to have it out right here, right now.

Stephanie tugged on his arm. "Please. Don't do anything about this now. Not here. The master won't allow it."

Reluctantly, he pulled his gaze from Constantine and followed Stephanie out of the room. Once in the hall, she led him deep into the shadows, far from the drone of voices, and leaned back against the wall. She tipped her head back to bare her throat.

"Bite me."

Valentino's fangs stirred at the sight. Would her blood satisfy him this time?

She reached for his shoulders and pulled him closer. "Please?"

He braced his hands on the wall, not wanting to encourage her by pressing his body into hers, and lowered his face to her neck. She sighed as his fangs pierced her skin. The warmth of her blood trailed down his throat and filled his veins, but once again, it only left him wanting something more.

Chapter Twenty-three

Sera felt ill.

The sight of the sexy, blonde mortal leading *him* away churned her stomach and unleashed a level of jealousy she'd never experienced before. It was silly to go on believing she didn't know the man. Clearly her body had stored some memories of its own if her reaction to looking at him was any indication.

It'd be nice if it would share the memories with her mind.

"You're staring, my pet."

She shifted her gaze away from the now empty doorway and met Constantine's blank stare. "Tell me his name."

He sighed and rolled his eyes. "Why?"

Sera shifted on the sofa and pulled the hem of her skirt over her thighs. She'd never been comfortable in miniskirts, but Constantine had arrived at her door with this outfit in hand, and she'd been too consumed by mixed emotions after feeding from Rick to argue when he told her to put it on. She knew she looked good, but that didn't make her comfortable.

"I want to know his name. Are you afraid saying it will bring my memories back?"

"You assume there are memories, my pet. What if there aren't? It is possible that I never put you under during the ritual and everything you did was of your own free will."

Sera didn't buy that for a single second. "Tell me."

"Fine," Constantine bit out. "Valentino. There. Satisfied?"

Valentino. Valentino.

Do you prefer, Val? The sound of her voice whispering the question echoed around her mind followed by the memory of Valentino's sexy chuckle. She closed her eyes and saw the flash of humor in his chocolate brown eyes and recalled how delighted he'd been to discover she knew his name. Even now, her cheeks heated with embarrassment as she recalled being teased for ogling his pictures on Captive Fantasy's website.

Captive Fantasy. Those two words shoved open a door to a whole other set of memories. She gasped and opened her eyes to find Constantine scowling at her. "I remember, you bastard." She got up, and he followed. "How dare you?"

He took hold of her arm and yanked her forward to hiss in her face. "You're better off without him."

"Am I? Do you hope keeping me away from him will make me forget how distasteful it is to be in your bed?" She didn't bother to keep her voice down and the drone of conversation ceased.

Constantine's eyes darkened. "Not here," he ground out.

"I don't care if everyone knows how much I despise you."

His fingers bruised her skin through the sleeve of her blouse. "Regardless of how you feel, I refuse to hand you over to that freak of nature." He shook her. "Understand?"

"Release her, Constantine." The master's voice sliced through the tension. The command was calm, but one couldn't ignore the fire behind it.

Constantine snarled softly and did as ordered. The hostile look in his eyes did not lessen, however.

Sera moved closer to the master and rubbed the sore spot on her arm. "You can't control me," she told Constantine. "Making me does not make you my keeper."

Constantine took a step toward her, but froze as the

master spoke again. "One more step, and you will be asked to leave this coven."

"Why are you protecting her? She's hardly a vampire, for God's sake. She won't even drink from a damn mortal." The disgust in Constantine's tone chilled Sera to the bone. He despised her just as much now as he had three hundred years ago. So why demand to control her? Why claim to want her all to himself?

His eyes settled on her face. "I look forward to finally making you into the vampire you should be, my pet. It's really that simple."

The master caught her as she stumbled backwards into him. He brushed his hands up her arms, then gently set her aside. "Go to your room, Seraphina," he ordered her softly.

"Don't you dare move," Constantine barked.

Sera was trapped between the will of two very angry vampires. A place no one would want to be. Very afraid, she stopped breathing and waited for one of them to make the first move.

"Are you challenging me, Constantine?"

"Your control over this coven? No. Your attempt to interfere with my property? Yes."

The silence in the large room reached a level that made Sera's ears ring.

"I told you to go to your room, Seraphina." The master repeated the command without taking his eyes off Constantine.

A cold hand slid over Sera's, and she jumped to find the queen at her side. "Come with me, my dear." Sylvia pulled her out of the fray and toward the doorway. She followed, too afraid to even glance back.

If possible, the silence had become even more deafening.

Once upstairs, and far away from the volatile atmosphere of the great room, Sera found the courage to speak. "What's going to happen?" she whispered, lest her voice travel. Vampires had exceptionally good hearing, after all.

Sylvia reached past her to open the bedroom door. With a little nudge, she guided her into the room. "Constantine will likely regret his little rebellion."

Sera turned to face the queen. "How can you be so calm?"

"My dear, I don't have a choice." She took Sera's hand and led her to the bed. "Now try not to upset yourself thinking about things you have no control over. Why don't you lie down and try to relax?"

Sera sat on the edge of the bed, but relaxing was not an option. There was something she needed to do, and with Constantine otherwise occupied, this might be her only chance. "Will you tell me which room Valentino is in?" Her question narrowed the queen's eyes. "Please?"

"No, I won't. It's not a good idea for you to go to him."

"Why? Because it'll upset Constantine? You have to know, I don't care."

Sylvia shook her head. "I'm not sure how safe it is for the two of you to be alone."

Twisting the comforter between her fingers, Sera tried to keep her growing impatience at bay. "Care to explain that?"

Sylvia sighed and came to sit next to her. The pleasant smell of orchids surrounded both of them. It was a soothing fragrance. "My husband is concerned about Valentino's transformation. It didn't happen naturally, and therefore, it's hard to say what sort of vampire he will be."

"He took my blood and changed. Isn't that the way it happens?" To her knowledge there was no other way.

Sylvia again shook her head. "No. It's much more complicated than that. Until the master knows more, you should keep your distance."

"He won't hurt me, if that's what you're worried about. Constantine might have erased most of my memories, but I know that for a fact." Sera got up and began to pace off her nervous energy. She needed to see

Valentino. It was a thick, heavy craving, growing stronger with every second that ticked by. If Sylvia refused to tell her where he was, she'd simply search until she found him.

"That would waste too much time, my dear."

Sera had forgotten *that* little talent. She glanced at the queen. "Please tell me." Desperation would make her beg if need be. She dropped to her knees and gripped the edge of the bed on either side of Sylvia's legs. "Please. I've seen you with your husband; I know you understand what it means to feel truly connected to someone. I think I felt that with Valentino, and it isn't fair to let Constantine steal it away." She boldly took her queen's hands. "Please help me."

Sylvia's green eyes were a little sad, but she nodded. "All right, my dear. I'll help you, but once you go to him, you are on your own."

"He won't hurt me." In her heart, Sera really believed that.

"And if he isn't alone? Won't that hurt?"

An image of the blonde mortal formed. The girl had led Valentino out of the room as if she had every right to do so. Where had they gone? And to do what? Unease tightened Sera's gut. "Just tell me where he is." She'd deal with what she might find when she got to him.

Please Lord, let him be alone.

"The master gave him the room in the attic. It's very secluded and very private."

Sera smiled at that. If the circumstances were different, and one of them wasn't a queen, she'd kiss Sylvia on the cheek. Instead, she squeezed her hands and whispered a thank you before hurrying from the room. Unsure of exactly where to go, she let her instincts guide her. Eventually she found a door near the end of the hallway that housed a narrow stone staircase stretching up into a black abyss.

Her heart flipped over, and she pulled the door shut behind her without making a sound.

Every step took too long and by the time she reached the top, she was nearly hyperventilating. She needed to calm down, for heaven's sake. There was nothing to light the way, but she could see just fine. Amidst the organized clutter along the back wall, she noticed a heavy wooden door. Careful not to make a sound and wishing she had slipped off her heels, she approached and stared at her trembling hand as she reached for the doorknob.

She took a deep breath, prayed again that Valentino would be alone, and opened the door. It squeaked on old hinges and announced her presence, whether she wanted it to or not. She froze and looked around the room. A good size bed rested along one wall, flanked by two nightstands. The pieces looked ready to crumble to dust, they were so old. Across the room, stood an ancient looking wardrobe, and next to it, Valentino.

Sera's hand slid off the knob. "Am I intruding?"

He shook his head, sending his hair over his forehead and into his eyes. He made no move to brush it away. Was he trying to hide from her?

"Can I come in?" She cupped her throat and felt the flutter of her pulse. When was the last time she'd been this nervous? Most likely, never. Valentino made her head spin and heart race, two rare occurrences for her even before she had become a vampire. He stood next to the time-beaten wardrobe, looking like an untouchable fantasy. But she had touched him, and she very much wanted to do so again.

"Does this mean you remember?" His voice only added to the emotions building within her.

Sera shook her head, then nodded. "Yes and no." Oh, it was too hard to explain. His shirt lay open over his chest, and she drank in the sight of his exposed skin. Memories of how it felt to touch that sleek, golden flesh teased her. "I remember some of our time together."

"Sera?"

She pulled her gaze from his chest. "I want to remember more." She wanted to remember it all.

Without a word, he took off his shirt and let it fall to the floor, leaving him dressed in only the fluid, black, silk pants that did little to disguise his lengthening erection. "Come here."

Sera licked her lips and focused on Valentino's face. The look in his eyes melted her and made it impossible for her to move.

He chuckled and held out his hand. "I said, come here." He crooked his finger at her and finally shook his hair out of his eyes. "You aren't afraid, are you?"

Yeah, to be honest, she was. She basked in the warmth of his gaze and decided to be completely honest. "I'm terrified. I don't know what to do."

He spread his arms out and leaned back against the wardrobe. "I'm yours, baby. Do whatever you want to."

Chapter Twenty-four

Sera stepped into Valentino's room with all the boldness of a mouse. The timidity clashed with the almost feral look in her eyes, however. She swept her gaze over his body, as if trying to figure out where the best place to start might be, and it was all he could do not to offer a few suggestions. He lowered his arms and hid his impatience at her slow approach.

A lifetime seemed to pass before she halted in front of him. She lifted her gaze to his and scraped her teeth over her bottom lip hard enough to leave red marks but no blood. Thank God. He wouldn't be able to handle that temptation right now. He opened his mouth to say something to put her at ease, but she reached for him and the words got trapped in his throat.

Her fingers dusted over his chest on her way to explore the tense muscles in his arm. She traced the vein in his bicep with her index finger. "Did you feed?"

"Yes." The word sounded raw and forced.

She peeked up through her lashes. "Did you do anything else?"

"No, I don't want anyone but you."

Her lids eclipsed her eyes, and pale color washed into her cheeks. "That woman looked very interested."

"Yes, she was." He gave in and reached out to cup her chin. He tilted her face up until she was forced to look at him. "I'm done having sex with women just because they want me, Sera." Something shifted in her gaze. A memory?

"You told me that before."

"Yes, I did. My life at Captive Fantasy is over. I want to be your man, and only your man."

She moved her hand to the center of his chest. "Yeah, I'd like that." Her fingers walked down his body until they were wrapped around the hard length of his cock. "I'd like that a lot." She squeezed him through the silk, and he didn't do a damn thing to stop her.

A little smile formed on her lips, and she released him to hook her fingers into his waistband. She watched his face as the silk pants slithered over his hips and down past his raging cock. "You said I could do anything I want, right?"

He nodded, unable to speak past the anticipation.

She shoved his pants to the center of his thighs. The sound of silk against flesh filled the air and heightened his lust. "I want to do something I've never done before," she whispered.

His cock jumped, the tip hitting her belly and causing her to gasp. "It's ready for you, baby."

Blushing, she dropped her gaze and knelt to slide his pants all the way off, which brought her gorgeous mouth right where he wanted it. She moistened her lips and stared at the thick head of his cock. It oozed cum, and he fisted his hands at his sides when she flicked her tongue out to lick it away. Jesus Christ, she had no idea how close he was to grabbing her head and shoving her forward so he could feel the back of her throat.

He suppressed the urge and bit back a growl as she wrapped her cold fingers around him. She stroked him from root to tip until more cum beaded on the head. Again, she licked it off, then shocked and pleased him by taking the fat tip in her mouth. She hummed softly and slid her mouth down further.

Good God.

Valentino leaned his head back on the wardrobe and prayed for control. This was what he had craved his whole life. This feeling of standing on a ledge seconds before the world fell away. One little slip and he'd dive head first into unimaginable pleasure. All because of Sera's warm mouth and wet tongue. He'd had women on their knees for him that were skilled enough to moonlight as prostitutes, but nothing compared to the innocent suction of Sera's mouth.

Kicking his pants away from his feet, he widened his stance and leaned fully against the wardrobe. The rough wood dug into his spine and ass, but it wouldn't matter if he was on a bed of nails right now. He'd suffer any form of discomfort as long as Sera kept sucking him. And she did.

The cool brush of her fingers slid toward his balls, and hesitantly, she cupped his heavy sac and then began to massage him. All the while, her mouth grew bolder. She scraped her teeth up his cock to let him feel the sharp tips of her fangs, then soothed the path with quick flicks of her tongue.

"Sera."

She hummed around him instead of pulling away to answer. One hand stayed between his legs while the other moved to grip his thigh. She squeezed his muscles and scraped him with her teeth again.

"Sera." The sensations threatened to drive him crazy, but he didn't want to come in her mouth. Not yet. He blindly reached for the back of her head, and tried to pull her away. She held on, sucking hard on the very tip before gripping it with her teeth. He hissed at the slight pain and glanced down to meet her gaze.

She shook her head while still holding him.

"Keep it up and you're going to make me come," he warned her.

She bit a little harder, then lowered her gaze and slid her mouth down his length. She couldn't take all of him, but it was enough to silence his protests.

"Fine," he ground out. "You win." He kept his fingers tangled in her hair, but did nothing to stop her as she proceeded to give him the best blow job he'd ever had.

When every muscle in his body was tensed and ready to explode, she took her mouth off of him, flattened his cock against the taut surface of his belly, and licked him from the center of his balls upward. She caught the cum as it trickled from his slit.

"If you finish now, will we be able to have sex?" she asked as her lips brushed over the pulsing vein on the underside of his cock.

He struggled to answer. "Yeah." He could come for her all night if that's what she wanted.

"Good." That one little word was all the warning he got. She jammed her hands against his hips to pin him to the wardrobe, then angled her mouth down to swallow all but a few inches. Her throat fought the intrusion and he heard her stifle a gag, but it didn't stop her. With the tips of her fangs gliding lightly up and down his flesh, she sucked him into her mouth over and over again, until both of them were panting with the need for something greater.

"Sera," he growled low in his throat and held her head still. He began to thrust into her mouth, setting the rhythm that he knew would work the best. She dug her nails into his hips and held on. A few times he went too far, and her throat closed around him and she gagged slightly, but not once did she struggle against the hold he had on her hair.

He was so close.

She took a hand from his hip and snaked it between his legs to clasp his balls. She moaned around a deep thrust and then gave his sac a light squeeze. He tightened painfully, then exploded in her mouth.

"Oh God..." Try as he might, he couldn't temper the rate of his release, and his semen shot straight down her throat, giving her no choice but to swallow every drop.

Sweat dripped into Valentino's eyes and beaded across his upper lip while he waited for the world to stop spinning. It took a while. Finally, he released Sera's hair and lifted his shaky hand to his own to scrape the damp locks from his eyes. She looked up with a smile and licked her lips like a satisfied pussycat. Oh God, his body hardened all over again.

"Did I do that right?"

Was she nuts? He couldn't think of words to express just how right she'd gotten it. Gripping her shoulders, he hauled her to her feet and slammed his mouth over hers. She gasped in surprise but parted her lips to let his tongue thrust inside. She tasted like him.

Still ravaging her mouth, he walked her back toward the bed until she hit the edge of the mattress. With one last long drag on her bottom lip, he ended the embrace and shoved her backwards. Her short skirt rode up to the tops of her thighs as she struggled to land gracefully.

Her legs were bare, and as she wrestled with the skirt, he caught a flash of black panties. His mouth watered at the sight. He reached for the skirt and tore it in half from hem to waist.

Sera squeaked, and her eyes grew huge in her face. "What are you doing?"

He dragged the ruined skirt away from her body and threw it to the floor before giving her blouse the same harsh treatment. This time, she giggled softly. "You aren't going to destroy all of my clothing are you?" She grabbed his hand as he reached for her bra. "Let me get undressed. Please."

He crawled on top of her and buried his face in her neck. "That'll take too long, and I want to be inside you now." He found the flimsy material of her thong and shredded it with ease. It lay in tatters over her pussy, and he didn't bother to toss it aside. He sucked at her neck and nudged his hard cock between her legs.

"Spread your legs, Sera."

She did.

****

Pinned to the bed under the weight of Valentino's sweat dampened body, with his teeth harmlessly nipping her neck, and his cock impatiently nudging her opening,

Sera could only close her eyes, arch her back, and pray she didn't scream.

Valentino thrust into her with one single move, forcing her to take all of him at once. It was too much, and it felt too good. Her body sucked him in but then began to fight the rough invasion. Her muscles cramped and stretched in an effort to hold him in and push him out. The battle left her breathless.

"Ah...no..." She squirmed under him and pushed at his shoulders. "Wait," she gasped. "Slow down."

He loosened his hold on her neck and withdrew his cock until only the slick head breeched her. Her hips reared up of their own accord to coax him inside again. Maybe her brain wanted her to go slow, but it wasn't the organ winning the war. Hooking her feet around his thighs, she forced him down, and he thrust home again. Her ass sank into the bumpy mattress until she felt the hard press of bedsprings. Valentino pulled out and thrust back in, time after time, with no sign of relenting.

Sera did her best to prolong the experience, but it was no use. Each time his cock slid home, he banged the upper reaches of her womb, and when he withdrew, the friction burned the walls of her vagina. She was on fire. It was too much for any girl to take. Reaching up, she fisted her hands in his hair and managed to lift his head from her neck. His eyes seemed unfocused as they met hers.

"You're driving me crazy." She forced the words out on a ragged whisper.

He nodded within her grip, his expression reminding her that he had once made her come with just his voice. "Yeah. I know. That's sort of the plan."

Before she could speak, he aimed for her mouth and shoved deep inside her pussy one last time, smacking her ass with his balls and spreading her legs wider with the hard ridge of pelvis. He swallowed her scream, and she absorbed another full load of semen.

That should have been it, but it wasn't.

Sera barely had a chance to remember her name

before Valentino pulled out fully, slithered down her body, and put his face between her legs. The first flick of his tongue made her scream, and she was thankful they were three floors up in the attic. She clawed so violently at the threadbare blanket under her that shredded fabric gathered under her nails.

"Valentino, please!" She couldn't take it anymore. Already she felt the chill seeping into her veins, and before long, her need for blood would rush to the surface and destroy this wonderful encounter. If he brought her to orgasm again, she'd lose control, and he was the only one around to bite.

He lifted his head and met her gaze across the length of her body. "I want you to remember, Sera." He took hold of her hips and lifted them a little ways off the bed. He blew lightly on her pussy and smiled when she cried out. "I want you to remember everything I've ever done to you."

She nodded, unable to speak. The moment she'd placed her hand on his bare skin, the memories had come back. His smell, his touch, his taste—all of it was indelibly imprinted on her soul. How she had managed to forget for even a moment was a scary testament to Constantine's power.

"Do you remember how excited you were the first time I bit you?" Valentino's voice pulled her into focus.

She closed her eyes and groaned. Oh yes, she remembered. Memory became reality as Valentino's teeth snared her clit. He sucked it deep in his mouth, then released it to scrape the smooth line of his chin across the sensitized flesh. She trembled and took a step closer to another orgasm. Oh no.

"No one else knows you like it rough, do they?" he asked her between nips of his teeth.

Sera shook her head, not strong enough to lift it off the mattress. She pressed her knees wide and angled her hips higher. Valentino took the hint and buried his face right where she wanted it. With his hands holding her ass off the bed, and his arms keeping her legs open, he worked her inside and out until the blanket ripped under her nails and her voice rang out around the room.

The climax left her numbingly cold and very close to the edge. She pried her eyes open just as Valentino crawled back up her body to settle between her legs. His crooked, close-lipped smile and wicked eyes let her know he wasn't through with her yet. This had to stop.

"Val—"

He kissed her to shut her up.

Sera surrendered to the swirl of his tongue inside her mouth and the taste of her body on his lips. Pulling back, she licked the moisture from his chin and tangled her hands in his hair to arch his head further back.

He complied with a soft chuckle. "Gonna bite me, little vampire?"

Sera didn't answer. She lifted her shoulders off the bed to reach the tempting chords in his neck and dragged her elongated fangs up and down the thickest one. He chuckled again and shifted to brace his weight more fully on his hands. His lower body pinned hers to the mattress, but his chest hovered above her. She missed the slick feel of his skin, but her need for blood outweighed everything else at the moment.

Right before she sank her teeth into his thick artery, the queen's warning came back to haunt her. The woman believed Valentino might be dangerous. Did she mean physically or had she been referring to his blood? If Sera gave into the urge to drink from him, would he poison her again? Would she die this time?

A cold chill of real fear crept over her, and she pushed Valentino away with a little cry of anguish. He rolled to his side, then sat up to shoot her a confused look. "What's wrong?"

Sera shook her head and rolled into a ball with her back to him. She squeezed her eyes shut and tried to concentrate on something other than the erotic temptation of warm blood filling her mouth.

Valentino laid his hand on her hip. "Baby, what's wrong?"

"Don't touch me," she bit out. "*Please*, don't touch me." Her hunger had escalated to the point where she was shaking. Pretty soon, it would hurt. "I need blood," she finally whispered.

"Take mine."

The sight of Valentino's perfect neck flashed behind her lids, and she groaned again. "Mortal blood."

"You're afraid mine will still make you sick?"

His wounded tone didn't make things any easier. "Please. Go get someone else."

His hand slid off her hip, and the mattress dipped as he got to his feet. "Who do you prefer?" There was something buried in that question that forced her to roll over and meet his gaze. His eyes stared through her.

Oh God, he hated her for rejecting him. She'd do her best to explain, after she had blood. "Rick." Pain stabbed at her heart as the name tightened Valentino's already rigid features. Nodding once, he turned away and snatched up the silk pants on his way out. He didn't glance back before slamming the door behind him.

Chapter Twenty-five

Rick followed Valentino into the room a short time later, wearing an expression that let Sera know she'd made his night by sending for him. Well, he had ruined hers.

She sat up under the covers she'd pulled over her tattered clothes and tried not to let her gaze stray toward Valentino. Of course, she failed. How could she not look at him if he was in the room? It just couldn't be done. Never mind that Rick—and all his towering, blond hotness—was dressed again in tight jeans and no shirt, he paled in comparison to the glowering man at his back. Valentino was shorter by a few inches and not nearly as bulky, but she'd dare any man to come within shouting distance of his beauty.

Rick certainly didn't.

"You called for me, mistress?"

"Don't call her that," Valentino barked before Sera could even part her lips. He stepped behind Rick and shoved him toward the bed. "She needs blood. Shut up and feed her."

Rick's sea-green eyes settled on her face, and he arched a pale brow. "Is the pit bull staying?" The comment earned him another rough shove in the back.

Sera tucked the blankets under her arms and patted the space next to her. "Please, don't make this any more difficult than it already is." She felt Valentino's gaze and met it. "You don't have to stay."

His expression was all the response she needed. He

wasn't about to leave.

Rick sat on the edge of the bed—a little closer to her than necessary—and reached for her shoulders. His fingers had barely closed over her skin before Valentino was beside him.

"Don't touch her."

Rick glanced toward Valentino. "Look, buddy, she told you to leave."

"She told me I didn't have to stay. Not the same thing. Now take your fucking hands off of her or I'll feed them to you."

Sera stared at Valentino's face. Anger pooled in his eyes, turning them the color of deep, dark chocolate. Her body reacted to the sight with a surprising jolt of lust. She should not be turned on right now, for God's sake. What was wrong with her?

His gaze shifted and clashed with hers. The intensity didn't dim, but it changed to something entirely different. Something that promised really naughty things were going to happen the moment they were alone again.

Sera broke eye contact and Rick's light grip on her shoulders. "Just put your head back and let me feed." He seemed surprised by the blunt request but did as instructed.

His skin stretched over the column of his throat, and her fangs finished their descent from her gums. Careful not to touch him, lest Valentino go off like a stick of dynamite, she scooted closer and placed her mouth against his pulse. The bite she'd given him earlier seemed a good place to feed from now, and with very little effort she broke the skin and called his blood to the surface. He didn't even flinch.

Thankfully, it was over quickly, and she pulled away with new life humming in her veins. Rick shuddered as she swiped her tongue over the wound, but he refrained from making any comments. Smart guy.

His gaze met hers as she licked the last drop of blood from the corner of her mouth. "Does this mean you've decided to make me your servant?"

"No." It was Valentino who offered the sharp reply.

Rick stood up and stared down his nose at Valentino. Dislike clung to ever pore on his body, and he fisted his hands at his sides. Heavens, was he tempted to hit Valentino? She couldn't let that happen. She got out of the bed, careful to keep the ragged blanket around her body, and stepped foolishly between the two bristling men.

Valentino lowered his gaze to scowl at her, but she turned her back on him to address Rick. "Calling you here was an act of desperation. Nothing more."

His disappointment bothered her. "Yeah, okay." He flicked his gaze past her. "Seems you've gotten rid of one heavy-handed keeper just to acquire another." He looked at her again. "I wish you a lot of luck." He turned toward the door, but Sera lashed out to grab his arm.

"Wait."

Valentino growled softly behind her, but she ignored him. "What do you mean? Has something happened to Constantine?"

Rick glanced at Valentino for a second before telling her. "The master punished him for his rebellion."

Sera released Rick's arm and looked over her shoulder. "What does that mean?"

Valentino shrugged and crossed his arms before glaring at Rick. "Tell her what it means."

Sera rolled her eyes. She'd have to get used to this new badass Valentino, but first things first. She glanced at Rick. "Just tell me whatever you know."

He nodded once. "There's really only one way to punish a vampire, and that's to deny them blood." He shrugged his muscular shoulders. "I assume Constantine is now locked away somewhere, wishing he'd kept his mouth shut."

Sera gasped then tried to hide the sound behind her hand. It was too late. Valentino took hold of her from behind and snapped at Rick to get the hell out. Rick shrugged once more, then sauntered from the room.

Valentino whipped her around, and the blanket drifted to the floor. "Do you actually feel sorry for him?" The anger was back in his eyes, and it was all for her this time.

Sera didn't know how to answer. Constantine had *made* her. Regardless of how much she loathed him, she couldn't deny the bond they shared. Putting all that into words didn't seem possible with Valentino's fingers biting into her shoulders, so she shook her head and averted her gaze.

He shook her. "You're lying, damnit!"

Sera glanced back up. "Please don't yell at me."

Valentino snatched his hands off her shoulders to rake them through his hair. His lips parted, but instead of speaking, he dragged in a deep breath that expanded his chest and feathered across her face when he exhaled. It made her shiver, and she wrapped her arms around her nakedness.

"I'm not going to hurt you." His tone was back to normal.

"I know." Sera laid her hand on his chest, feeling his heartbeat. It was fast and hard, more mortal than vampire. "Just tell me why you're so angry."

He covered her hand and gripped her fingers tight. "I don't want to see even a glimmer of sympathy on your face for that bastard. Let him rot. He deserves it for the way he treated you."

Sera stared at their joined hands. Her skin was so much paler than Valentino's, and she wondered if he'd eventually lose the golden hue. Part of her hoped he didn't. "I'm not sorry to hear that he's indisposed."

Valentino hooked a finger under her chin and eased her face up. His eyes were back to the comforting milk chocolate color that was so easy to drown in. "Just tell me what he means to you. I deserve to know that much, don't I?"

"He means nothing." Saying the words let her hear the truth behind them. Constantine had ceased to mean anything the moment he shut her out of his life. She'd survived without him, and damn well, all things considered. A little smile pulled at her lips, and a giggle tickled the back of her throat.

Valentino didn't look as amused. "What's so funny?"

Sera stepped closer and wrapped her free hand around his waist. She snuggled into his chest and inhaled the fragrance of his skin. He smelled like sex. His silk pants brushed her bare thighs, and her body let out a silent wail of need.

"Sera?"

She glanced up. "I find it a little humorous that I've wasted over two centuries believing I somehow needed Constantine in my life. Not that I wanted him there, but I convinced myself it was his right." She frowned as Valentino's gaze narrowed. "That doesn't make sense, does it?"

"Yeah, but it's not exactly humorous."

"Is annoying better?" He nodded, and her smile grew. "Everything I've ever done was because of him. Not drinking from mortals, stifling my real desires, hating sex—"

"You don't hate sex."

"I did before you came along. I was too afraid of losing control." She buried her face in his chest. It was easier to be open and honest if she didn't have to stare into his eyes. "I was terrified of becoming the sort of vampire Constantine wanted."

"Why?"

"I was afraid he'd come back for me." It was a fear she'd laid down with everyday, but one she needn't worry about anymore. Was this what liberation felt like? If so, she liked it. She snuggled closer to Valentino, and he wrapped his arms around her. "I still don't enjoy drinking from mortals though."

"Unless it's my neck," he teased.

In response, she slid her cheek against his chest until she could lick the hollow of his throat. "You're too delicious to resist, and that isn't my fault."

He dug his hands in her hair and eased her back to see her face. "But you're afraid to take any more of my blood, aren't you?"

"The queen warned me that you might not be the usual breed of vampire. Until we figure it out, I should play it safe." Never mind how much she wanted to sink her teeth into him even now. Just the proximity of his neck drove her mad, and she wasn't even thirsty anymore.

"Does that mean I have to watch you feed from Rick again? Not sure I can or want to do that."

Sera fought back a smile. "Jealous?"

Valentino tightened his arms and lifted her off her feet to kiss her. "Jealous enough to want to do some serious damage to him," he said once he'd thoroughly branded the inside of her mouth. "I didn't like it." He set her back down and kissed the top of her head. "I didn't like it at all."

"It's what we are—"

"No, that's Constantine talking, and we both know it. My Sera lived a happy life sipping synthetic blood from a silly mug. We'll get the hell out of this place and see that you have all the fake blood you need so that you never have to sink those sexy fangs into a neck again."

It sounded nice. Real nice. "And what about you?"

He cupped her face and kissed her forehead. "What about me?"

"My blood made you sick, so it's possible you can't ingest the fake stuff. If that's the case, you'll require a servant to feed from." The thought did not sit well in her stomach. How could she watch him feed from another, knowing the ecstasy to be found in his bite? She couldn't do it. She refused to do it.

"I'm not so sure your blood would have the same effect on me now."

Sera frowned at that. "Why?"

Valentino pulled her close and buried his face against her neck. "I've fed twice and I'm still hungry. Is that normal?"

"No."

He licked her skin, making her shiver. "I think I need *your* blood."

The thought of having his fangs inside her was unbearably tempting. "And if you're wrong?"

He lifted his head from her neck to kiss her. mouth. His gaze met hers. "Then I'm wrong." He began to peel the ruined shirt off her body. When he reached for her bra, his touch was gentle, and he took the time to slide the straps down and unhook the clasp.

"What are you doing?" The jab of his erection through his pants made her breathless.

"Since you're all full and happy with blood, I see no reason not to fuck you again."

His bluntness squeezed her insides, and she pressed her thighs together to trap the moisture there. "I didn't say I wanted to do it again."

He had her naked now, and he scooped her off the floor and into his arms. "You have until we get to the bed to say yes." It took two strides to get there. He arched a brow and looked down at her. "Well?"

Sera giggled and ducked her face against his chest. "Yes."

"Say it louder."

She lifted her face and stared at the sensual promise of his mouth. "Yes."

"Yes what?"

She growled in frustration and squeezed her eyes shut. "Don't you dare make me say it."

His lips brushed over her eyes. "I want to hear it. I want to hear you say, 'Fuck me hard, Valentino.' Can you say that?"

She squirmed in his arms, and the musky scent of her arousal intensified. His sharp intake of breath let her know that he could smell it. Ah, the joys of being a vampire. Wait until he realized he could see in the dark and hear through walls.

"Sera, I'm not a patient man."

She opened her eyes. "Since when?"

"Since I'm not paid to be." He moved her away from his chest and held her suspended over the bed. If he dropped her, the mattress would likely break.

She squealed and gripped his arms. "Don't you dare drop me."

"Say it."

An unwelcome voice shattered the moment. "Hate to interrupt, but the master says you should come downstairs immediately."

Sera peered around Valentino's shoulder as he gathered her back against his chest. Nadia stood just inside the door, looking more than a little amused. She smiled, but it failed to reach her eyes. "You aren't supposed to be here, are you, Seraphina?" She shook her head and tsked. "Shame on you."

Valentino set Sera down, but kept his body between her and Nadia. "Why does the master need to see me?"

Sera didn't miss the direction of Nadia's gaze. It settled hot and eager on the front of Valentino's pants. She licked her pale lips nice and slow before answering. "Not my place to spread gossip. I was told to get you, and here I am." She swept her gaze upward, not missing a single inch of exposed skin. "What exactly *are* you?" she asked.

Sera laid her hand in the center of Valentino's back and felt him stiffen. "Last I checked, I was a vampire." The coldness of his tone chilled the room.

Nadia seemed unaffected. She shook her head, and her brick-red hair slithered over her shoulders like live snakes. "No. You're too...too *something*." She waved her hand in the air, making the rings on her fingers clank together. One housed a large sapphire that winked as she moved. "You might drink blood and have fangs, but you're not a vampire. I'd bet my favorite servant on that."

Valentino shrugged under Sera's hand. "Tell the master I'll be down."

Nadia leaned against the door frame and crossed her arms. "I'll wait."

Valentino strolled across the room, turned Nadia around, and pushed her into the hall. "No, you'll tell him I'll be right down." He shut the door on her irritated expression, and turned back to Sera. "We really need to get the hell out of this place."

Sera could not agree more. "I'll go down with you, but not like this."

Valentino fetched his silk shirt off the floor and handed it over. "It'll have to do."

The cool fabric fell to mid-thigh, and Sera rolled the sleeves twice to expose her wrists. Not ideal, but it smelled like Valentino and it covered everything that mattered. Vampires weren't prudish, and she doubted anyone would bat an eyelash at her appearance.

Valentine combed his hair with his fingers, then reached out to do the same for her. His smile concerned her.

"What's wrong? Do I look like hell?"

"You look like you've had great sex a few times."

Sera rolled her eyes and shoved him out of the way. "Wonderful." She headed for the door and glanced back. "Let's get this over with."

Chapter Twenty-six

Sera was awfully glad to be holding Valentino's hand as they stepped into the master's study. The imposing vampire sat behind his desk and glanced up when they halted just inside the door. He didn't look very happy. In fact, the word pissed came to mind. Wonderful.

"Sit down." He waved at the same two chairs she had occupied with Constantine, and she and Valentino moved to obey. She put their linked hands in her lap and noticed that the master settled his gaze on them. He frowned and looked up. "You were warned to stay away from him, were you not?"

Sera nodded, and Valentino squeezed her fingers.

"Care to explain your disobedience?"

As much as she wanted to, she didn't dare tear her gaze away from the master's probing blue eyes. Not only did he look pissed, he seemed exhausted. His hair was more tousled than usual, and his skin looked too pale. A little blood might be a good idea. His gaze narrowed, and she quickly masked her thoughts and opinions. Oops.

"I find it hard to stay away from him." Sera shrugged, thinking that answer was good enough.

The master flicked his gaze to Valentino. "Did she bite you?"

"No." Valentino glanced toward her. "And I didn't bite her."

The master nodded once and then shoved his chair back to stand. He was dressed casually in black jeans and a black crew-neck sweater, but the attire didn't lessen the aura of power around him. "You two seem intent to doom one another, and I have half a mind to just let you do it."

Sera peeked out the corner of her eye and caught the angry shift of Valentino's features. She squeezed his hand to keep him from speaking out, and thankfully, he took the hint.

The master braced his hands on his desk and leaned toward them. His gaze remained on Valentino. "You should be aware that the coven received three visitors tonight, brought here at my request."

"Who?" Valentino's fingers flexed under Sera's.

"Two of them don't matter, but the one, you may wish to have a word with."

"Who?" Valentino said again.

The master straightened and nodded toward the door behind them. "See for yourself."

The leather chairs groaned and crackled as they spun around. Sera didn't recognize the white-haired, bespectacled man in the doorway, but the energy pouring off of Valentino told her he certainly did. She glanced over and then wished she hadn't. The anger he had focused on Rick was nothing compared to what shot out of his eyes now.

"Hello, CF19."

****

Valentino's body went through a range of emotions as he stared at Dr. Reynolds. The strongest being anger. "What are you doing here?"

The doctor looked to the master. "I was *invited*, you might say." He refocused on Valentino before going on. "Did he tell you that Raphael is here as well?"

Jesus, why?

Valentino twisted around to meet the master's gaze. "What is going on?"

"It's rather simple, Valentino. This is the only man capable of deciphering what is going on inside you. It seemed logical to bring him here."

"And Raphael? Why is he here?"

The master shrugged. "Insurance."

Valentino shook free of Sera's hand and lunged out of his chair. "Where is he?"

The master didn't even flinch. "He's safe. For now."

"What the hell does that mean?"

"It means, if you cooperate with the doctor, your friend will leave here uninjured and devoid of any recollection of having visited." The master crossed his arms. "Like I said, insurance."

"You said there were three people." Sera's interruption was almost too faint to hear. "The doctor and Raphael are only two. Who else is here?"

Her question earned her the master's full attention. "There was a woman with Raphael. She insisted upon coming along, I'm told."

Sera made a horrible choking noise and looked up at Valentino with frightened eyes. "Becca. It has to be Becca."

"Red hair, very little clothing, and a fiery mouth?" the master asked.

Sera's nod looked painful.

Valentino sat back down and reclaimed her hand. He laid it on his thigh and stared hard at her profile. She looked straight ahead, not blinking, not breathing, not anything.

"Your friend won't be hurt, Seraphina." All the anger the master had directed at Valentino was gone as he addressed Sera. "She's been taken to a guest room and made comfortable. You have my word on that."

****

Sera couldn't focus on the voices talking around her. Becca was here. Somewhere in this very house was the person she had lied to for two years. What on earth would Becca say to all this? How could any of it possibly be explained?

The sound of her name jerked her into awareness. She blinked and glanced at Valentino. He offered a comforting smile. "Do you want to go to Becca?"

Yes and no. She wanted to make sure her friend really was all right, but did she wish to face her? No. Confessing she'd never had a real orgasm was nothing compared to coming clean about being a vampire. God, Becca would kill her.

"I think it would be best if you leave us, Seraphina."

She looked at the master. "What's going to happen to Valentino?" She didn't like the look of the doctor, and she really didn't like the tension in Valentino's entire body. None of it boded well.

"He'll undergo a series of tests," the master explained, "that will help us determine how best to deal with his vampirism."

That didn't sound good. Sera alternated her attention between the doctor and the master. "I don't like how that sounds."

Valentino squeezed her hand and captured her gaze as it slid toward the doctor. He leaned closer to whisper. "It'll help us figure out if I can drink your blood."

Sera squirmed in her chair, aware of the study filling with the smell of her desire for Valentino. Wonderful.

"There will be no need for you to do so within the coven." The master's voice made her jump. "You'll both choose servants to provide what you need."

Valentino looked away. "We don't plan on staying."

Sera held her breath when the master crossed his arms and glared at Valentino. "I've already dealt with one rebellious idiot tonight, don't make me do it again." There was little doubt he meant Constantine.

Valentino didn't back down. "You can't force us to remain here."

The doctor spoke up from the doorway. "Let us test his blood first and go from there."

The comment diffused the rising tension in the room, and the master nodded at Sera. "You will find your friend in the room next to yours. Go to her."

She knew a direct order when she heard one. On shaky legs, she stood up. Valentino tugged on her hand,

and she leaned back down as he lifted his face. She kissed him, not caring if the master liked it or not. "I love you," she whispered against his lips.

He pulled back and snaked his free hand around her neck. "Say it again."

She smiled. "I love you."

"Are you saying that because you believe we'll never see each other again?"

"Maybe," she answered truthfully. "But it doesn't make it not true."

He nodded and pulled her face close to kiss her again. Someone in the room cleared their throat, but Valentino didn't seem inclined to let the sound interrupt their embrace. Eventually he took his mouth away and released her hand. "Go to Becca. I'll be fine."

Sera left before she could decide not to. Once in the hall, it hit her that Valentino hadn't returned the sentiment. Was it possible for him not to feel the same way she did? She refused to consider that as she made her way up the steps to Becca's room. Outside the door, she hesitated. Maybe she should get dressed first?

The knob turned, taking away any chance of escape, and Becca's scared face peered around the edge of the door. "Oh my God, Sera!" She threw the door open and nearly jumped into her arms. "What is going on? What is this place? Why are you here? What are you *wearing*?"

Sera extracted herself from Becca's chokehold and guided her back inside the room. She shut the door and leaned against it. At least Becca didn't look harmed in any way. Her bright red hair was a little messed up, and her white tank top looked as if it had been slept in, but all in all, she seemed fine.

"Are you okay?" she asked just to be sure.

Becca nodded and plopped down onto the bed. The room was decorated with silks and velvets in shades of burgundy and beige, and the sumptuous décor made Becca look like a cheap hooker in her tiny, denim, mini-skirt, tank top, and wedge sandals. "I'm fine, but a little confused."

"Tell me what happened. How did you get here?"

Becca crossed her legs and her arms. "I was with Raphael and suddenly two guys burst into the room and hauled him out of bed. They were really scary, Sera." She shivered before going on. "Anyway, I screamed and jumped in front of the door. Raphael told me to stay out of it, but I threatened to keep screaming until they either told me what was happening or let me go with them."

"Clearly they went for option B."

Becca nodded. "They let me get dressed and then everything after that is fuzzy. I woke up in this room. Why are *you* here?"

"That's a really long story," Sera hedged.

Becca's green eyes narrowed. "Whose shirt is that?"

Lying was normally futile with Becca involved. "Valentino's."

Becca looked intrigued. "Is this his place?" She glanced around the room with obvious interest now. None of her earlier terror lingered. "Is this some sort of surprise party or something?" She settled her wide eyes back on Sera. "Did you two secretly get married? Is that why you've missed work?" She frowned suddenly. "Mr. Henry wasn't pleased, by the way. If you try to come back now, he might not let you."

Sera took a deep breath. "Becca, I'm a vampire and this house belongs to the coven."

Becca snapped her mouth shut, but it popped right back open. "Ha-ha."

"It's true." Sera moved away from the door and joined Becca on the bed. In situations like this, there was really only one way to prove her point. She faced her friend and smiled.

Becca swore and jumped off the bed. "Jesus Christ! Are those fangs!" She cupped her hand over her mouth and looked around the room as if expecting someone to laugh at her outburst. A few seconds passed and she fixed her gaze back on Sera. "Are those fangs?" she asked in a more controlled tone. "*Real* fangs?"

Sera nodded. "I'm not going to bite you, Becca."

"This isn't for real." Becca shook her head and sat back down on the bed. "Sorry, good trick, but I don't believe in vampires. And if I did, you wouldn't make a very good one."

Okay... "So, how do I prove it to you?"

Becca shrugged. "I don't know. Do something vampiry."

"I don't think that's a word."

Another shrug. "Can you levitate?"

Sera almost laughed out loud. "No, sorry."

"Turn into a bat?"

"No." Nothing like being reminded of any shortcomings all at once. "I can't read or control minds either." Not anymore, anyway. For just a moment, she'd been able to glimpse inside Valentino's thoughts, but then the ritual and Constantine had taken that from her.

Becca stared at her, clearly a non believer. "We both know you can see yourself in a mirror. Vampires can't do that."

Sera left the bed and walked over to the tall, pedestal mirror. She met Becca's gaze in the reflection. "Yes, we can." For good measure, she waved.

Becca frowned and got up to join her. "You aren't a vampire, Sera."

Sera sighed. "Name one time you've seen me out in the sun."

"I never see anyone during the day. I'm in school."

Sera grabbed Becca's hand and held it between her cold palms. "Why do you think I'm so cold?"

Becca shrugged. "My grandmother had very cold hands and she was most definitely not a vampire."

That was it. Time to pull out the real proof. Sera looked in the mirror and caught Becca's eye. "Watch this."

In her mind she conjured the sleek line of Valentino's neck. She thought about the feel of his pulse under her tongue, the smooth surface of his skin, and the first surge of blood into her mouth. The moment she felt her fangs start to extend she curled her lips back and let Becca witness the phenomena. The color bled from Becca's face, and her eyes rolled back into her head. She fainted before Sera could catch her.

Damn. That had gone badly.

Chapter Twenty-seven

Sera had plenty of time to think while Becca remained unconscious. She had moved her limp friend to the bed and pulled the covers over her. It might be wise to call for some help, but she didn't think Becca would wish to wake up with a strange vampire hovering over her, so she stayed in the room with her friend. The shock had to wear off eventually.

In the meantime, there was nothing to do but think, and there was really only one thing to think about.

Valentino, and the fact that he hadn't said he loved her. Maybe he'd felt uncomfortable saying such a thing in front of two other men? Maybe it was some macho, hide your feelings thing? Maybe he really didn't love her?

Sera sat on the floor, across from the bed, with her head against the wall and her eyes closed. Becca's steady breathing echoed around the room. Valentino's silk shirt was pulled over her upraised knees, but her bare feet stuck out. The room was cold. Or maybe she was cold? Yeah, she was very cold. Just the suggestion that Valentino might not feel the same made the blood in her veins feel like ice. It wouldn't be fair, after all this time, to fall in love with a guy that didn't love her back.

Not fair at all.

Becca moaned on the bed, ending Sera's depressing thought pattern. She got up and crossed the room just as her friend opened her eyes. "How do you feel?"

Becca frowned and pressed a hand to her forehead. "I had the strangest dream," she mumbled. "I was in a

230

strange house, you were there, and you told me you were a vampire."

Sera hugged herself and gazed down at Becca. "It wasn't a dream."

Becca lowered her hand from her face and stared. "Was I brought here to be killed?"

"My god, no!" Sera reached for Becca's hand, but it was snatched away. Okay, fine. "Why would you think such a horrible thing?"

Becca struggled to sit up. "There's only one logical reason for me to be in a house full of vampires. Blood. I've been brought here to be sucked dry, haven't I?"

Sera rolled her eyes. "You watch too many movies."

"Then tell me what's really going on?"

Before Sera could, there was a light knock at the door and then it opened without either of them calling out. Valentino peeked in, spotted Sera, and entered. Sera's whole body reacted to the sight of him, but she tore her eyes away as Becca let out a low sound of feminine approval. She looked at her friend, only to find her friend staring hungrily at Valentino. She'd never get used to seeing that look on other women's faces. She just knew it.

"Am I interrupting?" he asked, still hovering just inside the door.

Sera looked back. "No. This is Becca, by the way." She gestured toward her mute friend. Valentino flashed the kind of smile that undoubtedly had made him a favorite at Captive Fantasy. Sera heard Becca sigh.

"Becca, this is Valentino," she added, though it was hardly necessary.

Despite the fact that she'd just been unconscious for close to an hour, Becca slid off the bed and floated toward Valentino. She held out a hand. "Hello. Lovely to meet you in person."

Valentino shook her hand and shot a quick look toward Sera, who shrugged. "Thank you," he said to Becca.

"You're much more gorgeous in person than on the

website," Becca went on. "Though so is Raphael."

Sera moved forward to put a halt to the conversation. "Becca, not now." She gripped her friend's shoulder and received a hostile glare in return.

"Did you bring him here to feast off of him?"

Sera removed her hand and shook her head. "An hour ago, you told me that if vampires did exist, I wouldn't make a good one, and now you're accusing me of bringing Valentino into my lair to feast on him like some animal. Make up your mind, Bec. You either believe in us or you don't."

Becca's green eyes narrowed. "I don't know what to believe, but I know that something weird is going on." She turned back to Valentino. "Have you seen Raphael?"

"Yeah, I have."

Sera watched Valentino closely as he spoke. His gaze shifted and met hers, and she knew without being told that they needed to speak privately. Now.

"Will you excuse us, Becca?" Sera had a hard time taking her eyes off Valentino. "Valentino and I need to talk privately."

Becca arched a brow and propped her hands on her hips. "I don't think it's a good idea for you to be alone with him. You might bite him or something."

Valentino spoke up before Sera could tell Becca to mind her own damn business. "I'll be quite safe," he said. "But thank you for your concern."

Becca whipped her head around. "What if she attacks you?" She moved toward him and gestured at his bare upper body. Despite becoming a vampire, he still bore the scar of Sera's first bite. It wasn't as ugly as it had been, but it stood out against the golden skin of his neck. Most likely, it would never completely go away.

"You've already got marks," Becca said. "Are they from her?" She turned to pin Sera with an angry look before Valentino could defend himself. "I thought you were little miss prude? You've actually *bitten* him?"

"None of this concerns you," Sera told her.

"So you have," Becca concluded. "During sex?" Her tone shifted from accusatory to really curious. "So that's how it happens? You drink and fuck at the same time?"

Sera had had enough. She grabbed Becca's shoulders and physically moved her back toward the bed. "You need more rest, I think."

Becca fought her as best she could considering Sera had decided to employ a little vampire strength. Hadn't Becca wished for a demonstration? "I don't need to rest," she protested.

Sera pushed her down onto the bed. "Well, do so anyway." She turned toward Valentino and caught him attempting to hide a smile. He failed, so he ducked his head and let the fall of his hair hide it for him. She took a step, but Becca's frantic voice stopped her.

"Where are you going?"

Sera glanced back at the bed. "I'll be right next door, and I swear, you won't come to any harm." She reached down and brushed a thick lock of red hair from Becca's forehead. "No one wants to hurt you, Becca. You have to believe me."

"But I'm mortal and full of blood. Isn't that some sort of temptation?"

"Most of us do pretty good fighting temptation."

Something flashed in Becca's eyes, letting Sera know that her friend probably wouldn't fight too hard against a sexy, male vampire. Thank God Constantine was locked away somewhere. He never could resist easy prey.

****

"She's something else," Valentino said about Becca once he was alone with Sera in her room. She rolled her eyes and wrapped her arms around his waist to hug him. He hugged her back and kissed the top of her head. "What's this for?"

She shrugged and the movement brushed the silk of her shirt over his bare skin. "Can't I hug you?"

Valentino tightened his arms around her back. "Yeah, you can." They embraced in silence for a few more moments, then Sera started to squirm. He loosened his hold, and she stepped out of his arms. She ran her fingers through her hair and fixed her gaze on his chest. He suspected something was on her mind, and he knew he was right when he saw her teeth hook over her bottom lip.

He reached out to tap the tip of her nose. "What's wrong, baby?"

She glanced through her lashes. "Why didn't you say it back?"

He had no idea what she was talking about, and before he could say as much, she tossed up her hands and stalked away from him. At that moment he realized how much easier it was to seduce a woman than to actually figure out her mind.

Sera sat on her bed and glared at him. "You said you saw Raphael?"

"I take it we've changed the subject now?" Better safe than sorry. Her glare was the only answer he got. "Yeah, I've seen him, and he's fine. In fact, he's handling this a whole lot better than your friend."

"Maybe he believes in vampires?"

"I told him what you were, so seeing all this shouldn't be a surprise."

She shot off the bed and flew toward him. Her agitation knocked the oversized shirt off one creamy shoulder. She didn't stop to fix it. "You told him? Who else did you tell? And why would you do such a thing?"

Valentino grabbed her around the waist. "Whoa. Calm down, for God's sake. Can we finish one conversation at a time?"

She huffed and yanked the shirt into place. "Fine."

Valentino maintained his grip on her waist and walked her back toward the bed. As he tried to get her to sit down, she flipped out again and started smacking him on the chest.

"Don't you dare think you're going to calm me down with sex."

"What?"

She balled her fists and hit him hard between the pecs. "In fact, I might never sleep with you again."

He let her go and stepped out of reach. "Obviously we need to talk about something before I tell you what happened after you left the study. Care to tell me what that something might be?" She moved toward him, and he retreated. "Stay where you are."

She glared at him some more and crossed her arms. "Tell me what, if anything, I mean to you."

Awareness dawned on Valentino like a new day. He reached up to brush his hair back and also to stall for time. So this was the problem. She'd said she loved him, and he hadn't said it back. Now she looked at him as if he were something he'd scrape off his shoe. Nice, real nice.

"Well?" she snapped, when he'd obviously stalled a second too long.

"If I say it now, you'll never believe me."

She seemed confused for a moment. A short moment. "You don't know that."

He nodded and tried to silence the chuckle he could feel building. "Yeah, I do know that. You'll wonder for the rest of your life—which is a really long time, I might add—if I said it because you forced the issue. That doubt will eat away at you until you can't stand it, or me, anymore."

She shook her head and took a little step toward him. He didn't retreat this time. "That won't happen."

"Sera, baby." He took hold of her waist again and pulled her closer. She braced her hands on his chest so that only their lower bodies touched. It was enough to set him on fire, and the blush bleeding into her cheeks let him know she burned as well. "I'll say it when you least expect it. How does that sound?"

She trailed a finger up his chest to trace the line of his collarbone. Her touch was so light it almost tickled. "When will that be?" She focused on her hand, not his face, so she missed his smile.

"If I tell you, it won't be unexpected."

She was quiet for awhile as she continued to trail her finger over him. From his collarbone, she went toward the hollow of his throat, then up over his adam's apple. "It doesn't count if you say it during sex."

Valentino dropped his head back as her finger traced the line of his jaw, then delved into his hair to find his ear. God, who knew one finger could feel so erotic? "I'll keep that in mind."

She had all her fingers buried in his hair now at the back of his head. Her grip wasn't gentle as she forced his head up to look him in the eyes. "You do realize that telling me you'll say it when I least expect it, means you love me. If it didn't, you'd have no reason to say it at all."

"Nice of you to realize that." He dipped his head and caught her parted lips. He could still taste the lingering flavor of Rick's blood on her tongue as it thrust forward to meet his. The sooner he got her out of here, the better, because the only taste he wanted in her mouth was his.

He made love to her mouth for awhile and then dug his hand in her hair to ease her face away. She sighed and licked her lips as her eyes drifted up to meet his.

"We need to talk," he reminded her.

"Can we talk in bed?"

All the blood in his body shot right to his cock. "Jesus, Sera." He shoved her away and reached for the front of her shirt. He fumbled with the buttons, but was careful not to do any damage. It slithered to the floor, leaving her naked and trembling. He wanted to drop to his knees and worship her.

She placed a hand on his shoulder and pressed down. "On your knees," she ordered him.

Valentino cocked a brow. "What's with the Mistress Seraphina act?"

She applied more pressure to his shoulder, and he gave in to sink to his knees. Her gaze followed him down. "I'm trying to learn to be more assertive." The stain on her cheeks indicated she still had a ways to go before she mastered her shyness.

Valentino lightly clasped her hips. "I'm yours to command, mistress."

Her lips parted, and her fingers dug into his shoulder. She stared down at him, clearly at a loss as to what to say or do next. God, he adored her.

"What do you want?" He was close enough to her pussy to feel the heat of her arousal. Mixed with the heady fragrance, it was enough to drive him mad, but he'd wait for her to take the lead. He did, however, lower his face just enough to feel her curls brush over his chin. She tensed and let out a little gasp.

"I want that," she finally said.

"You can do better than that, Sera."

She tightened her jaw and stared at some point across the room. "I want you to use your mouth." More color stained her cheeks. "Please."

"Where do you want my mouth?"

She looked down, clearly exasperated. "I want it," she paused to lick her lips. "I want it down *there*." She gestured with the hand not digging welts in his shoulder.

He should take pity on her, but it was too fun to make her squirm. He brushed his chin over her again. "Here?"

She nodded and gripped both his shoulders now. "Valentino, please. You're being cruel."

"Am I?" He lowered his gaze, and his hands to her pussy. With his thumbs, he spread her lips apart to expose her clit. She inhaled sharply and drew blood with her nails. The smell filled the room and made his nostrils flare. "Never let it be said that I'm cruel to women." He bent forward and sucked her clit deep into his mouth. She shuddered and moaned out loud.

Kneeling might work great for women, but Valentino wanted better access. Moving his hands back to her hips, he glanced up her body to find her watching him. "Turn around, bend over the bed, and spread your legs."

Her eyes widened, but she did as he asked. She visibly shook as she braced her hands on the shiny comforter. Still on his knees, he simply scooted up behind her and spread her open for his tongue. She cried out and filled his mouth with the sweet taste of her cum. Relentlessly, he licked and sucked at her until her knees buckled and she begged him to stop.

He sat back on his heels and ripped the front of his pants down away from his cock. Taking hold of Sera's waist from behind, he guided her down astride his thighs and watched her body take him inside. She had yet to stop convulsing from her orgasm, and her muscles gripped and released every inch as it slid deeper and deeper. She lurched forward and took hold of the edge of bed with his name spilling from her lips.

"Just hang on," he told her.

He heard the comforter snag under her nails as she obeyed. He waited for the last pulse of her climax to fade, then he lifted her up and slammed her back down. She shrieked and the comforter tore some more. Over and over, he pounded her down on top of him, and finally she lost her hold on the bed and reached down to grab his knees. Sweat beaded down the center of her spine and he strained forward to lick it away. She shivered under his tongue.

"Val…"

"Hmm?" he hummed against her spine as he licked away more sweat. He could feel her vagina tightening.

"I want to feel your teeth." The words were barely a whisper, but she'd managed to say them, and he couldn't refuse her.

With one final lick, he scanned her pale back and then latched onto the back of her left arm. He bit into her muscle, and she climaxed with a soft cry.

Chapter Twenty-eight

The room came into focus for Sera as she drifted down from her high. Valentino's bite on her arm weakened and then disappeared all together. He shuddered one last time underneath her before dropping his forehead against her back to let the throbbing and twitching of his cock subside. Each pulse made her catch her breath and forced her to fight the urge to ride him all over again.

"I don't think I can move," he said against her.

Sera didn't think she could either. "We still need to have that talk." She flexed her fingers around his knees and noticed how badly she'd wrinkled the delicate silk. Oh dear. The pants were likely stained beyond repair, too. The thought brought fresh heat to her cheeks.

Valentino encircled her waist with one arm. "Grab the comforter."

Sera didn't ask why. She took hold of the smooth cover and then suddenly fell backwards. She landed spooned in front of Valentino. He put his lips to her ear. "The bed would be better, but I don't think I can walk." He dragged the comforter over them and snuggled closer.

Sera wiggled her ass against the dwindling bulk of his erection and gave a little sigh. "This is just fine." She closed her eyes and contemplated drifting off to sleep, but Valentino gave her a tight squeeze.

"Hey," he said in her ear. "We have things to talk about."

Sera didn't open her eyes. "So talk."

"Dr. Reynolds was able to determine some very interesting things about me."

That got her attention. She shifted onto her back and pulled Valentino's arm across her belly. She tried to make her head comfortable on the wood floor, but failed. Valentino smiled and worked his other arm behind her head. She settled onto the bulge of his bicep, careful where she put most of her weight. "This will put your arm to sleep."

"I'll live."

"What did the doctor find out?"

"In spite of what some might believe, I am a vampire."

"Yes, I know." Sera reached over to touch a finger to his lips. "I felt the bite."

He smiled. "Did it feel good?"

She snatched her hand away and lowered her gaze. "Stop teasing me."

His chuckle filled her ear as he nuzzled close to her. "I like teasing you. You should know that by now." He kissed her ear and then pulled back. "But in all seriousness, I'm not the normal kind of vampire."

Sera propped herself on her elbows and looked down at Valentino. He rolled onto his back and laced his hands together behind his head. He looked like he was waiting for her to ask, so she did. "What kind are you?" Who knew there were different *kinds*. Not her.

"I'm the kind who shouldn't drink human blood." His brown eyes twinkled up at her. "Fancy that."

Sera didn't understand. "You've already had human blood though. You told me you fed from that woman."

He nodded. "And I did, twice, to be exact."

"I didn't need to know that."

He took an arm out from behind his head to reach up and cup her cheek. "She didn't taste as good as you."

Sera sat up completely and twisted to face him. "Women don't like hearing things like that."

Valentino dropped his hand down to her waist, and

then further still. "All right, I'll never tell you how good you taste, ever again."

She swatted his hand and scowled at him. "You know what I mean."

He smiled again and propped his arm back under his head. "Yeah, I know what you mean. But back to the good doctor. It seems it's your fault." He winked at her. "My aversion to human blood, that is."

Sera pointed at her chest. "Me? What did I do?"

"You made me, baby. Your diet of synthetic blood, mixed with whatever the hell used to flow in my veins, has turned me into a vampire that can't get full on mortal blood. I can drink it, and it won't make me sick, but it won't satisfy me either." He shrugged his shoulders and gazed up at her. "To be honest, I've been hungry and miserable since my damn fangs grew."

"I don't think you'll find any synthetic blood in this house." But he needed to feed. Sera frowned, wondering if the queen could somehow help them.

"Hey?" Valentino rolled over, propping his head in one hand while reaching out with the other to take hold of her. "I have what I need right here, as it turns out."

Sera stared at their joined hands. "Meaning?"

Instead of answering, Valentino lifted her hand to his mouth and turned it wrist up against his lips. He licked the tracing of veins visible through her pale skin, and she dragged her gaze toward his. "Let me bite you, Sera."

Her insides clenched, and her lips parted, but not a single sound came out. Valentino chuckled softly and scraped his fangs along her wrist. She gasped and sucked her bottom lip into her mouth. She couldn't let him do this. "I haven't had synthetic blood since I got here. What if you can't drink from me?"

"I've already bitten you tonight, and I feel fine." He looked up with his mouth still pressed to her wrist. "So, may I?"

Sera could only stare.

"I'll take that as a yes." He opened his mouth and

241

sucked gently at her skin before piercing her vein.

She nearly collapsed from pleasure, but Valentino took only a tiny bit of blood and drew away before she wanted him to. She blinked at his smiling face. "Why did you stop? Did it taste wrong?" She pulled her wrist away, staring down at the small wound.

"It tasted just fine." He reached for her and licked the marks. "Better than fine, but I have the rest of forever to bite you whenever I want to. I'll drink my fill later, after you've had yours."

"Oh..." A sudden swell of emotion clogged her throat. Tears burned her eyes, and she ducked her head to hide them.

"Hey." Valentino pulled her down and snuggled her against his side. "You're supposed to be happy, unless the thought of spending eternity with me terrifies you."

Sera shook her head, burying her nose in the scent of his skin. "No. I can't imagine what I'd do without you." Nor did she wish to think about it.

"You'd go back to hating sex," he teased.

Sera swatted him, and he hugged her tighter, drowning out the sound of his chuckle in her hair. "Just tell me one more thing," she said after he finally calmed down. "Tell me the master granted us permission to leave."

"As a matter of fact, the master insists that we do."

She worked free of his embrace and levered up to look at him. "Why?"

"He likes to do things the old fashioned way, I think. Synthetic blood isn't his style, and maybe he's afraid we'll influence some of the others."

"So, we're being kicked out?" Once again, she was being labeled a freak among her own kind. Lovely.

But this time, I'm not alone.

"Yeah, we can be freaks together," Valentino commented.

Sera stared hard at his face. "Why did you just say that?"

He looked confused. "Say what?"

"About being freaks together?"

"Because it's what you were thinking about."

Oh no. "You can read my mind?"

"You can't read mine?" His surprise was all the answer she needed.

Sera pulled her knees to her chest and dropped her forehead down. "Why don't I have any neat talents?" Even the ability to turn into an icky bat would be nice.

Valentino chuckled and walked his fingers up her spine. "You have a few."

She peered back at him. "Name one."

His eyes darkened, and he shoved the comforter down past his waist to expose the erection tenting the front of his pants. "You have the talent to make that happen, anytime, anywhere."

Heat crept into Sera's face. "That is not a talent." Or was it?

"Oh, yes it is, believe me." While she stared, he eased his pants past his hips. "Close your mouth, and come here." He grabbed her and pulled her down next to him. Rolling on top of her, he brushed kisses across her face. His hair drifted into her eyes, but she didn't care. Down below, he nestled hard and heavy against her opening.

"Want to do it again?" He asked the question between wet kisses. There was no denying that he was ready and willing.

Sera squirmed and fought down her rising desire. "We can't have sex twenty-four hours a day for the rest of eternity, Valentino." Despite her words, she gripped his back and spread her legs. He slid inside, and she arched up with a sigh.

"Why not?" He pressed his mouth to her neck, and she felt the tips of his fangs.

Yeah, why not, indeed?

Epilogue

San Francisco...

"I have something for you."

Sera looked toward the door as Valentino strolled into the apartment. A quick glance at the clock showed her he was home early. Always a good thing. It meant more time in bed before dawn claimed them.

With a smile on his face, he shrugged out of his leather jacket and tossed it and his keys on a nearby table. Tonight he was dressed in tight, black leather pants that were cut low around his hips and a see-thru black tee. The outfit left little to the imagination.

Sera's mouth watered at the sight, and she forgot all about the book she'd been reading. One would think she'd be used to such a display by now.

For the past six months, Valentino had been running the *new* Captive Fantasy. Instead of offering state of the art sex, it was now just a simple male strip club. If such an establishment could be called "simple." Most of the guys Dr. Reynolds had created had stayed on, and Raphael was now the co-owner. Several additional strippers had been hired off the streets because Valentino had wanted diversity. Whatever he was doing over there, it worked, because there was always a line out the door every night.

Sera had never stepped foot inside, but Becca—now a waitress at the club and determined to be Raphael's girlfriend—told her more than she needed to know almost every evening on the phone. Supposedly the women were gorgeous, horny, and full of money. Yippee.

When Valentino had mentioned Dr. Reynolds abandoning the club and returning to Russia, Sera had made her opinion perfectly clear. He could own the place, but he couldn't work there. Sometimes he tended bar, hence the drool worthy outfit tonight, but he didn't go near the stage. She didn't need Becca filling her ear with stories of how much money got stuffed in his g-string. No thank you.

He walked into the living room and dropped a kiss on her forehead. "Miss me?"

"You smell like cigarettes and easy women." She wrinkled her nose in distaste and set her book aside.

Straightening, he tucked his hair behind his ear, smiled and then pulled a box out from behind his back. "I'll shower after you open this."

Sera took the plain white box and pulled at the black ribbon. Valentino slid onto the couch next to her and propped a booted foot on his knee. Stretching his arm out behind her, he snagged the ribbon out of the air. She glanced at him while opening the lid. "What is it?"

He trailed the long ribbon over her shoulder. "Just open it. It won't bite."

"It's not my birthday."

He rolled his eyes and pushed the box toward her. "Open it."

Looking into the box, she frowned then reached inside the blood red tissue paper. She pulled out a large coffee mug and spun it in her hands to read the words "Got Blood?" They were written in drippy red, and the mug was black. Cute.

Valentino flicked the ribbon to gain her attention. "I thought it could replace the other one you use all the time. I've never enjoyed the saying, to be honest."

Sera didn't know what to say. As far as gifts went...well, it wasn't exactly a diamond ring, but she couldn't blame him for not liking the "my ex-boyfriend is a vampire" mug. She'd gladly toss it and all memories of

Constantine out in this week's trash.

Setting the box aside but keeping the mug on her lap, she leaned over to kiss him. "Thank you," she said against his lips.

He smiled and then pulled away. "I have one more thing to give you." His eyes sparkled.

"I think you've given me enough for one night."

He cupped her face, and his expression grew frightfully serious. "I love you."

Sera dropped the mug. It bounced over her knee and onto the soft carpet with a dull thud. Gasping, she whipped around to make sure it hadn't broken. Suddenly the mug was her favorite thing in the world, because every time she looked at it she'd remember this moment.

"Hey," Valentino said.

She looked over her shoulder and memorized the look on his face, the fall of hair over his eyes, the slant of his lips...everything that made him, Valentino. Was it possible for her heart to just burst? "I love you too." For some reason, she felt like crying.

Valentino reached for the mug. The brush of his body sent the threat of tears into hiding, making her want to crawl onto his lap and thank him properly and thoroughly. A soft chuckle let her know he'd read her mind.

He set the mug in her lap and kissed her cheek. "Now, I'll go get a shower." But he didn't leave. Instead, he moved his mouth to her ear. "And when I'm all clean," he purred like only he could. "I expect you to lick your way to my mouth."

Sera caught her breath and gripped the mug. "Starting where?"

"That's for you to decide, baby."

About the author...

L. Rosario's interest in vampires began when she devoured Anne Rice's Interview with a Vampire. Until she actually gets the opportunity to interview one of her own, she'll content herself with creating steamy stories featuring sexy vampires and oh so willing victims.